TWENTY
YEARS LATER

Jenna Fiore

CONTENTS

CHAPTER ONE

Jayda

"These Miami boys sure are hot," Kaileen said, eyeing one of the baristas.

I elbowed her. "Kaileen! Shh. Isn't he a little young for us?"

"So?" She raised a brow.

"Jayda?" the young girl at the counter said. "Here's your mocha frap, extra whip, extra chocolate."

As she put the cup on the counter, she looked up at me, and her jaw dropped.

I knew then that she had recognized me. It didn't happen often, but it was always kind of sweet *and* weird when it did.

"Omigosh," she started. "You're Jayda Jenkins, like *the* Jayda Jenkins, who wrote Chassidy Rising!"

I smiled, a little embarrassed but also

flattered. "That's me."

"I adore your books. Please, please, *please* tell me when the next one is coming. You left off on such a cliffhanger. I'm *dying*."

I had to laugh at her enthusiasm, but Kaileen took over. "Well, dear, I'm her agent, and her next one is *supposed* to be in by the end of the year. Then we need to edit and all that stuff. So it might be a whole other year."

Her face fell. "A whole year?"

I nodded. But really, I had just released the last one a few months ago, so I didn't feel all that guilty about it. But I certainly understood what it felt like to have to wait on something you loved.

"Sorry, sweetie," I said. "I'm working as quickly as I can."

She sighed. "I understand. I'll just keep re-reading."

Her face suddenly lit up as she looked behind me at something. Curious, I turned around to see what had caused that reaction and bumped right into a solid wall of muscle.

Oh, whoops.

Glancing up, I took in a chiseled jawline complete with sexy stubble and sensual, full lips before my eyes peeked all the way up into a pair of soulful, brown eyes.

Those eyes. I knew those eyes. What on earth?

Those eyes went wide, and my gut clenched while my heart nearly leaped out of my chest.

Alex Hernandez! Alex Hernandez stood in front

of me!

My mind went blank, and I felt my jaw go slack. My gosh, he looked hot, even hotter than in high school when I'd been so madly in love with him *all four years*.

"Jayda?" he asked.

I nodded, still not able to speak. Somewhere in the back reaches of my brain, I could sense Kaileen staring between us. But my heart couldn't calm down enough to pretend to have any manners for introductions.

"Wow," he said with that deep, sexy voice that made my knees wobbly. "I can't believe it's really you. I haven't seen you since graduation night."

Taking a shaky breath, I tried to speak, but nothing came out.

"You must be here for the reunion, right?" he asked, his eyes searching my face.

What? What was he even talking about?

"Reunion?" I heard Kaileen say.

That finally snapped me out of my stupor. "Um, no," I managed to utter.

Those stunning eyes grew wider once again. "You're not?"

Had I maybe heard disappointment in his voice or just imagined it? "I had no clue there was even a reunion going on."

He smiled at me, and my heart did that fluttery thing I'd attempted to capture with words so many times in my books. "Yes, tonight," he said. "And if you don't have plans, I think you should be my date."

What in the world was going on? Was *the* Alex Hernandez asking me on a date? Was I hallucinating? Or had I entered into some other dimension? My brain just seemed to get even dumber, and I had no clue what to say. This couldn't really be happening.

"She'd love to go," I heard the slightly amused voice of Kaileen say.

"W-what?" I sputtered in her direction. "Don't we have, you know, things to do tonight?"

She gave me a look that I instantly recognized, like she was scolding her toddler. "No. We do *not* have things to do tonight."

"Great," Alex said. "Hey, if you have a second now, maybe we could catch up."

"Um, um," I said. Yikes, I was acting like an idiot. Seeing this god was transporting me instantly back to my dorky, insecure teenage self.

"Yes, she has a second," Kaileen said.

Why was she answering all of his questions? "Um, Kaileen, can I talk to you for a minute? Over there?" I pointed to a quiet, empty corner.

She nodded, then said to Alex, "We'll be right back."

We huddled in the corner, and now, I *really* felt like a damn teenager—whispering and giggling with my friends while staring at Alex Hernandez.

She gave me that look again. "What is going on with you, Jayda? Why are you acting so weird all the sudden?"

How could I even explain it? "That guy... that guy right there?" I resisted the urge to point as my eyes darted back and forth between Alex and Kaileen.

"Yeah?" she asked in an exasperated voice.

"He was the hottest, and I mean *hottest*, most popular guy in our whole school."

One perfectly groomed eyebrow shot up. "So?"

"So I can't go on a date with him," I tried to explain. "To my twenty-year reunion, no less."

"Why the hell not?"

"Because..." I sighed in frustration. "Because I get completely tongue-tied whenever I'm around him, whenever I even see him. And apparently, twenty years hasn't changed a thing. You saw what an idiot I turned into."

She gave me an epic eye-roll. "Yeah. It was hard *not* to see that."

I felt my right eye twitch. "So you see? There is no way on earth that I can go out with him."

She put her hands on my shoulders, capturing all of my attention, her gaze burning into mine. "Get yourself together, girl. You are a grown woman now, a mom, a hugely successful novelist. You are not an insecure teenager anymore. You owe it to the teenage girl still inside you to go on that date. You are going, and I will not take no for an answer."

I closed my eyes, trying to imagine it, walking into whatever big room and seeing all my old classmates. Oh, God, I didn't think I could do it.

"Did you go out with him in high school?" she asked, interrupting my momentary panic.

"Are you kidding me? He never would have asked *me* on a date. We were friends, though, and had quite a few classes together."

"Well, as your agent *and* your best friend, you are going. You'll have a few drinks, and you'll be totally fine," she said, waving her hand in dismissal.

I sighed again because I knew there was no chance of winning this argument, and a part of me kind of did want to go. I hadn't turned out all bad. Plus, didn't a petty side of me want to go to see how all the super popular girls had fared, in hopes that they hadn't aged well?

"But I don't even have a dress," I realized, mentally rifling through my suitcase for the writers' conference I was mentoring at this weekend.

Kaileen pointed to an upscale outdoor shopping center nearby. "See that? I'll go there and get a head start shopping while you have your coffee with Mr. Hot and Popular. Then you can meet me there. Okay?"

Nodding, I released a pent-up breath.

"You can do this, Jayda. God knows, you really need this. After everything you've been through, you deserve to have a little fun. Just remember who you are *now* and not that teenage girl you used to be. Okay?"

I nodded again as she shoved me forward in the direction of Alex, who was sitting at a small table near the back.

"Wait," she whispered, making me pause. "Should I make an appointment with a hair-ripper?"

"Excuse me? What?"

Her eyes traveled up and down my body. "You know, to get things taken care of, just in case."

I felt my face turning crimson at the thought of what she was not so subtly implying. "No! I just went a few days ago as a little splurge before this trip. Besides, *that* is not going to happen."

"You never know," she said, wiggling her eyebrows at me.

I laughed, shaking my head at my crazy friend. "You are unbelievable."

She pushed me back toward Alex, saying, "You go get that fine specimen of a man."

CHAPTER TWO

Jayda

"Hey," he said, smiling as I approached.

"Hey." Why was I so out of breath?

I sat down across from him, the morning sun blaring through the window, illuminating our faces. His nose looked like it had been broken at some point, and he had a small scar above his forehead, all just adding to his sexiness.

So not fair. Why did men have to age so well?

"You look the exact same as you did in high school," he said.

Was he serious? "Thank you?"

His eyes lit up as he chuckled. "That's supposed to be a compliment."

"Oh, well, thanks then." I paused. "I was pretty dorky in high school, so I wasn't sure."

Alex's laugh rang out again. "You were *not* dorky. And you're certainly not dorky now."

That laugh was contagious, and I felt myself relax just a little. But the teenager in my mind still screamed, "I'm having coffee with Alex Hernandez!"

"So," he said, observing me over the rim of his coffee cup. "You'll go with me to the reunion?"

Inhaling a deep breath, I answered, "Sure."

His eyes narrowed. "And why don't you sound very enthusiastic about it?"

I hesitated a moment, thinking about how to articulate my fears.

"Is it because you don't want to go?" he asked. "Or is it because you don't want to go with *me*?"

Be still, my beating heart. Alex Hernandez thought I didn't want to go with *him*? Oh, the irony. As he watched me, I tried to conjure up some kind of answer in my swirling head. "Well, first of all, it's not *you*. I just..."

"You just what?"

"Well, it's, um, I haven't been to a reunion yet." I'd ignored the few invitations I'd received many years ago. "And I really never planned on going to one."

"Why not?"

How on earth could I explain it to him? Could Mr. Hot and Popular ever really fathom what I was feeling?

"I guess I just think being around those people from high school will take me right back to that place. You know?"

"What place?" he asked, his brow furrowed in confusion.

Did he really not understand? "That completely awkward and insecure teenage place where I used to dwell in high school."

Now his face registered surprise. "You felt insecure in high school?"

I felt my eyes widen. "Yeah. Just a little. Didn't you?"

He looked out the window as he thought. "Hmm. I guess." Then those eyes returned to mine. "But you're not insecure now."

"Right. That's true." He did have a good point. I could do this. I *would* do this.

"Sorry," he interrupted my little internal pep talk. "I should have asked if your husband was in town to see if he wanted to go too."

"Oh," I said. It was kind of strange the way he had said that, like he knew I had been married. But maybe it was just that I still wore my wedding band. "My husband actually passed away four years ago."

After staring at me for a moment, he finally said, "I'm really sorry to hear that."

"Thanks." I released a deep breath I hadn't been aware I was holding inside.

He played with his coffee lid before looking at me again. "That must have been really hard."

"It was." It still is, I wanted to add. Being a single mom was incredibly challenging. Going it alone truly sucked.

Those brown eyes stared into mine, seeming to reach into my depths. "Do you mind if I ask how he died?"

I shook my head. "I don't mind. He had something called an aortic dissection."

"Oh, that's awful."

Nodding, I took a sip of my drink as I felt a lump develop in my throat. This was something I wasn't used to talking about anymore. Everyone around me already knew, and I didn't have to tell the whole terrible story.

"You don't have to talk about it if you don't want to. I'm really sorry," he said.

"No. No. It's okay." Those eyes showed so much concern that I found myself wanting to share it with him. "When I was two months pregnant, he needed emergency open-heart surgery. And well, the recovery was rough, but it seemed like he would pull through. But then, three weeks after our daughter was born, he had another emergency. And that time..." I had a tough time getting the words out. "That time, he didn't make it."

His breath came out in a whoosh. "That's unbelievable. I can't even imagine how hard that must have been... must still be. What was his name?"

"Blake." He nodded, and I decided it was time to change the subject before I embarrassed myself with tears. "What about you? What's your situation?"

Leaning back in his chair, he sighed. "So I kind of have a, um, complicated situation, I guess."

That was rather unexpected, and I wasn't sure what to say. Of course, I was beyond curious but didn't really want to pry. "Oh, okay."

He smiled. "Not sure you want to ask?"

Was he reading my mind or what? "I don't want to be too nosy," I confessed.

"You're not being nosy," he said after taking another sip of his coffee. "Actually, I have a daughter too. She just turned one."

"Aww, that's such a cute age."

His eyes lit up. "She's the light of my life."

That totally made my heart leap. I imagined this giant man holding his baby girl, and my insides melted. And I'm sure he had a beautiful wife to complete his beautiful family. "I bet she's adorable and has you wrapped around her little finger."

He busted out laughing at that. "Definitely."

For a moment, we didn't say anything. And I didn't want to ask about his wife. But I felt so awkward because he had asked me to be his date tonight, right?

Thinking back, had he literally used the word "date" earlier? I had been so shocked by running into him, I couldn't even remember.

"So you're probably wondering about a wife..." he said.

I nodded, amazed again at him guessing my thoughts.

His chest rose and fell in a big sigh. "She left soon after Gabby was born."

I gasped. Then feeling bad, I covered my mouth with my hand. "That's... wow, I'm so sorry to hear that."

His lips compressed together, he gave a small nod. "Thanks. She just—she just didn't have any maternal feelings."

My mind whirled. But wasn't it post-partum? Surely, she would change her mind once all her hormones settled down. I couldn't remember how long that took really.

"You're probably thinking post-partum depression," he continued. "But it was more than that."

I stared at him, still not sure what to say in an effort to not sound *too* curious. This conversation had taken a seriously intense turn with both of us discussing our previous partners so quickly. But life could be cruel. And apparently, we had both experienced some awful events in the years since high school.

"This might be TMI," he said. "But I've known you since I was fourteen, right?"

"True." I smiled, remembering freshman year when I had first seen him in our English Honors class.

"So I didn't get married until a few years ago." He looked out the window briefly before returning his gaze to me again. "I really wanted a wife and a family, and I just got tired of waiting, you know?"

I nodded.

"But I picked the wrong person," he said in a low voice.

I couldn't believe he was confiding in me like this. "I'm so sorry to hear that."

"Thank you." His eyes were filled with regret, making me wish I could hug him. "In the end, we weren't meant to be, unfortunately, and having a child only made things worse."

"That... I don't know what to say really," I admitted. "Just I'm sorry that happened to you."

"Thanks. I truly appreciate that." He smiled softly. "But it's not all doom and gloom. I have amazing parents who help me out and take care of my baby girl, especially since work is so busy."

"It's so nice to have parents like that. I have that too. Thank God."

He inclined his head in agreement. "Definitely. Glad you have that too."

There was a moment of hesitation, and I was dying to know what he did for a living, even though I already had a feeling. "So, Alex, let me guess... you said you work a lot. I would bet the farm that you're a doctor."

Letting out a laugh, his amused eyes met mine. "What makes you say that?"

"I don't know. Maybe the fact that you were incredibly smart and got into Harvard."

"Well, yeah, you guessed it. But can you guess what *kind* of doctor?" He tilted his head, awaiting my answer.

"Hmm, let me think. Gynecologist?"

He laughed again, this time even louder. "Nope. Interesting guess, though. But I'm actually an orthopedic surgeon."

"Wow. Okay. That's pretty amazing."

He shrugged. "Just lots and lots of school."

"I'm sure you're being modest."

Smiling, he seemed uncomfortable and asked, "What about you? What keeps you busy besides being the incredible mother I know you are?"

Oh, this man. He was smooth. I realized I needed to watch my heart around him or I'd completely lose it... again.

"I'm a writer," I finally said.

His eyebrows shot up. "Really? What kind of writer?"

"I write young adult fiction."

"No way," he said, his eyes widening even more. "That's amazing, Jayda."

The way he said my name set off flutters deep in my belly that I tried not to think about too much. "Thanks. That's why I'm here actually."

"What do you mean?"

"I'm here for a writers' conference at the Marriott."

As if on cue, the young girl from behind the counter came over to our table. "Ms. Jenkins, I'm so sorry to bother you again. But can I get a picture with you?"

I laughed to hide my embarrassment. "Sure."

She leaned down next to me and aimed her phone at our smiling faces. "Thank you so much," she said, dancing away. "I can't wait to show my friends."

Alex stared at me, shaking his head. "I always knew you'd do something incredible."

I felt my cheeks flush. "Nah, not really. What *you're* doing is incredible, helping people, fixing people."

"But you've created something that apparently people adore." His eyes on me were intense. "What's your book called?"

Why, oh, why did he want to know that? "Um..."

"Come on. Please tell me." He flashed that sexy smile, making those butterflies flutter around. How could I resist that?

"Well, it's a series, actually, called Chassidy Rising, about a teen girl finding her powers. I just wrote the fourth one. And the next one will be the last."

"So you're like the new Stephenie Meyer."

I couldn't help but laugh. "No. Not even close. But I do all right."

His eyes narrowed. "Okay. So Chassidy Rising. Chassidy Rising. I've got to remember that."

"Please don't," I begged.

"Chassidy Rising. Chassidy Rising," he repeated, a light in his eyes that took me all the way back to high school trig when he'd sat next to me and used to make me giggle with his teasing.

"You really haven't changed. Still love to annoy me."

"Always," he said, his eyes staring into mine and something in his voice sending shivers down my spine.

His phone buzzed, breaking the spell that had descended on us, and I was glad. It was too intense. Being around him was almost too much. Everything felt magnified. Everything somehow felt more significant.

"Oh, man, I hate to do this, but I have to run. I'm actually on the reunion committee, and I'm supposed to check out the space right now and make sure everything looks okay for tonight."

"No problem."

We both stood up and started for the door. Once we tossed our trash out, he turned to me. "You're at the Marriott next door, right?"

"Yep."

"I'll pick you up in the lobby at six-thirty then. All right?"

"Sounds good." I nodded, gulping as I turned to go. This was really happening.

"Oh, and Jayda?"

I looked over my shoulder at him. "Yes?"

"I'm going to read your book today."

He winked at me and walked away, leaving me stunned. Alex Hernandez was going to read my book? About a teenage girl?

I didn't know what to make of that. Was he

teasing me again? Or was he serious? After all these years, this guy still did things to me, and I had no idea how to feel.

CHAPTER THREE

Jayda

P acing inside the Marriott lobby, I looked at my phone again.

6:45 P.M.

My heart sunk even more. Was Alex Hernandez seriously standing me up?

I felt sick. I *already* felt sick, but this... this made it unbearable. Cursing my high heels, I walked over to the bar and ordered a glass of wine. Something, anything, to take off the edge, I hoped.

As I sipped my drink and eyed the doors, I wondered, how long did a person wait? Thirty minutes? An hour? That seemed too long.

I decided on thirty minutes. That's how long I'd give him to show up.

As I waited, I thought of every teenage movie I'd ever seen where there's a cruel prank played on some poor nerdy girl who got all dressed up for the prom. I so felt like that girl right now.

No one had ever stood me up before, and I really couldn't believe he would do that. Something had to have happened, right?

6:50 P.M.

As the minutes ticked by, my mind spiraled into that dark, insecure place I'd inhabited in high school. It hadn't been torture like some kids, I knew. No one had really picked on me or bullied me.

But I'd had a weird relationship with my best friend where she always led the way, and I followed. And she hadn't been very nice about it. She had lorded it over me a ridiculous amount of times. Being an unconfident girl, I had let her, and that unique torment had made those years hell.

6:55 P.M.

Five more minutes and I was out of here. I took a shaky breath. In some ways, I was glad. I didn't really want to see my ex-best friend, Melanie, anyway. We had lost touch years ago, and I had no intention of rekindling that "friendship" anytime soon.

I stared at the door and watched a beautiful couple decked out in their finest as they headed out for the night. God, how I missed that. Not that Blake and I had been big out-on-the-town people. We were much more likely to cuddle up on the couch with popcorn and wine.

But I just missed having that *person*, that one person in the world I could always rely on to love me no matter what.

6:59 P.M.

That was it. I was done waiting. Maybe in high school, I'd have given him longer. But no way. I wasn't in high school anymore.

After setting my wine glass down on the bar, I headed for the elevators. Just as I pushed the button, I heard a shout behind me.

"Jayda! Wait!"

Whirling around, I saw Alex running toward me, taking my breath away in his black suit and black shirt, open at the collar. He was here! I didn't budge, though, deciding in an instant to let him come to me.

He rushed up, out of breath. "I'm so sorry. You must have thought I was standing you up."

All I could do was nod as he stared into my eyes, and I tried to squash the rush of tears before he could see them.

"I'm so sorry. Gabby spit up all over my shoes, then had a huge meltdown right as I was trying to leave." His eyes were creased with concern. "And I didn't even have your phone number to let you know I'd be late. Please forgive me."

I let out a big exhale. "Of course. We should have exchanged numbers. But yes, of course, I forgive you."

"Oh, thank God." He sighed. "Thank you for waiting. Although it looked like you had just given up." He nodded toward the elevator door as it opened.

"Yep, you were close, buddy." Smiling, I pressed my thumb and forefinger together. "This close."

He grinned back, making those ever-present butterflies wiggle around. "Looks like I was just in time. And thank God for that because I'm finally about to take the great Jayda Jenkins out on a date. And I can promise you, it'll be a night you'll never forget."

Those butterflies went crazy. What on earth did that mean exactly? I had no idea what to say.

He looked at me, *really* looked at me, taking in my new little black dress and heels. "Damn, you look good."

"Thank you," I managed to say.

When his eyes returned to my face, there was heat in that gaze, and I felt singed just looking at him. Oh, my. This man had a lifetime of practice at being a player, making me wonder if I might be his latest victim.

We headed out into the night, Alex guiding me with a gentle hand on my back that seemed to burn right through me. He pointed at a sleek black car. "That's me."

I thanked the valet who held the passenger door open for me as I tried to slide in with some kind of modesty wearing this dress. Definitely not something I was used to anymore, considering I practically lived in yoga pants and hoodies.

"Nice car," I said while buckling up. "I remember you used to like fast cars. Looks like some things never change."

He grinned at me as he drove off. "Yep, still like a fast car. How do you even remember that?"

"Well, it's a little fuzzy because I may have had a drink or two. But I remember being in the back of my friend David's car one night in high school. I think it was him. Anyway, at a stoplight, we pulled up next to you and some friends. And when the light changed, you guys both just took off and raced. It was beyond thrilling... and terrifying to go that fast. But of course, you won."

He laughed. "Me? I'm not sure about that."

"Yeah, and another time—"

"There's another story?"

"Sure is. This one involving my dad."

"What?" His smile turned into a frown. "Oh, no."

"Oh, yes." I gave him my best mom face. "So my dad was driving me to school one day, for some reason, and I remember being late and annoyed that he wouldn't go faster. And then, zoom, there you go, speeding by us on the left—"

"Crap."

"In a no-passing zone."

We both laughed. "That sounds like something I'd do as a teenager. I was such an asshole."

"That's pretty much what my dad said."

He cringed. "Whoops."

"I didn't tell him I knew who the asshole was, though. Kept that to myself."

"Good. Thank you for that."

He pulled into a large, upscale hotel, the bright lights making a path to the front where valets waited.

"The reunion's here?" I asked, surprised by the shortness of our ride.

"Yes. We could have walked, but I figured it might be uncomfortable in your shoes."

That was seriously thoughtful. The player had definitely grown up… a bit at least.

The valet held the door open, and again, I had to shimmy out to where Alex was waiting for me. He offered me his elbow, and I gladly looped my arm through his, excitement and adrenaline shooting up and down my body.

He looked at me as we headed into the glitzy lobby. "You all right?"

"Mm-hmm. Sure," I said, my voice a little higher than usual as he led me down a long hallway.

"Everyone's going to be so happy to see you."

I nodded, not so sure about that.

He leaned closer to me, his breath near my ear, sending those butterflies into a frenzy. "No one's going to eat you. I'll make sure of it."

What this man did to me. I didn't have much time to think about it or recover my composure because we rounded a corner and went into a big room, straight from my nightmares.

There at the front sat a table manned by a woman who looked familiar. I supposed everyone was going to look that way tonight.

"Hey, Jessica," Alex said. "How's everything going?"

That's right. Jessica Sinclair, one of the queen bitches.

She eyed Alex's large frame and smiled. "Great. Now."

"Sorry I'm late. Had an incident with the little one."

"No problem." Her gaze turned to me, and her eyes went wide. "Jayda? Jayda Jenkins?"

I smiled, surprised she recognized me. "That's me."

Her eyes darted to my arm linked with Alex's, and a small frown appeared on her face. "Wow, I can't believe you're really here. You know, this is like the fourth reunion we've had."

Things were taking a weird turn. "I had no idea," I sort of lied. I'd known about a few but definitely not this one.

"Right. Well, I'm glad you could finally make it." She looked down at all the name badges in front of her. "Oh, I don't think you RSVP'd so I don't have a badge for you. And you didn't pay—"

"Jess," Alex interrupted. "I'll take care of it later. But could you just write her name on a badge maybe?"

"Sure. No problem." She scribbled my first name on a blank name badge, then looked up at me. "Is it still Jenkins?"

"Yes," I said.

"So you never got married, huh? Interesting."

What was that supposed to mean?

"She's a widow," Alex said, grabbing the sticker from her. "Thanks for that."

As he whisked me away into the room toward the bar, I thought about that phrase—a tiger doesn't change its stripes—and realized this was going to be one long night.

CHAPTER FOUR

Jayda

T hank goodness for the open bar. Even though it was tempting to go full throttle, I decided I'd just stick to wine. The last thing I needed to do was embarrass myself at my twenty-year reunion.

"Sorry about her," Alex said as he handed me my glass.

"You have nothing to apologize for."

"Yeah, but I dragged you here."

Someone behind us screamed. "Oh, my God! It's Jayda!"

I squeezed the stem of my wine glass so hard I thought it might break as a small group of women came rushing over, Melanie in the lead. They stopped a few feet from us, taking in the sight of Alex standing right beside me.

After a brief awkward pause, Melanie dashed forward, arms outstretched, and nearly crushed the life out of me. "Jayda! I can't believe you're really here."

I had to smile at their reaction, like I was some kind of rock star that had just arrived at the big class reunion. We took turns hugging as I struggled to remember the names of the other four girls who had been part of our larger group of friends.

Melanie grabbed my hand. "Come on. Come on. Grab your drink and let's go talk. We have *so* much to catch up on."

After my reluctant glance at Alex, she pulled me to a table in the far corner, the rest of the crew following, and we all settled in as a DJ blasted music from our high school years.

Leaning forward in her chair, she said, "So first off, are you seriously here with Alex Hernandez?"

I laughed that this was the first thing she wanted to discuss. "Well, first off, Melanie, it's great to see you, and you look amazing." Glancing at them all, I took in their eager faces that were so carefully made up for the night. "You all look amazing actually."

"You do too," someone said, a woman named Anne if I remembered correctly.

"Thank you."

"So?" an impatient Melanie asked. "What's the deal with Alex?"

Shaking my head because some things never changed, I said, "We just bumped into each other at a coffee shop earlier today, and he invited me to come tonight."

Melanie looked slightly disappointed but then perked up. "Well, I hear he's single now, so you never know."

Everyone else nodded in agreement.

"You guys." Rolling my eyes, I decided to change the subject. "So what's up with everyone? Do you all live here? Married? Kiddos?"

The group of us caught up for hours, going through several bottles of wine and tons of appetizers. Even though I saw glimpses of the old Melanie, she had really grown up a lot, as we all had hopefully.

Taking a moment to eat some dinner, I looked around the room as my friends continued their discussion. Everyone looked pretty much the same, although perhaps with a few added pounds and more lines on their faces plus thinning hair on some of the guys.

I caught Alex's eyes on me from across the room, and when he smiled at me, my heart did a little dance. Something about being in this environment, with flickering candles casting shadows on the walls, just made him even sexier.

But I was soon distracted by another old friend who wanted to chat... and another and another. While it was wonderful to talk with everyone, and a few people even knew about my book series from their teenage daughters, the emotional toll became overwhelming.

At some point in the conversation, the topic

of marriage would come up, and I had to retell my story about Blake over and over—and then deal with the awkward condolences and have to almost comfort the other person.

Taking my wine glass with me, I snuck out to a large patio area I had noticed earlier for a little break. The muggy night air hit me even though it was October, and the scent of the nearby ocean took me right back to those high school days.

I had only lived in Miami for four years, moving here from Southern California right before freshman year. Not knowing a soul, no wonder I had clung onto my dysfunctional friendship with Melanie when she had befriended me in PE class. The other option had been to have no friends—which wasn't really an option for me personally.

A sudden noise startled me, and I turned to see Alex walking my way, something about the look on his face making me sigh. He was so incredibly dreamy.

"Hey," he said. "Sneaking away?"

"Maybe." I took a drink of my wine. "Just needed a breather."

The closer he walked, the faster my breaths came until he was right in front of me. The music spilled out from the open door, serenading us with a sexy, slow song.

He took my glass out of my hand and put it on a nearby table. "Dance with me?" he asked.

Looking into those sensual eyes, there was no

way I could say no. "Sure."

I hesitated, not sure how to even dance with a man anymore. It had been so long. So incredibly long. But Alex held out his hands to me, and I stepped forward into him. As his arms came around me, a million sensations washed through me.

He smelled amazing, his grip strong on my hips the way I liked it, sending sparks through my body. I didn't dare look at him because I just couldn't handle it. So I kept my eyes on his shoulders and leaned into him a little. Our bodies barely touched, but I still felt the heat. The sensational heat. Holy crap.

When he drew me in closer, I thought I might die, and now we were flush together. I almost laughed as I remembered that church phrase for teen dances—leave room for the Holy Spirit.

But the urge to giggle quickly faded as he pulled me in even tighter until I couldn't feel where my body ended and his started. His warmth poured into me, flooding me with a hunger... a hunger I hadn't felt in a very long time. If ever.

That was a terrible thing to think! I closed my eyes against the guilt, confusion whirling through me about what I was feeling.

"Just let go, Jayda," Alex whispered against the top of my head. "Let go."

How had he known?

His hands on my hips guided me with his body

as we moved together to the slow beat of the music whirling around us. I looked up at him, and that was my first mistake, because those kissable lips were the first thing I saw, those seductive eyes staring down at me.

I swallowed hard as the unbelievable thought entered my mind that Alex was going to kiss me. And then he did—hesitant at first, his lips barely touching me, like he wasn't sure how I'd react. But God, those lips felt incredible. More than incredible. Sublime.

Stretching myself up as high as I could, my arms tightened against the back of his neck, hoping for more pressure. And he didn't disappoint. His lips pressed into mine, and thank goodness he was holding me so tight because my knees nearly gave out.

"Jayda?" a slurred voice called out. "Are you out here?"

"Feels like high school again." Alex laughed as he gently released me.

Still stunned, I watched as Melanie wound her way through the maze of oversized tropical plants and cushy chairs to where we stood.

"There you are," she said, her eyes glancing between Alex and me, taking in my now flushed face. "Oh, whoops, I'm so sorry if I interrupted anything."

"No. It's fine. Really," I assured her.

"I just—I just was scared you had snuck out like you used to do in high school all the time."

She narrowed her eyes at me. "And I didn't want you to leave until I had your number."

"She *was* about to sneak out I think," Alex said, grinning.

I elbowed him. "Shh."

"Hmm, okay," she said, eyeing Alex as she grabbed her phone.

We exchanged numbers quickly, and after she gave me another hug, she took both of my hands in hers. "Listen, I want to say something to you."

Alex edged away from us, which she immediately spotted.

"No, Alex," she said. "Please stay." Her eyes turned to me again as she took a heavy breath. "Look, I just wanted to tell you how sorry I am for being such a bitch in high school."

I gulped, shocked by her words.

"You were the best friend I ever had," she continued. "And sometimes... well, sometimes I really treated you like crap."

She looked down, unable to meet my eyes, and all those long-ago feelings of resentment I'd kept in some hidden part of my heart just flitted away. Gone. After so much time.

I squeezed her hands, making her glance up at me. "You know what? That really means a lot to me. Thank you for saying that. That couldn't have been easy."

She nodded, her eyes watery. "Well, it's the least I can do. I've thought a lot about it over the years."

"We had some good times too," I reminded her. "Don't forget that."

"I won't ever forget." She let out a hiccup, and we all laughed. "Oh, dear, I think I better get some water."

I let her hands go. "Good idea."

She headed for the ballroom but turned back toward me with a smile. "So *now* you can sneak out of here."

CHAPTER FIVE

Jayda

After she disappeared through the door, I looked up at Alex. "You know, I think I'm going to head out. It was really fun but, well, big day tomorrow."

He nodded. "I get that. I'll grab the car."

"No, no. I'd like to walk back. I'll just tiptoe right out there." I pointed to the courtyard beyond the open patio. "You should stay and have fun."

"Are you trying to get rid of me?" His sexy smile lit up his face.

"No, I'm—"

He leaned closer, making my heart rate tick up a notch. "Nice try, Jayda. But I'm not going to let you walk back alone at night."

I hesitated, feeling bad that he was leaving the reunion before it was over, and thought about going back in. But as a highly introverted person, there was only so much of parties I could take. Even *with* alcohol. "Sure," I finally said.

We both stayed quiet as we stepped into the courtyard, the music fading behind us. And soon, we were out on the bright Miami streets, cars blasting by us, beats bouncing in celebration of a Friday night.

"You holding up okay?" Alex asked.

"I am," I said, warmed by the thoughtfulness in his voice.

"Thanks for being my date tonight."

I smiled up at him. "It was actually really nice."

"Good. I know you were dreading it."

That cracked me up. "I wasn't dreading it."

"Yes. You most definitely were," he argued between laughs.

"Okay. Yeah. I kind of was," I admitted. "But I'm glad I went."

"Me too." He paused a beat, then said, "I bet it was nice to catch up with Melanie and the rest of your friends."

I sighed. "Yeah, I wasn't sure how that was going to go. But she's changed a lot since high school."

"Hopefully, a lot of us have."

Feeling bold, I asked, "What about you? Have you changed much?"

Our eyes met as we crossed the street in front of my hotel. "More than you know," he said.

What on earth did that mean?

The front of the hotel was hopping with

people coming and going, valets running past, luggage being hauled in. Alex walked with me into the lobby, and I prepared to say goodnight. But he stopped suddenly, a serious look on his face.

"Will you have another drink with me?" he asked. "We barely had a chance to talk tonight."

That was true. My friends had definitely monopolized the night. "Sure," I said.

His eyes. Oh, my, those eyes looked intense like I had just agreed to... I didn't know what.

"Good."

He took my hand in his, causing my heart to flutter, and led me to the nearby bar where we ordered some wine. The glasses were filled to the rim, and I tried not to let any liquid slosh over the side as we found a little table in a secluded corner of the lobby, hidden by plants.

After we sat down, Alex made a toast. "To you. To tonight. And to the future."

"Cheers," I said, while carefully clinking my glass to his.

Our eyes met above our drinks, his heat melting me even from across the table.

"So," he began, "would you believe I don't even know where you live?"

"Right." I couldn't help laughing. "I guess we never got to that. Well, I live in Maine now."

His eyes widened. "Whoa, that's a long way from Miami."

"Just a little, right?"

Nodding, he gave me that Alex smile. "Where in Maine?"

"In Portland, right by the water."

He whistled. "By the water, huh? Can't take the Florida girl out of you."

"That's the truth." I laughed. "But I've only lived there for the last four years. So I still feel kind of new."

"Where were you before that?" he asked.

"I lived in Cobble Hill, Brooklyn, for a long time, basically, since I got married, soon after college."

His eyes looked thoughtful. "You were married a long time."

"Mm-hmm. Twelve years. Blake was my college sweetheart. Well, we met our junior year. But once we started dating, that was it."

"That's amazing," he said.

For some reason, I found Alex easier to talk to this evening, and I had no problem telling him about my past. "Then after he died, I moved to Maine to be near my parents who moved there a while back."

"Don't they kind of have it wrong? Going from Florida to Maine?" he teased, a glimmer in his eyes. "Shouldn't it be the other way around as you get older?"

I laughed as I took another sip of my wine. "That's exactly what they say. They travel a lot in the winter, though, now that they're retired."

"You must get a lot of snow."

"So much snow. But I adore it. It's so nice to curl up inside, fire blazing, a hot beverage, writing. That's the life for me, at least when my daughter's not around. Otherwise, I'm out there freezing my butt off building snow princesses."

He burst into laughter. "Snow princesses. I love it. So tell me about this daughter of yours. She's four?"

"Four going on fourteen."

"Oh, man." Alex let out a sigh.

"Yeah. Her name's Audrey, and she is a bleepin' handful. Smart and very strong-willed. Like *every single day*, I have to pick my battles with her because *everything* is a battle if I let it become one."

"Really? Is that what I have to look forward to?"

I nodded with empathy. "Yep, probably. But it's made me creative in how I approach life. She's stretched me to the limits of my humanity and made me become a better person. And even though it's been incredibly tough at times, and I have literally pulled out my own hair, I wouldn't trade it for anything in this world. The love I have for that kid... well, there are just no words."

His eyes held an emotion I couldn't name, and he didn't say anything for a long moment. In the silence, I took another sip of my wine, wondering why Alex was so strangely quiet. Maybe I'd been hogging the conversation and needed to change the subject.

"Sorry, I've been chatting away all about me, me, me. What about you? What about your life now?"

That seemed to snap him out of whatever had consumed his thoughts. "Oh, my life's not very exciting. I work while my parents take care of Gabby. And when I'm not working, just trying to be a good dad."

Something about the way he said that made me all mushy inside. "Do you have your own practice or how does that work?"

"I'm in a sports medicine clinic with other doctors. So it's a group of us. And then if surgery's needed, I work with several of the local hospitals and go wherever the insurance takes the patient."

"Ah, I see. I bet that's interesting. Do you work a lot?"

"Actually, not as much anymore because of Gabby. A few days a week. It just doesn't seem as important now."

"I totally get that."

He swirled the wine in his glass, and I realized he hadn't actually consumed very much of it. "Hey, can I tell you something?" Alex suddenly asked me.

The butterflies in my belly swished around at his serious tone. "Sure. Of course."

I took a sip of my wine as I watched him clasp his hands together on the table. "So in high school, I don't know if you remember, but I was kind of..."

"Kind of Mr. Hot and Popular?" I blurted out.

Oh, no. Had I really just said that?

He cracked up. "That's definitely not what I was going to say."

"Yeah. Sorry. Just a joke." *Not really.* I needed to stop writing these teen romances and move on to the adult genre.

"I was going to say I was a complete idiot."

This was an interesting turn of conversation. "No way," I disagreed. "You were totally cool. Everyone loved you. Girls *and* boys."

"I don't know about that. But..." He seemed to struggle for the right words. "Well, basically, I was just a horny teenage asshole."

I nearly choked at that. "Excuse me? What did you say?"

His eyes were bright with amusement. "Yeah. A horny teenage boy who just wanted to date a certain kind of girl, you know?"

What on earth was he trying to say? "Okay."

"You're looking at me like I'm crazy."

"No. I'm, uh, just trying to figure out where this is going."

"Well," he began, rubbing his hands together in thought. "I have a confession."

My heart started beating in double time. "You do?"

His eyes boring into mine, he cleared his throat. "I always had a major crush on you."

What in the world? Did I seriously hear that

right? Or was the wine doing things to my hearing?

"Jayda? You okay?" he asked, concern lacing his voice as he studied my face.

"Um, yeah. Just... I don't think I heard you correctly."

Alex chuckled. "Yes, you did. But I'll repeat it just in case." He leaned closer, making the breath leave my lungs. "*I had a major crush on you.*"

Good God. I was going to faint. Alex had a crush on me? Like me? Jayda Jenkins? "Um, me?" I looked over my shoulder. "Are you sure?"

His wide smile did things to my core. "Yes. You. Jayda."

I slid my wineglass away. "Okay. I think I better stop drinking now."

Those eyes of his burned into mine. "Even back then, despite my complete stupidity, I knew you were the whole package."

Utterly speechless, my head started to swirl with his words.

"You had everything. You were incredibly smart and funny. You had the sweetest, kindest personality. And..." He hesitated a moment. "You were absolutely beautiful."

I felt like I was in some alternate universe right now along with the heroine in my books. How many times had I daydreamed about hearing these very words from him in high school?

"W-why didn't you ever—" I stammered,

unsure how to complete the sentence.

"I was just too stupid to do anything about it," Alex said, sighing. "But the real reason, ugh, I don't even want to admit it."

"What?" *My word, what?* I reached for the wine glass again.

"Well, you were kind of a good girl." Leaning away, he had trouble making eye contact. "You know what I mean?"

I laughed out loud, surprising him.

"You think it's funny?" he asked, eyes bright.

"So in other words, you thought I wouldn't give up the goods, huh?"

He shook his head, grinning. "I guess that's one way to put it."

I couldn't stop laughing. This was seriously something right out of a teen romance. Good girls and bad boys. But twenty years later. Just to make him squirm, though, I had to admit something to him. And I had to make it good.

"What's so funny?" he asked.

"Well, Mr. Hot and Popular, the joke's on *you*."

"What on earth do you mean?"

He looked so confused, I took pity on him and decided to be as blunt as possible. Leaning forward, capturing all of his attention, I said, "Well, I had a crush on you too."

Alex swallowed thickly, and I moved even closer.

"And," I continued, savoring this moment, "if you had ever asked me out, I would have done everything, *everything*, with you."

He released a loud groan. "Are. you. serious?"

"Yep." I smiled. "On the first date probably."

Burying his face in his hands, he let out another noise of frustration. "I am *such* an idiot."

Now, I started to feel a little mean. "Not anymore."

Lifting his head, he met my eyes, his own filled with regret. "Not anymore. Hopefully," he answered.

The air around us pulsed with a weighted silence while we stared at each other, something electric passing between us as our faces moved closer.

A loud burst of laughter from the front doors startled us apart.

"Should we get out of here?" he asked, his narrowed eyes surveying me.

"Definitely," I said, standing up and trying my best not to wobble in these heels.

Taking my hand, his strong grip steadied me. "Can I walk you upstairs?" he asked.

"Please."

As we wordlessly passed through the lobby, I felt like I was traveling through another world, a strange world where Alex Hernandez was escorting me to my room, but also a somewhat familiar world where I didn't want to let him go.

The noise as we waited by the elevators made it hard to talk. And besides, my thoughts consumed me as I remembered what Kaileen had said right before I'd walked out my door earlier.

Don't you dare pass up a chance to sleep with that man.

Tonight was my one and only chance to finally be with Alex. And there was no way I was going to let him walk away.

The elevator dinged, and hand in hand, we moved forward.

I just really hoped he didn't pull the "You've been drinking" or "You have an early morning" card and try to be all gentlemanly with me. But as the doors closed and we were finally all alone, I found out that Alex was no gentleman.

CHAPTER SIX

Jayda

Right after I pressed the fourth floor button, he spun me around, pulling me to him. His lips came down on mine, truly kissing me this time, taking my breath away. I grasped onto him, afraid I might crumble from the intensity of his mouth taking, giving, teasing.

Those lips.

But we were interrupted too soon by the elevator door opening. As we broke apart and headed into the hall, I was so dazzled I couldn't remember my room number. But it came back to me while I dug around in my little purse for the key card. I fumbled with the lock as Alex put a firm hand on my back.

Once I opened the door, I whirled around to look at him, unsure what he would do. "Want to come in?" I asked, my heart in my throat.

His eyes burned into me. "More than anything."

As the door shut behind us and I said a silent thank you to Kaileen for getting us separate rooms, Alex turned me around to face him, the dim light from the lamp casting shadows on his gorgeous face.

"You're sure about this?" he asked.

I swallowed hard. "Absolutely."

The intensity in his eyes almost scared me. And for a second I had a doubt, a weird nagging feeling that I was cheating on my late husband, that I was doing something wrong.

But I didn't have time to think further about it as Alex pressed forward, leaning his body into mine. That scorching heat melted me and turned my brain to putty.

His mouth was on me, this time his tongue touching my lips, just barely teasing, barely tasting. As I met his tongue with mine, he groaned like he was in pain, and our kisses grew hotter, needier.

"You have no idea how long I've wanted this," he whispered against my mouth.

I wanted to say the same thing back, but the words wouldn't come out. I was so lost in a haze, so lost in the spell he had cast.

His rough hands roamed my body, down my neck to my hips, where he tugged at the material of my dress. "I want this off. I want to see you, touch you, taste you."

Those words made me tremble. No one had seen me without clothes for so long.

With nimble fingers, he worked the hidden zipper in the back, and he slowly helped me out of the dress, tossing it onto the nearby chair. I stood there in my black bra and panties, a wave of vulnerability washing over me.

Alex paused for a minute, his eyes taking in my body while I held my breath. Then he looked at my face again. "You're absolutely gorgeous."

His words nearly made me cry as overwhelming emotions swept through me. Wrapping my arms around his neck, I kissed him then, giving him all of my passion since I couldn't actually voice how I was feeling.

Our tongues tangled together, both of us breathless with our lust. Alex tugged at my lower lip with his teeth, making me gasp with need and desire, before his lips crashed against mine once more. Tilting his head, he took the kiss deeper, slanting his mouth again and again like he couldn't get enough of me, his hands gripping me tightly to his hard body.

I could barely think. Or breathe. All I could feel was Alex and this inferno blazing between us. His hot hands branded my flesh everywhere he touched me.

Above all, I wanted to see him naked and feel him against me. Skin on skin. As if reading my mind, he pulled away from our kiss, tossing his suit jacket to the chair, both of us fumbling with his buttons in a race to get his shirt off.

I gasped when his flawless chest was revealed before my wide eyes—strong, muscular, and tan. He was beyond perfect, and I couldn't believe that he was actually standing here in front of me right now.

In awe that I finally could touch him like this, my hands explored every inch of his hard chest, his big arms, and broad shoulders as he watched me with sultry eyes, breathing heavily. I paused for a moment to feel where his heart pounded in time with mine, our gazes locked together in the heat and emotion of the moment.

Grazing my fingers down his abs and then lower to the waistline of his pants, his breath hitched before his hands stopped mine. "It's been a long time, sweetheart, and I'm not sure how long I can last," he whispered near my ear.

I smiled at this player admitting something like that. "That's okay. You don't have to take it slow with me."

A half growl escaped his lips as he unfastened his pants, letting them drop to the floor to reveal his black boxer briefs, his enormous erection straining against the fabric. *Oh, wow*. Alex Hernandez definitely lived up to his reputation, and I had serious trouble breathing, especially when I looked up to see the fire in his eyes.

"Come here," he said softly.

I pressed myself to him, intoxicated by the feel of his hardness against me. We stayed like that for a moment, savoring the closeness, breathing each other in as I felt his heart beating against my cheek.

He lowered his mouth to my neck, kissing a path to my ear, nibbling and tasting along the way. Barely able to stand up anymore, I clung onto him even more.

Suddenly, he picked me up, my shoes falling to the floor, and he walked me over to the bed where he sort of dropped me. I laughed as I tumbled onto the bed on my stomach.

"Damn, not as smooth as I used to be," Alex said, joining in my laughter as he removed his shoes and socks, never taking his eyes off me, looking like he was about to eat me alive.

When he joined me on the bed and started kissing his way up my legs and then my back, all my giggling died away as his mouth, those lips, made me forget everything. The coarseness of his five o'clock shadow tickled and scratched against me, only adding to the flames whipping through me.

His hands moved to the clasp on my strapless bra, and my heart somehow sped up even more at revealing myself to him. It seemed like forever ago since I'd felt this nervous exhilaration at being with someone for the first time.

Then his fingers caressed the sides of my breasts, making me shiver with need and desire. I rolled over slowly, leaving my bra behind, desperately wanting to feel his hands on me. His breathing turned ragged as he stared at me, his eyes full of wonder. I felt a blush rise up my chest to my face that I tried to ignore.

Alex finally looked back to my eyes. "More beautiful than I even imagined," he said.

His mouth and hands descended on my breasts, worshipping me, loving me, as ecstasy shot to my core with every movement. Kissing his way down the valley of my cleavage, his fingers caressed one breast, kneading, exploring, while his lips moved to my other breast. His tongue teased around my nipple, making me throb with want.

Arching my back, I needed more. "Alex..." I murmured, hoping he could sense my desire.

Those eyes met mine as he lifted a finger to his mouth, licking it before gently grazing my nipple, making me wild. Leaning back down, he breathed warm air over my breasts, one at a time, my skin responding instantly with goosebumps.

"What do you like?" Alex asked, his voice husky.

"Ev-everything you're doing."

His low chuckle greeted my ears as he lowered his head once more, raining kisses on my chest, still not giving me what I needed the most.

Writhing beneath him, I tried again. "Alex, *please*."

And he didn't disappoint. His tongue flicked my nipple, his heated gaze on my face as his mouth finally latched around me, sucking, white-hot electricity shooting down my spine.

"Ohhh," I moaned, slightly embarrassed at how loud I was.

I squirmed in pleasure as he lavished attention on my breasts, taking his sweet time, building up my anticipation into a feverish peak. While his lips and tongue hypnotized me, his hands drifted down to my hips, slowly moving my underwear down my legs.

He raised his head to look at my lower body as I froze, waiting to see his reaction.

"God, these curves. You have curves for days," he said. "I've thought about these curves so many times. You don't even know."

His words left me absolutely breathless.

Once again, his mouth returned to my body while he kissed a path down my stomach toward my thighs. Squeezing my legs closer together, I worried about where his mouth might go next. I had never felt one-hundred percent comfortable with *that* and could never quite get over my self-consciousness.

Alex worked his way down one leg and started kissing a trail up the other, leaving me trembling with the way his lips felt against my sensitive skin. When he reached my hips, he looked up at me, those eyes searing into me, his hands placing slight pressure on my knees.

"Jayda, please. Let me taste you."

I didn't know what it was. Maybe it was the wine, maybe it was this man, but I felt myself relax at those hot words coming from him, and my legs fell open as he blatantly stared at me for a long moment, a lusty sound vibrating from the back of his throat.

Something about it all made me a quivering mess. But that was nothing compared to the feeling that swept through me as he moved even closer to the center of my heat, his stubble grazing along my inner thigh.

My hips bucked as his lips made contact with me, kissing me softly. But when he used his tongue to lick me, I thought I might pass out.

"You taste like heaven," he murmured against me.

Those words... this man. My brain wouldn't even work anymore as pure pleasure took over everything else.

His tongue plundered my depths, hitting me like a lightning bolt before finding my most sensitive spot. And then, wow... just wow... he feasted on me, the combination of tongue, lips, and sucking nearly sending me to the ceiling.

Was this what I'd been missing? Something told me it was Alex. Just Alex.

As he continued his sensual assault, the fierce fire inside me built, and I knew I was close. I wanted to touch him. I *needed* to touch him. Both my hands reached down to grab his hair as I arched my back, pushing my hips even further toward his mouth.

I couldn't get enough of this man. And maybe

he felt the same because his grip on my bare flesh only intensified while his tongue stroked me relentlessly, sending me into pure oblivion.

"Alex... Alex, I..."

"Let go, sweetheart," Alex said, the vibration of his words completely sending me over the edge. I floated off the bed as wave after blissful wave crashed through me, and I hung on for dear life, in awe at what Alex did to me.

After the last wave had crested, I finally opened my eyes to see Alex kneeling and staring at my face. Before I could even begin to be embarrassed, he said, "That was so damn hot."

I smiled at the amazing man before me. Somehow he knew all the right words to say to me, to make me at ease, to make me want him even more than I already did. It was almost like we were made for each... no, I couldn't say it. Couldn't even think it.

"Alex... that was..." I whispered, not able to complete my sentence.

But he didn't seem to mind my incoherence. His mouth returned to my stomach with lazy kisses and eventually my breasts again where he took his time with me. As the pleasure started to rise again, I let my hands explore him more.

Everything about him felt so good, from his hard chest to his arms flexing as he held his weight above me. I wanted to return the favor and I reached for his boxers, but again, his hand stopped me.

"If you touch me, I'll explode." He paused his kisses to grin at me. "It's like you've taken me back to being a teenager again."

I smiled back at him. "Oh, whoops. Sorry about that."

"Believe me, there's nothing to be sorry about," he said, returning to his kisses.

But I wanted more. Now. All those daydreams from so long ago... they haunted me, and I finally had the chance to make them come true. And I couldn't wait any longer.

"Alex, wait... I..."

That caught his attention, and he looked up at me. "You want me to stop?"

"Yes. No."

His brows narrowed in confusion. "I'll stop any time you want. You've already made me the happiest man alive."

Oh, my heart. Could he possibly be any sweeter?

"No. No. I don't want that." I paused, my heart suddenly pounding, the liquid courage from earlier slowly ebbing away.

"Don't want what?" Now he really looked bewildered.

I sat up so I could see him better, and I finally said the words that I wanted to say. "I want to feel you inside me."

His face... wow, his face looked like he might shatter. "Are you sure?" he said, his usually confident voice a little shaky.

"Yes. Please. Like now."

That blaze in his eyes scorched me for a long moment until he moved off the bed and started looking around.

"What are you doing?" I asked.

"Looking for my pants, my wallet, for protection."

I stopped him, though. "Wait, Alex, I'm on the pill." He paused to stare at me, and I continued, "And I don't have any ST—"

"Me neither," he interrupted, coming toward me with such a fierce look on his face that I couldn't draw a breath.

And then I really had trouble breathing as his lips closed in on mine in a red-hot kiss, like everything before had just been practice. The sizzling passion between us was almost overwhelming.

He paused to look into my eyes. "Say it again, sweet Jayda."

"Hmm?" I asked, confused.

"You know, what you said earlier."

My muddled brain had trouble processing his request. Was he talking about being on the pill? But then I realized what he wanted to hear, and I smiled. "What?"

He growled and tickled my stomach. "You know damn well what I want to hear, you little seductress."

Between the tickles and his use of the word seductress, I couldn't stop giggling. That was so not the word to describe me.

I struggled to get away from him as we both rolled around laughing, our bodies tangled together. His hands were soon replaced by his mouth, tongue, and teeth nipping at me. And I ended up on top of him, straddling him, only the thin fabric of his boxers separating us.

Our smiles faded as the room somehow felt overheated all the sudden. Or maybe it was just me. Or maybe it was the intimacy of the position. Feeling a bit like the seductress he'd accused me of being, I wanted those boxers off. I wanted to see *all* of him.

With shaky hands, I looked up at him and started to slowly remove his boxers. His stormy eyes blazed into mine. And I returned to staring at the sight in front of me as I pulled his boxers off completely.

Sweet mercy. This man.

My heart sped up at the thought of him, *every inch of him*, inside me. Kneeling down, I kissed my way up his hard length, relishing the taste and feel of him, his loud groan encouraging me. Savoring every moment, every sensation, I began to lick him while taking him into my hand, leisurely exploring him, his sounds telling me just how much he loved it, how much he wanted it.

"Jayda, please..."

"Hmm?" I hummed.

"Please stop torturing me."

I smiled as I crawled up over him, returning to my previous position, only this time with nothing separating us. Completely overcome with desire, I straddled his hips, beginning to rub myself against him, the electric sensation making me cry out. Not able to wait any longer, I decided to whisper those words he wanted to hear again.

"I want to feel you inside me," I said, staring into his eyes.

His body started to tremble along with mine as I guided him to my entrance, gradually settling down on him, feeling inch after blissful inch glide into me as we became one. When he was finally fully inside, he pushed his hips against me, and I gasped at the fullness, adjusting to his size.

We stared at each other, not moving for a long second, my mind whirling with the fever that was all Alex, all hot-blooded passion for this man filling me.

Letting out a shaky breath, I started to move, slowly at first, and Alex's eyes closed as his chest heaved up and down. I didn't know what was hotter, the look of sweet agony on his face or the way he suddenly grabbed my hands like he was holding on to a life raft.

In my mind, I couldn't believe this was happening. Alex, the boy I had crushed on for so long who had become *this man*, was inside me right now, making love to me with such sweetness and care I could never have imagined.

"Oh, God, Jayda, you are..." Alex said softly.

I leaned down to kiss him, increasing the pressure, increasing the pace, his hips meeting mine with every movement.

His hands moved to my breasts, caressing me, cupping me, then moved the length of my body, leaving behind fire wherever he touched. He sat up and held onto me, his arms clasping around me as we rocked our bodies together, swiveling our hips in a scorching hot rhythm, faster and then even faster as a raging wildfire built between us.

My breath hitched as I felt it—the tidal wave that was about to crash over me.

"Alex..." I whispered, not even sure what I was trying to say.

"Look at me," he said, his face so close to mine. I forced my eyes open. "Come with me."

Those words... those words and the raw emotion I could see in his eyes catapulted me off the cliff, making me lose all control.

He let out a shout, spilling his seed deep inside me as my body clenched around him, milking him. We clung to each other as, together, we rode the never-ending euphoria that rushed through our bodies.

Our steamy explosion seemed to last forever... with an absolutely gut-wrenching intensity that I'd never felt before. Finally, *finally*, the waves began to subside, and I still held on, shocked at what had just happened between us, stunned at how this man had made me feel.

I felt the moisture gather behind my eyes as my emotions overwhelmed me. And of course, I couldn't hide it from Alex whose face was only inches away.

He wiped a tear with his thumb. "Are you okay?" he asked, his eyes filled with concern.

I nodded, afraid to speak.

He kissed away a few more tears, then met my mouth with his, gently, sweetly, and I could taste the salt on his lips.

Pausing to tuck a strand of hair behind my ear, he then lifted me off of him, pulling me up close until we were lying down, my head snuggled into the cozy spot between his arm and chest.

As we cuddled together, his hands caressing me softly, he asked, "Why the tears, sweetheart?"

I sniffled, trying to get it under control, especially because I didn't really know why. No reason really. Or a million reasons. Extreme pleasure. Amazement. Elation.

But absolutely topping the list? Guilt.

A heart-wrenching guilt that I had somehow betrayed Blake. Not that I thought I had done anything wrong. He was dead. Gone from this world. My brain knew I hadn't cheated. My mind knew that I'd done nothing wrong. I'd never betrayed our marriage vows, and I had wholly honored "till death do us part."

But deep down in my heart, in my soul, I felt

awful. Because I couldn't help but compare Alex to everyone from my past, most especially Blake, since the guys before Blake were a little fuzzy at this point.

And what had just happened was beyond... well, beyond anything ever before. Like soul-shattering beyond anything.

Alex squeezed my arm and pulled me in closer. "Jayda? You're kind of freaking me out here."

"Sorry. Sorry. It's just... I'm going to be honest." I hated stupid misunderstandings just because people wouldn't have a potentially difficult conversation.

"What is it?" he asked.

I raised up my head to look at him. "I'm feeling a little guilty."

His eyebrows shot up. "Guilty? Why?"

Sighing, I wondered how to explain it. "I don't know. I guess I'm feeling kind of bad about my late husband," I whispered.

Alex stared at me for a long moment, then finally said, "God, Jayda, you're so damn sweet. That tender heart of yours has somehow managed to stay so kind. Always thinking about others and not yourself. Still."

I smiled at his unexpected response and his thought process. Of course, he didn't really get it. And I wasn't sure I had it in me to thoroughly explain it all as exhaustion crept up my limbs, my body completely sated.

**

Sometime in the night, I woke up to a fully dressed Alex kissing me lightly on my forehead. "I've got to go," he said as he handed me my phone. "You should set an alarm."

Shocked and confused that he was actually leaving, I couldn't find any words to say. So I just took my phone from him and set the clock for six-thirty.

He kissed my cheek. "Go back to sleep. Sorry for waking you up."

And with that, he headed for the door. I lay back down and pretended to close my eyes, wondering if he'd look back at me.

But he didn't.

He just quietly shut the door behind him as he left—leaving me stunned and feeling very much alone.

CHAPTER SEVEN

Jayda

Hours later, freshly showered with several cups of coffee in me, I met Kaileen downstairs in front of the conference room.

"Well?" she asked, her face lit up like it was Christmas. "What happened? Did you *do it*?"

I could always count on my best friend to make me laugh. "Yes. Yes, I did."

Her jaw dropped, and she smacked me on the arm. "Jayda Jenkins! I'm so proud of you for getting some!"

"Shh," I whispered. "We don't have to tell the whole writers' conference about my one-night stand."

Kaileen laughed. "So? How was it?"

"There are no words," I said as dramatically as possible.

She clutched at her heart. "Oh, my good

Lord..."

I wandered away into the conference room because I didn't really want to talk about it, and I certainly didn't want to reveal that he hadn't even spent the night.

Besides, in the shower that morning as I had washed him away, I'd decided to not let that bother me. I would take it for what it was—one amazing night with my high school crush that I would cherish forever along with all the other monumental memories of my life so far.

I was beyond grateful that the day ended up being crazy busy and I didn't have a minute to myself. People even talked to me in the bathroom, which was kind of annoying but also funny. I mean, these writers treated me like I was a celebrity, a boost to the ego for sure.

My emotions were literally all over, from elation to pure misery, and I wondered how just one night could so completely affect me like that. Every second replayed in my head all day long as I chatted with people about their writing.

Finally, the day was over, and I looked forward to a quiet dinner with Kaileen where I could unwind and then a video chat with my darling daughter before she went to bed.

The huge room had mostly emptied out, and Kaileen was by my side as we entered the hallway. I looked up, and my heart stopped because just outside the conference room, leaning against the wall and looking sexy as all get-out, was Alex.

"Whew," Kaileen whispered next to me, echoing my thoughts. "He is so fine."

Yeah, he was. Just like something I'd write in my books, he seriously gave me butterflies deep down in my belly, especially as flashes from last night whipped through my mind—the feel of his lips on my skin, his head between my thighs, his body entering mine.

Shut up, brain, before I mounted him right here in the hallway.

"Hey," he said in that deep voice that vibrated right through me. "Sorry for stalking you. I would have called, but I still don't have your number."

"Okay, that's it," Kaileen said in her mom voice. "Take out your phones right now and exchange numbers."

We both laughed at Kaileen, but we did as she said and didn't argue.

"So," Alex said when we were done, "what are you ladies doing for dinner?"

I glanced at Kaileen. "Well, I think we're just going to grab a—"

"Actually, I have a client to meet," Kaileen interrupted. "So you're on your own, hon."

I rolled my eyes at her. "Okay."

"Good. You're free," Alex said, a twinkle in his eye. "Would you have dinner with me?"

Feeling my cheeks burn, I said, "Sure. I'd love to."

"Okay," Kaileen said. "Now that we've got that settled, I'm going to head out. Enjoy your dinner."

She waved as she sashayed away in her own unique style.

Shaking my head, I met Alex's eyes. "She's not very subtle, is she?"

"As subtle as a sledgehammer." He laughed while reaching for my hands and pulling me closer to him. "I thought about you *all day long*."

My heart skipped a beat at those words from him. "Same," I managed to say.

Drawing me up against him so our bodies were flush together, he said, "Last night was the most incredible night of my life... by far."

My heart fluttered in my chest, and I took a shaky breath. It was hard to believe he really meant that, especially because I knew he'd been such a player and had been with some super hot girls.

He lifted my chin with his finger and stared into my eyes. "I really mean that, Jayda."

Something about the sincere look on his face made me believe him. And now, those flutters took over my whole body. I wanted to say the same thing back, but I couldn't. It just felt... wrong. So instead, I wrapped my arms around his huge chest and inhaled his own unique scent of sun and heat. *Alex*.

His arms came around me too as he kissed the top of my head. I could feel the steady beat of his heart against my face, and I thought back to the one and only time we had hugged in high school.

Graduation night. I remembered it like it was yesterday. On the football field, after we had all thrown our caps in the air, there'd been a feeling of jubilation that swept through us amongst the cheers from friends and families in the bleachers.

Alex had been sitting near me because our last names were close alphabetically. And between hugs from other friends, suddenly he was in front of me, arms outstretched. And believe me, I didn't hesitate to hug him back.

I still remembered how strong he felt, the amazing way he smelled, the feel of his arms around me. The feeling had been unbelievable. Just like now. Only this was here... in the present. But I wondered, for how long? Would I ever see him or speak to him again after I left tomorrow when the conference was over?

A noise behind us startled me as a few stragglers entered the hallway. I pulled away from his warmth and looked up at him, the tenderness in his eyes making me speechless.

"So," he said, "do you want to go to my place for dinner and relieve my mom from babysitting duties? Maybe get some takeout?"

Wait, what? "You want me to meet your daughter?"

"If that's okay with you."

I smiled. "I'd love that."

And the smile he gave me back melted my soul.

***

The drive to his house didn't take long, and I took delight in teasing Alex about his car.

"You know, as a dad, you should really consider getting something a little more practical."

He narrowed his eyes at me right before he rounded a tight corner. "Hey, my car is *very* practical. It's very safe too. I looked into it when Gabby was born."

I laughed and pointed to the back with its small car seat. "Not too long and you'll need a bigger one. And eventually, she'll have to face forward, and despite those little legs, she'll somehow manage to kick you in the back *repeatedly* as you're driving."

He groaned. "I was kind of hoping things would get easier as she got older."

I couldn't hold in my laughter. "Nope. And from what my friends say, it only gets more and more complicated."

"God help me," he said while pulling up to an attractive house shaded by towering palm trees.

"Nice house," I said, amazed at the difference between his Florida home and mine in Maine.

"Thanks," he said, sighing, as he turned off the car. "Bought it right after my ex Fiona and I got married. To be honest, I'd like to sell it. It's just never really, uh, never really been me."

"I get that." And I truly did. I knew firsthand how hard it was to live with memories.

As we walked up the front path, I felt a flicker of nerves at meeting Alex's mom and daughter for the first time.

Alex took my hand in his and gave me a reassuring squeeze. "I'm excited for you to meet Gabby," he said, opening the front door wide to reveal a lightly furnished living room with a bunch of toys littering the floor.

An adorable little dark-haired beauty came rushing over on her knees, not quite crawling, not quite walking. "Dadadada," she said.

Oh, boy, she was super cute.

Alex hoisted her up, and I felt a tug in my chest at the sight of this man holding his child. A woman who was clearly Alex's mom smiled at me and walked over, hand extended.

"I'm Lisa," she said as we shook hands. "You must be Jayda."

"Wonderful to meet you," I said.

"You too."

We were distracted by laughter as Alex tossed Gabby in the air and caught her over and over. Her shrieks mingled with her giggles, making one of the sweetest sounds in the world. Turning toward us, my breath caught at the light I saw in Alex's eyes, a jolt of electricity shooting between us. Carrying his girl, he started to walk my way, and Gabby held out her hands to me like she wanted me to hold her.

Alex's mom let out a gasp, and I glanced at her as she covered her mouth. "Sorry," she said. "Just Gabby doesn't really do that to anyone."

That made my heart melt, but it was nothing like when she reached out and I pulled her tiny body into my arms. It felt so amazing to hold a little one again. Audrey was getting too heavy to carry, and I missed that feeling so much.

"Hi," I said, whirling around with her as she flashed me smiles. "Ooh, look at those two little teeth you have."

She giggled and held out a chubby finger to my cheek while studying my face. It always struck me how babies could stare at you and seem to figure out your very soul.

As I cooed and danced with this sweet girl who hadn't yet grown into her sass, I felt two sets of very intense eyes on me and glanced up to see both Alex and his mother watching us.

"She's just adorable," I said. Neither one said anything... which was kind of strange. So I returned my attention to Gabby and started chatting with her. Poking her cute stomach, I asked, "What's this? Is that your belly?" I did the same to her arms and legs and tiny toes.

She giggled and giggled and looked at Alex. I started to hand her over, thinking she wanted to go back to him, but she clung onto me and didn't let go.

Lisa cleared her throat. "Well, I guess Gabby likes you," she said, her voice a bit strained.

I touched her button nose. "I like you too."

They were silent a moment longer, then Lisa said, "I'd love to stay and chat and get to know you better, Jayda, but I have dinner plans tonight and need to get going."

"That's too bad, but I understand."

I tried to hand off Gabby to her grandmother to say goodbye, but she wouldn't budge. Lisa just laughed and gave us a big group hug. Then she went over to Alex and embraced him too, whispering something in his ear that I tried in vain to hear.

She grabbed a nearby bag and headed for the door. "Nana loves you," she said, waving at Gabby.

I helped Gabby wave back, and then Lisa was gone.

Turning to Alex, I said, "Well, your mom seems really nice."

He nodded, and I couldn't read the expression in his eyes. I realized he hadn't spoken a word to me since we'd entered his house.

"Are you all right, Alex?"

He let out a deep breath and nodded again. "I'm fine. Really."

I gave him a funny look but didn't say anything. Still carrying Gabby, I started to walk around the living room, asking her about all the toys and stuffed animals. "What's this?" I pointed to some stackable rings.

Eventually, we ended up playing on the floor,

Alex soon sitting down on the messy couch watching us again.

"She's super sweet... and happy," I told him. "It's clear you've done an amazing job."

I glanced up at him to see his jaw clamped down hard like he was fighting some sort of powerful emotion.

Finally, he answered, "I appreciate that."

We played for a while with Alex joining in until my phone buzzed and I saw it was my own little cutie pie calling me.

"Hi, Mama," Audrey said, her tablet displaying a view of the ceiling.

I showed her Gabby who seemed fascinated at first by the energetic little girl bouncing around, but then she just wanted to eat my phone. We didn't talk long because Audrey suddenly had to go "winkle." But it was wonderful to see her beautiful face and hear her happy voice.

After I hung up, or rather she hung up because she loved pressing the red button, I turned to Alex. "So glad we got to meet each other's little girls."

His smile warmed me completely. "Me too."

Suddenly, my stomach made a loud rumbling noise, and I laughed with embarrassment.

Alex closed his eyes and shook his head. "Jayda, I'm so sorry. I'm the worst host ever. I invite you to dinner and then forget to feed you. Or even offer you a drink."

"Ah, don't worry about it. Sometimes I forget

to feed myself."

He jumped up, heading to the kitchen at the other end of the big room while I kept playing with Gabby. In a moment, he returned and handed me a glass of ice water.

"Thank you," I said.

"The least I can do." He rolled his eyes at himself as he whipped out his phone. "What do you feel like? Pizza? Chinese? Any old favorites?"

That jogged my memory. "You know what I'd love? Frankie's Pizza."

Alex cracked up. "Of course. I bet it's been a long time. What kind?"

"Just cheese would be amazing."

A few minutes later, after he ordered the pizza, Gabby started to get fussy. "Man, I'm really on a roll tonight. Forgot to feed my kid too. Dad of the year here."

I laughed as I picked Gabby up and followed Alex to the kitchen. "Well, I'm sure I'm totally disrupting your usual routine."

He turned to look at me. "Um, yeah, our routine," he said, grinning.

While I distracted Gabby as best as I could, Alex made some mac and cheese with peas, our pizza arriving right when he finished cooking. Since Gabby didn't want to eat in her high chair or go to Alex, I sat at the table with her balanced on my knee as I bit into a crispy square slice.

"I bet that brings back a few memories," Alex said while pouring me a glass of red wine.

"Oh, definitely. I can't even tell you how many times we grabbed a pizza and then went to the beach to eat it."

"Same here. Frankie's is legendary."

"I'm glad it's still here."

Alex watched as I helped Gabby with a spoonful of her dinner. "Thanks for doing that. She really likes you."

"Aw, she's sweet. And I don't mind. It's nice to have a little one in my lap again."

His eyes were bright with emotion, and we didn't say anything for a bit as we all ate. The coziness and the warmness of the scene seeped into my soul as I realized this was how it *could* be, how it actually *was* for some people. A partner to share all the moments with—good and bad.

I'd certainly had that... for years. But not in a long while. My heart began to ache at what I was missing, the loneliness of going it alone for the last four years.

Watching Alex take a sip of his wine, I dared to imagine the possibilities of this man sitting at our kitchen table every evening, this man to talk to at the end of the day and snuggle with all night.

I sighed quietly to myself because I just shouldn't go there since that would never happen. And even if it did by some miracle, I could never let it happen. Not after making that vow to Blake.

"Hey," Alex said, interrupting my spiraling

thoughts. "I keep meaning to apologize to you about leaving last night."

It took me a second to recover from my painful thoughts and figure out what he meant. "Oh, you don't need to apologize."

"Yes, I do. So Gabby spent the night at my parents and I just—I just feel terrible if she wakes them up in the middle of the night, you know?"

With that explanation, my heart suddenly felt much lighter. "I totally get that."

We shared a smile, our eyes connecting as those butterflies made a reappearance. This emotional roller coaster was unbelievable— utterly depressing thoughts a minute ago to pure joy just from his smile.

Gabby began making some very unhappy noises, and Alex picked her up from my lap.

"I think I'd better get you ready for bed." He glanced at me with regret. "Sorry. I'll be right back. Please make yourself comfortable. Maybe after she's asleep, we can watch a movie or something... if you're up for that."

I nodded. "Yeah. That sounds nice."

My pulse sped up at the idea of cuddling up on the couch with Alex and the possibility of what else it might lead to.

Slow down, Jayda.

Taking a deep breath, I studied the living room, looking around for clues as to how he lived. There were a few pieces of art on the walls, but they were sparse. And the way they were arranged was kind of odd, like something was missing.

I stepped closer to one and, yeah, judging by a nail hole in the wall, it looked like there had been something right next to it. Walking around, I noticed even more little holes in the walls. It seemed like his ex had taken her stuff with her, and Alex hadn't even bothered to redecorate. He'd probably meant it when he said he wasn't really into this place.

Alex soon returned with Gabby, who looked so stinking cute in her little unicorn onesie.

"I tried to get her to lie down, but it might be one of those nights where I have to rock her to sleep." He lifted one shoulder in a shrug. "She's just too wound up."

"Oops, my fault probably."

"Nah," Alex said as he sat in the chair. But Gabby had other ideas as she held her tiny hands out to me and started to fuss. "No, no. We can't ask the guest to rock you."

I laughed at his silly tone. "I don't mind. Really. It's been a long time. Audrey outgrew it soon after her first birthday, and I used to love it."

His eyebrows shot up. "Are you sure?"

"Absolutely." I nodded as Gabby fussed some more and started to struggle.

"It's a lot of work some nights," Alex warned.

"Challenge accepted."

Alex's grin was contagious. "Okay. Let's see how you do, Jayda Jenkins. My record is nine minutes." He handed a very annoyed Gabby to me. "Good luck."

She began to calm down the minute I started rocking her in the super plush chair. Watching us, Alex settled in across from me on the couch, a soft smile on his face.

"So do you sing to her or anything?" I asked as she played with my hair, not seeming the least bit tired.

"Sometimes. Just kind of depends."

I narrowed my eyes at him. "So you're not going to help me, huh?"

"You're on your own," he said, that teasing light in his eyes again.

"Thanks. You're a big help." I rolled my eyes at him, but he just grinned back.

A song or two would definitely help this very awake child, but I felt shy about singing in front of Alex. After a while, though, of a fidgety Gabby squirming and fighting sleep, I started to hum. With no luck on that front, the humming eventually turned into singing quietly. I remembered some of my made-up lullabies, and that seemed to do the trick of calming her down at least.

But those little eyes were determined to stay open, so I just kept on rocking and singing. Rocking and singing. And as I rocked and her tiny trusting body began to relax in my arms, I felt a pull, a longing, in my chest and realized between this man and this little darling, I was in deep, deep trouble.

CHAPTER EIGHT

Jayda

My own eyes started to get heavy, but I fought it and kept on rocking. Nine minutes had passed long ago. I looked up to see Alex still intently watching us, that fire blazing in his eyes, and I wondered what he was thinking.

But I didn't dare speak because Gabby's body started to have that heavy feel like she was finally letting go and welcoming sleep. I glanced down at that beautiful little face and noticed how similar she was to Alex with that same dark hair and eyes. It also made me wonder what his ex-wife looked like.

Soon, Gabby completely zonked out, and Alex rose up from the couch to gently take her from me. "Nice job," he whispered.

I smiled without saying anything because I didn't want to chance waking her up. Once they had left the room, I went to the kitchen and carefully filled up my wine glass, suddenly feeling anxious about being all alone with the big bad wolf. I giggled at my stupid little joke, definitely showing my nerves.

"What's so funny?" Alex asked as he entered the kitchen.

Oh, boy, how ridiculous was I? "Um, nothing really. I guess I didn't break your record, did I?"

"Not even close," he teased. "But seriously, that was... well, that was nice to watch."

His sexy smile sent me right to the couch to drink more wine so I could handle the heat Alex was throwing my way. He soon followed with his own glass and settled down at the other end of the toy-covered couch, facing me.

"So," he said, "I finished your book today."

"Y-you what?" I sputtered, nearly spitting out my drink.

He smiled with amusement. "I told you I was going to read your book."

I held my breath waiting to see what he'd say. For some reason, it felt so personal to have him read it. Complete strangers, no problem. But this man here, it felt like my soul had been spliced open to him.

"And..." he drawled, clearly finding enjoyment in torturing me. "It was incredible."

Finally releasing that breath, I had to wonder if he was just saying that because, of course, he would say that. Didn't he kind of have to?

"Really. I mean that," he said. "It's not my usual genre—" My laughing interrupted him. "But I loved it."

I felt my eyebrows shoot up into my forehead. "You did not."

He looked offended. "I did too, Jayda. I couldn't put it down. The mystery of it is what really got me and wanting to know what's going to happen and how on earth she's going to get out of this mess."

I actually started to believe him that he had enjoyed my teen paranormal romance.

"And I have to admit that I'm a little bit mad at you," he continued, those kissable lips in a pout.

"You are? Why?"

"For ending it on a cliffhanger. Please tell me you don't do that with all of them."

I laughed because he sounded exactly like some of my readers who sent me love/hate emails. "Um…"

"You do! Damn it!" He tossed a teddy bear at me.

"Guilty?" I cringed. "Please don't hate on me."

"Never, sweetheart. Never."

That word sweetheart coming from those tasty lips. Oy. Swallowing hard, I fought the urge to pounce on him. "So I'm sure you just loved the angsty teen romance aspect."

He leaned forward. "I live for that."

I threw the teddy bear back at him as we laughed together.

"So how did you get into writing anyway?" he asked.

"Well, I have you to thank in some ways." Oh, no. Why did I just admit that?

His eyes narrowed in confusion. "How so?"

"I, um..." I took another sip of wine as he moved closer.

"Okay. Now you *have* to tell me."

My heart pounding, I gulped more wine, looking down at the pile of stuffed animals between us. "Well, I, um, I used to have epic daydreams about you that were kind of like novellas."

He was silent, and I dared to look up, my cheeks flushed.

A grin lit up his face. "So glad I could help."

I launched a stuffed unicorn at him that he easily caught. "You can't take all the credit, though."

He lightly tossed the unicorn back at me. "Fair enough. I'll just be *part* of your origins story."

That elicited a much-deserved eye roll from me. "Right. Okay. Moving on. So I started creating stories in my head sometime in high school, and then I majored in English Lit in college which is kind of useless in real life. But anyway, Blake went on to law school, and I was able to get an MFA in creative writing."

His eyes widened. "Wow, that's really impressive."

"Not really. But I loved it. And that's where it

started."

"Wait." He frowned. "I thought it started with me."

This time it was a poor stuffed lion that I chucked through the air at him. "You're incorrigible."

"Ooh, the bestselling author throwing out the big words at me."

My cheeks were starting to hurt from all the laughing. "Don't even get me started, Doctor Hernandez."

"I should know better than to mess with the woman who created the kick-ass heroine of Chassidy Rising," he teased, that light shining in his eyes.

I shook my head at him. "That's for sure. I know some moves."

"I bet you do." His suggestive tone wasn't lost on me. "So how did you come up with the idea anyway?"

"It wasn't easy actually," I admitted. "I had to work at what kind of story I wanted to tell. But I've always liked the genre and just really wanted it to be about female empowerment for young girls, first and foremost, and everything else is secondary."

"I totally get that," he said, nodding.

"And fortunately, Blake was able to support us while I struggled with trying to write the first book."

His eyes softened. "That's really great that you

had that."

"It was." I didn't know if it was weird to talk about my late husband with this man I had just slept with last night. But it kind of slipped out anyway. "And he always encouraged me, even though I so often felt like it was such a waste of time and why was I even bothering to write it. But he patiently read through it all and gave me a million pep talks."

Alex watched me for a long moment. "You really miss him, don't you?"

I nodded, my eyes watering at the tenderness in his voice. "He was my best friend."

Oh, boy, was I really going to cry about Blake in front of Alex? And then he was right next to me, wrapping his arms around me, pulling me in close to him.

"Sorry," I said, my voice muffled against his shoulder.

"Don't be sorry."

His arms squeezed me in tighter, and I tried to breathe through the tangle of emotions I was feeling, something I'd been doing for years. As he held me close, I thought of those early days right after Blake had died when I was a tortured mess of hormones and grief and how I had cried pretty much all day every day.

Thankfully, those times had eventually passed, and the pure agony had gradually lessened to a dull ache. But the tears still bombarded me at the strangest times, like a certain familiar look from Audrey, a song at the grocery store, or sympathetic words like Alex had just offered.

My own arms went around him as I sought comfort from his big solid body that felt so strong, so healthy, like he was indestructible. And I selfishly started to crave that closeness, that intimacy, with him.

Slowly, I lifted my head and dared to glance at him, unsure of what I'd see. But when our eyes met, he seemed to look into my very soul with such sweetness and compassion that the tears threatened to come back.

But instead of giving in to the sadness, I leaned forward, determined to show this man in front of me how grateful I was for his thoughtfulness. I brushed my lips against his almost in an invitation, and his low groan was my answer. For a moment, our mouths moved together slowly as I savored the taste of him, the wine on his lips.

His tongue traced my lower lip, and his hands moved to my cheeks, drawing me nearer. Our kiss turned into something different, something fierce and fiery. He hauled me onto his lap, and the angle was even better as our kisses became more heated and carnal. My head was spinning at what this man was capable of, how he made me feel, how he made me abandon all other thoughts.

Leaning his forehead against mine, Alex paused, his breathing heavy. "God, what you do to me."

I closed my eyes at his words, almost the exact thing I had been thinking. He leaned back, and I opened my eyes to see him staring at me.

"What?" I asked, suddenly feeling self-conscious.

"Just thinking how beautiful you are, how sweet you were with my daughter, how much I... how much I want you."

That ache in my chest spread throughout my body as the need for him became something alive. "I want you too."

Those words set off a firestorm as his mouth returned to blazing kisses and his hands explored my body. He stood up with me in his arms and slowly carried me down the hall, holding me against his strong chest, kissing my cheeks, my forehead, and then my lips again. I could feel his heart pound along with mine in anticipation.

We entered his bedroom, where he gently let go of my legs and pulled my body flush with his. I stood on my tiptoes as my arms reached around his neck, my hands in his hair drawing him closer, wanting more, wanting all of this man.

He nibbled on my lip, sending shockwaves down my body while his hands worked the buttons on my shirt, his fingers brushing against my bare skin adding to my trembling.

A muffled noise from down the hall made us pause, looking at each other, frozen and waiting to see what would happen.

"Dadadada?" Gabby called out.

Alex sighed the sigh of a very frustrated man. "Sorry."

I shook my head. "Don't even worry about it. I've so been there."

More noises came from Gabby's room, and Alex looked uncomfortable, dragging his hand through his hair. I wondered whether to leave, suddenly feeling kind of awkward and in the way.

I reached for my cell in my back pocket. "Maybe I should get going."

"Please don't go," Alex said, his deep voice vibrating through my body.

While I debated what to do, Gabby's fussing grew louder.

"Will you wait for me?" he asked, his eyes pleading.

The sensual promise in his voice was impossible to resist. "Sure."

He let out a sigh and kissed me softly on the lips. "Thank you." Pointing to the closet, he said, "Feel free to grab a t-shirt or something more comfortable."

I nodded as he rushed off to help a very loud Gabby. Still feeling a little strange, I opened the closet and saw a bunch of nice shirts hanging up but no comfy t-shirts. Next, I noticed some drawers and tried opening those. Lots of boxers thrown in there and... was that a pair covered with Santas? I stifled a giggle.

With the next drawer, I hit the jackpot—tons of casual shirts. I pulled out a worn Dolphins t-shirt and slipped it on, debating whether to take off my bra or not. Still undecided, I sat on his bed and noticed a small video baby monitor similar to the one I had. I flipped it on and smiled at the sight of Alex walking around holding Gabby, singing something in a slightly off-key voice.

Watching him and listening to him, my heart swelled with a million emotions. I couldn't help but think back to all those sleepless nights when Audrey had been an infant waking me up to nurse. I had been such a zombie from lack of sleep and the crushing loss of Blake.

Those days were a blur of pain, exhaustion, and longing to share those nights with my husband, to have some kind of help and support with a newborn. I realized Alex had probably felt the same way, and I wondered exactly when his wife had left him. Hadn't he said very soon after Gabby was born?

I felt a surge of empathy with him that we had both experienced something so similar. And I imagined him alone in the kitchen in the middle of the night, heating up a bottle of milk, feeling that same bone-weary tiredness and loneliness.

Holding the monitor in my hand, the minutes ticked by, and Gabby was still very much awake. My own eyes grew heavy as I wondered how long it might take, remembering some of those three-hour, middle-of-the-night sessions I'd endured with Audrey, trying to get her back to sleep.

If that was the case, maybe I should sleep here after all. I certainly didn't want to take off and disappear without telling him. Finally deciding to remove the bra and stripping down to just the t-shirt and my underwear, I set the alarm on my phone then slid under Alex's soft sheets.

As I rested my head on one of his comfy pillows, I could hardly believe where I was—in Alex's bed! How many times had I thought about this very thing? Maybe not with him helping his daughter get to sleep down the hall. But still!

Burying my head in one of his pillows, I breathed in his masculine scent that surrounded me and seeped into my soul. *Alex.* I brought the sheets up higher and clutched them around me, closing my eyes, imagining it was him.

I must have eventually drifted off because, sometime later, I half-awoke to a warm arm around my stomach and a hot, hard body pressed right up behind me.

CHAPTER NINE

Jayda

My heart hammered against my chest, and now I was fully awake, fully aware of Alex cuddled up next to me, spooning me, just like I absolutely loved. I couldn't believe how amazingly well we fit together, his tall body perfectly outlining mine.

Was he awake? His slow, steady breathing told me he was asleep, and I wondered how long he'd been there.

I snuggled even closer, trying to memorize the feel of him, his strong arm tight against me just under my breasts, squeezing me into his powerful chest. The feel of his breath tickling the back of my neck, making my hair flutter with each exhale. The feel of his muscular legs tucked up under mine.

Not able to help it, I did the thing I really wanted to do. I nestled my bottom closer to him, wanting to feel him up against me. And that's what did it. I felt him stir, felt his arm pull me in even more, his head moving against my hair with a deep breath against my neck that gave me instant chills.

"Sorry I woke you," I breathed out with barely a whisper in case he wasn't really awake.

"Don't be sorry," he whispered back. His face nuzzled in closer. "Sorry I took so long."

He planted a long, slow kiss on the back of my neck, and any words I wanted to say were lost to me as the sensations poured through me. Our bodies were flush together, my back into his front, as we both started to move, somehow getting even closer.

I reached around with one arm to feel him and realized he wore no shirt, just his boxers. He let out a breath as I touched him, his skin hot, almost like a fever raged in him.

His lips continued with open-mouth kisses on my neck, forging a scorching path upward, the roughness from his whiskers making every nerve ending crackle with electricity. When his mouth reached my ear, my heart began to pound. What was it about this man? He set off fireworks in me with his every touch, unlike anything I'd ever felt before.

He sucked my earlobe into his mouth, setting my core on fire. When he bit down, I let out a loud moan, quickly clamping my hand over my mouth. We both froze, waiting, listening for the space of several heartbeats. But nothing. No sounds from down the hall or from the video monitor that cast a slight glow over us.

"Your fault," I whispered, smiling.

And then he did it again, biting even harder, making me nearly cry out again. But this time, I was able to swallow back the sound.

"Oh, it's like that, huh?" I asked.

I laughed at the game he was playing and decided to play my own version. Since it was difficult to roll over with his heavy arm pinning me in place, I did the only thing I could think of—I pushed my ass all the way back so his hardness pressed right up against me. I started to move, increasing the friction, eliciting a heavy groan from him that made me giggle at the lusty noise in my ear.

"Oh, really? You think that's funny?" he whispered, his hot breath near my ear fanning the flames of my need.

His hand started to move, at first barely brushing against my stomach, then under the t-shirt, skimming my skin and moving upward. My breath hitched when he reached the sensitive skin just under my breasts. He paused, making me light-headed with anticipation. Then his big, warm hand grasped me fully, his thumb brushing against my hardened nipple, making me gasp. I arched into him, wanting more, needing more.

"The way you fill my hand makes me so *damn*

hot," he said against my neck.

He squeezed and caressed my breast, and then he moved on to the other side in a full-on sensual assault as his lips sucked that sensitive spot right below my ear and his body moved against mine. His hand moved lower and slipped under my panties to grasp the bare skin on my bottom, his hot grip branding me.

Oh, fuck me.

"If you say so," he breathed.

Oops, had I said that out loud?

I didn't even have time to think about it because overwhelming desire for this man pounded through every cell of my body, demanding release, demanding all of him. Reaching back, I felt for his boxers but he was already reading my mind and taking them off, so I shimmied out of my undies as well.

And then his body met mine again, this time bare skin on skin, his hardness pressing into me from behind. *Oh, God.* My whole body started to tremble as we rubbed against each other in a moment of fiery passion.

"Jayda," he said, his voice rumbling through my back. "You are so..."

He didn't finish his sentence as I reached for him and guided him into me, pleasure ricocheting from my center all the way to my fingers and toes. We both groaned as he pushed into me slowly, inch by inch, stretching me, filling me. And when our bodies were fully connected, we both paused a long moment, the only sound our heavy breathing.

"...hot," he finally said, his voice low and strained.

I needed to hold on to something to keep me from floating off into the stars, and I found his other hand under the pillow. We clasped our fingers together in a tight grip, grabbing onto each other.

With his free hand, he grasped my hips, hard, and we both began to move, the feel of him thrusting in and out of me almost too much to handle. I bit into the pillow, the sweet and pure pleasure pulsing through my veins, setting my whole body ablaze.

Alex buried his head in my neck, his breath coming out in gasps against my shoulder, his muscles tense and rigid. Our pace increased as the fire burned bright between us, our bodies sliding against each other.

"Alex..." I whispered, feeling close to release.

He reached down to touch me, stroking me into oblivion, as our hips moved together in a wild frenzy, pushing me over the edge into white-hot ecstasy as we both shattered apart and tasted heaven together. His groan in my ear matched mine while I smothered the sound in my pillow. His arm squeezed me tighter to him as we rode out every last bit of pleasure, overheated and breathless.

"God, woman," Alex mumbled.

I laughed into the plump pillow, elated at the passion we'd shared together.

This time, for some reason, I didn't feel that same awful guilt like before. Well, maybe some. Definitely some. But not the gut-wrenching, bring-tears-to-my-eyes kind. Maybe because I had accepted the fact that this weekend spent with Alex was a once-in-a-lifetime experience, and I would just go back to my regular life soon enough.

With Alex still inside me, his body nestled up tightly to mine, I let my eyes close.

CHAPTER TEN

Jayda

The second and last day of the writers' conference flew by in a whirlwind of busyness. Again, my night with Alex replayed in my head the whole time like some kind of erotic movie.

And whenever I stood up or sat down, my soreness reminded me of the multiple times we'd had sex during the night plus the hot, steamy quickie in the shower early in the morning before I had to leave.

On the airplane that evening, I squirmed in my seat, trying to get settled in. At least Kaileen and I had splurged for first class where the seats were wider and more plush. Finally, feeling somewhat comfortable, I took a deep breath and realized I was kind of depressed. Not just kind of. *Very* depressed.

My old life suddenly seemed bland—endless

days of loneliness stretching ahead. Writing alone. Parenting alone. Sleeping alone.

Oh, no, I had never thought of this. After experiencing the heaven of Alex's arms, how could I go back to my very boring existence? And it wasn't just the sex. It was everything—his eyes, his kindness, his teasing. It was having another grown-up to talk to late at night. But not just anyone. It was *Alex*.

Returning from the bathroom, Kaileen sat down next to me and checked her phone.

In the stillness before we started taxiing, another feeling abruptly made itself known deep down in my belly—weird yet familiar little twinges and cramps, a pulling and stretching sensation.

My heart stopped, and all the sudden, I couldn't breathe as I remembered the last time I'd had that feeling.

When I'd been pregnant with Audrey.

My whole body started to shake, and I began to twist my wedding band.

Kaileen glanced at my hands. "What's wrong? You only do that when you're freaking out about something."

"Huh?" I asked, totally lost in my panic.

She pointed at my fingers still frantically turning my ring. "That."

I looked down and realized what she was talking about. "Oh, yeah. Sorry."

Turning a bit more in her seat, her narrowed

eyes stared at me. "So what is it? Obviously, you've got something going on."

"Well, I..." What could I say? She would think I was absolutely insane.

"Come on, Jayda. Just spill it," she demanded.

Quickly, I peered around to see who might overhear us, but the plane wasn't very full. The only person I could see was one young guy who sat in front of us with his headphones on.

Kaileen raised her eyebrows at me in a silent question.

"Well," I tried again, swallowing hard. "I think... I think I'm pregnant."

She surprised me with a sudden burst of laughter. "What? I know that man is sex on wheels. I mean, his name even rhymes with sex. But you literally just had sex and you think you're pregnant already? After only one weekend?"

I nodded, feeling kind of ridiculous. But even so, those little cramps deep in my abdomen persisted. And I decided to confide in Kaileen and tell her something I hadn't told her before. "I'm... well, I'm weirdly fertile," I whispered.

Her brows shot up so high, they practically disappeared into her hairline. "You are? What on earth do you mean?"

After glancing around again, I continued, "I got pregnant with Audrey after just one time. And I knew the very next morning I was pregnant because of this same little twingey, crampy feeling I'm having right now."

She pulled back in shock. "Why didn't you tell me all that?"

I thought about all of her fertility struggles. "Because I know it wasn't exactly easy for you."

"You're too kind." She squeezed my hand, pausing for a minute as she thought. "But didn't you use a condom?"

"No," I admitted. "I'm on the pill."

"You are?"

I nodded, bewildered and overwhelmed.

"I'm finding out all sorts of things about you," Kaileen said. "I mean, can I ask why you're even on the pill? No offense, but it's not like you're out picking up dudes every night."

Once again, I peeked at the guy sitting in front of us, worried that he was getting an earful of some very private girl talk. But he was bobbing his head to his music, completely oblivious to us.

"It's because I have extremely heavy periods that knock me out for a few days if I'm not on the pill," I confessed in a low voice.

"Really? You poor thing. I had no idea." Her tone was sympathetic but also kind of hurt.

"It's just not something I go around telling people," I tried to explain. "To be honest, it's been so long, with the exception of the one time I was trying to get pregnant, I don't even think about it."

"Well, that makes sense." She fussed with her seatbelt while the pilot came on to tell us we'd be delayed taking off. When he finished, she turned to me again. "So if you're on the pill, how on earth could you get pregnant? How effective is the pill anyway?"

"Good question."

Kaileen whipped out her phone as I rested my head against the back of my seat, not daring to think about the future if I was indeed pregnant with Alex's baby. Good Lord. After a few minutes of my mind whirling in circles trying to comprehend this insane possibility, she spoke up.

"Okay. It says here... well, we all know the only one-hundred percent effective method is abstinence."

"Right. A little too late for that," I said, remembering the look on Alex's face as he first filled me.

"Not helpful. I know." She laughed. "Okay. It says the pill has a ninety-one percent effectiveness rate. Reasons for pregnancy are usually due to a missed pill, especially in the first week of a packet when the blah, blah, blah." Kaileen turned to look at me. "So did you miss a pill?"

I thought back over the last couple of weeks and groaned, putting my head in my hands. "Yeah, actually, I'm pretty sure I did."

To be honest, I wasn't exactly the best about remembering to take the pill. It's not like I had to worry much about getting pregnant. Until suddenly I did.

"Okay. Take a breath, Jayda. It's one missed pill. What about..." She looked back at her phone. "Did you throw up or get food poisoning or anything like that?"

Thinking back, there was actually a weird night recently where Audrey had thrown up spaghetti after dinner and then that made me get sick too. "Oh, God, yes."

Oh, wow, so I had somehow missed two pills? And then slept with sex on wheels with no condom? I put my head down between my knees and started to breathe, trying to stop the panic that pumped through me.

Kaileen put her hand on my back, moving in slow circles. "Jayda, Jayda, Jayda, you've got to chill, though. You don't even know for sure you're pregnant."

Yeah. I was pretty sure. But I didn't say anything, and after a few minutes, I sat back up, still attempting to calm myself.

"You want to get a morning-after pill when you get back?" Kaileen asked, searching on her phone again. "It says some you can take up to five days after sex. But the sooner the better."

The plane finally started to back out from the gate, and soon, we were heading down the runway as my mind fought for some kind of control amidst this mental hurricane. Releasing a deep sigh, I thought about the possibilities.

How unbelievably complicated would it be to

have this baby? Of course, I'd have to tell Alex. And of course, he'd want to be part of this child's life, forcing us to manage this baby with two different households that were so far apart. How would that even work?

And then the other possibility—the morning-after pill. Stopping this soon after I landed.

Oh, I didn't know what to do!

"Jayda, you have a little while," Kaileen said. "Just chill and maybe by the time you get home, you'll know what to do."

That's true. I did have hours, including a layover in New York where I'd say goodbye to Kaileen before getting on my plane to Maine.

"And besides," she went on, "you get in late and can't do anything about it till tomorrow anyway. If you decide to do anything at all, that is."

She was right, of course, but if I was being honest with myself, the reality was I already knew what I was going to do.

I nodded at Kaileen's words, leaning back in my seat and hoping to rest. When I closed my eyes, the only thing I could see was Alex, like a movie playing on the inside of my eyelids. Alex laughing. Alex holding his daughter. The look in his eyes just before he kissed me. The pleasure on his face as we came together.

Oy, I had it bad. One weekend that had utterly changed my life.

CHAPTER ELEVEN

Alex

"S hi—" I stopped myself from cursing as I burned my hand on the hot pan while trying to hold a squirmy, grumpy Gabby with the other.

"Sorry, sorry, little squirt." I bounced her around a few times and tried to make her laugh by swinging her. Gabby started to cry. Nothing worked. Maybe she was just hungry?

"See? Mac and cheese on the way." I stirred the cheese in, and Gabby seemed interested... for a second. Then the crying got even louder.

Crap.

I hurried and grabbed a bowl, spooning up a serving. Man, I hated it when Gabby cried. Every single time, it felt like my heart was breaking a little.

"Okay, here comes the airplane." Still holding her, I blew on a spoonful to cool it down. "Gotta start the engine first. Vroom-vroom."

That stopped her. I aimed the spoon and made a big show about bringing it in, closer to her. Thank God she seemed into it, and the crying stopped. She opened her mouth a little.

"Coming in for landing."

Crash. She swatted the spoonful away, and it landed on the floor with a loud clatter. And then the tears started again. Even worse this time.

I let out a huge sigh. Not exactly what I needed after a long day of surgery.

Giving up on food, I put her against my shoulder and walked her around. Any time I tried to put her down, the crying turned into screams. So walking it was. Around the living room. Down the hall. Detour through the bedrooms. And back again.

It seemed to help. The crying quieted down. But whenever I stopped or even slowed my pace, it came back full force. So I kept on going.

And as I walked and walked and walked, my mind drifted back to two nights ago... when *she* had been here. When she had made it all look so easy. When she had brought a warmness and light into this dismal house that had never been here before. Ever.

Shaking my head, I sighed again. Since we'd said goodbye yesterday morning—was that just yesterday? It felt like forever ago already—I'd tried not to think about her. Tried not to think about what could be. Because it just couldn't be.

I lived in Miami, and she lived in Maine. We were both tied down by family. There was no way it would work. So what was the point in even thinking about her? But damn it, every time I tried to think of something else—work, baseball, Gabby—my mind went back to Jayda. *Every single time*.

Thinking about how she crinkled her nose when she laughed. Thinking about how her greenish-blue eyes seemed to change color, how soft her skin felt, how her long hair tickled my chest, how her breasts—

No. I couldn't go there right now.

But beyond the absolutely mind-blowing sex that I couldn't think about at the moment, what really got me was dinnertime with her and Gabby—how she'd effortlessly fed Gabby on her knee while eating her own meal and how she hadn't even seemed to mind it. Actually, it seemed like she'd enjoyed it.

And then later, my God, when she'd rocked Gabby to sleep. She had really wanted to do it. Not just pretending. Not just going through the motions. And her sweet voice as she sang her made-up lullabies...

Damn it.

I swallowed against the strange lump in my throat and focused on Gabby again. She had at least quieted down, and her eyes were doing that heavy blinking.

Glancing at the clock on the stove as I walked by, I saw it was a little early to go to sleep. And she hadn't even had any dinner. What kind of night was it going to be? One where she woke up hungry at two o'clock in the morning.

You'd think after a year of being a single dad, I'd have some sort of routine or schedule. But the truth was we were kind of all over the place. Just barely squeaking by. As I put Gabby down in her crib, I thought of something Jayda had said. She'd told me that Gabby seemed really happy and that I was doing an amazing job.

An amazing job? It was nice that she thought so. But I wasn't so sure.

Seeing Jayda with Gabby that night, seeing the way Gabby had responded to her, seeing her so effortlessly interact with her, I didn't know what to make of it.

All I knew is that I wanted *that*.

Looking at Gabby sleeping so sweetly, I realized I wanted a mom for her. And I wanted a wife, a *real* wife. I tried to remember the exact phrase that had been said in my wedding vows to Fiona—something about doubling the joys and halving the sorrows.

That was it. I'd never actually had that with Fiona. And I really wanted that. But damn it, what I wanted more than anything?

I wanted Jayda. And *only* Jayda.

And that was when I decided to say screw you to the distance, screw you to the complications, and picked up my phone to call her. But looking at the phone, I realized it was probably too early. Most normal parents would be in the middle of the dinner to bath to bed transition.

So I decided to kill some time and hit the treadmill while I watched SportsCenter. I had trouble concentrating and only half-watched it because thoughts of Jayda kept running through my head.

I'd been such an idiot in high school... and through most of my twenties. I remembered when I turned thirty, I had this sudden urge to settle down. I saw my older brother with his wife and kids when they came to visit at Christmas, and I'd had a strange feeling of jealousy. I'd done a massive internet search around that time, looking for Jayda, thinking back to my high school crush and how I'd always thought she'd make a great wife someday.

Well, it'd been a little late for that. Obviously. Of course, she'd moved on.

I hadn't found much about her online—she must not have published her books yet. But the one thing I'd found? She'd been married since the age of twenty-two. Some guy—now I knew it was Blake—who'd been way smarter than me had met Jayda and seen what an absolute catch she was. And he hadn't let her go.

With that depressing thought, I noticed the

time and thought I'd give her a call.

Taking a long breath because I was suddenly kind of nervous, I picked up my phone and tried her. My heartbeat accelerated as her phone rang and rang and rang. But finally, on the fifth ring, she answered.

"Hello?" she said, sounding breathless. "Alex?"

"Hey. Yeah. It's Alex. I... I hope it's not a bad time." Damn, I felt like a teenager calling a girl for the first time.

"No, no. Not at all," she said quickly, a question in her voice like she didn't know why I was calling.

"Well, I just wanted to make sure you made it home okay."

"Yes, I did. Thanks. That's really nice of you."

"Sure. Of course. So... how are you? How was your day?" I asked, wishing I'd thought a bit more about what I was going to say *before* I called.

"Oh, I'm fine," she said, her voice a little high. "Just a day of rest, laundry, and getting back to the routine, you know?"

Yeah, I did know. After that weekend that had rocked my whole world. "Mm-hmm. I get that."

"How about you?" she asked.

"Nothing too exciting here. Just worked today and then a quiet night with Gabby. Well, actually not such a quiet night. But we survived it." I glanced at the monitor and saw a peaceful sleeping baby, thank God.

"Ooh, that sounds rough," she said with

empathy. "What happened?"

I chuckled. "Yeah, actually, it was pretty rough. She cried a lot and wouldn't eat a thing."

"Hmm. What'd you try to feed her?"

"Mac and cheese."

A sound came through the phone that resembled a smothered laugh. "Again?"

"What? It's her favorite," I defended myself.

This time she didn't try to hide her laughter. "Right. But she might appreciate a little variety sometimes."

I sighed, thinking about what else I could feed her besides the usual few foods I knew she liked.

"Sorry," Jayda said. "I don't mean to laugh. It's actually pretty cute."

"Cute, huh?" I'd take that.

"Yeah, cute," she said, her tone a little shy.

Man, I really wanted to see her face, see if she had that adorable blush that crept up from her chest to her cheeks. Next time, I'd definitely do video.

She cleared her throat. "So anyway, I can email you some food ideas, you know, some links if you'd like. Not that I'm an expert or anything."

"Yeah. That'd be great. Thanks. I appreciate that." There was a pause, and I tried to think of what else to say.

"But at this age, you can also just feed her a little of whatever you're eating too," Jayda said. "If I remember correctly."

"Hmm, I can try that. I mean, I usually just

pick dinner up on the way home, like Greek, Cuban, or something like that."

"Ah, nice. Are you a guy that actually eats vegetables?" she teased.

"What are vegetables?" I joked back.

As we both laughed, I wished again that I could see her. Ah, hell, who was I kidding? I wished I could be there *right next to her*. But I wasn't.

"Well, I'm one to talk," she said. "I'm probably the worst cook in the world."

"No way. I don't believe that." There was something Jayda was bad at?

"Oh, yes. I'm super impatient and burn everything," she admitted. "I even burned hard-boiled eggs once."

"You did not. How is that even possible?"

"I forgot to set the timer, and all the water boiled off. I heard this weird popping noise from the living room, and I came running in to see burnt eggshells that were exploding."

I couldn't hold in my laughter. "I had no idea."

"Well, now you know. But there's one thing I'm really good at."

"Oh, yeah? What's that?" Although I knew of a few things she was really good at.

"Pancakes. I make killer pancakes."

"Really? Interesting. I'm pretty good at pancakes too actually," I bragged.

"Really? Hmm." Again, she had that teasing tone.

"You say that like you don't believe me."

"No, I do. I just wonder who'd win in a pancake-making contest between us."

"Oh, definitely me," I said.

She giggled in that way that I'd loved since the age of fourteen—one of the reasons I had always teased her. I heard a noise from the monitor and saw Gabby stirring. Sighing, I realized I was probably in for one of *those* nights.

"Are you all right, Alex?"

Man, I loved the way she said my name. "Yeah. I just think Gabby's about to wake up. She's probably starving."

"Ah, well, I hope you have better luck feeding her this time."

"Me too." I really hoped so. Gabby moved more and started making some noises.

"I'll let you go and deal with it before she gets too upset," Jayda said.

"Okay. Yeah. I guess I better get on it." There was a brief silence as I hesitated, not wanting to say goodbye.

"Well, thanks for calling me," Jayda said. "It was really nice talking to you."

"That *was* nice." More than nice. "Same time tomorrow?" It just kind of slipped out, and I could almost hear her mind processing that.

"Yeah. I'd like that," she finally said.

"All right. Goodnight, Jayda."

"Goodnight," she said in that sexy, soft voice that made me want more.

As I walked down the hallway to a now-awake Gabby, I realized I wanted a whole lot more of Jayda. Much, much more.

CHAPTER TWELVE

Alex

The next day, I had a few post-op appointments in the morning and thought I'd take Gabby to the beach in the afternoon when she woke up from her nap. I needed something to take my mind off of Jayda.

I just couldn't stop thinking about her. And I couldn't wait to call her again tonight. But a big part of me also wanted to hold back because, again, what was the point? Why make it even harder by calling her?

When I came home from work, my mom greeted me at the door. "Shh," she said with a finger to her lips. "Gabby's asleep."

I nodded and came in, expecting her to take off right away like she usually did. But she hung around the kitchen while I made a sandwich. "What's up, Mom?" I said, feeling a little suspicious.

"I don't know. Why don't you tell me?" she asked in a tone I hadn't heard in a long time.

A bit wary, I glanced up from slicing a tomato. "What do you mean?"

"I mean, you've been acting strange the last couple of days."

"I have?" I asked, surprised to hear that. "How so?"

"Just like you have something on your mind," she said, eyes narrowing in on me.

"Hmm. Not sure what you're talking about." I turned away from her to grab the turkey deli meat from the fridge.

"Alexander Xavier Hernandez, don't even try that with me. I'm your mom."

Oh, damn, the whole name, huh? "It sounds like I'm about to be grounded for two weeks," I joked, remembering all the times I'd been in trouble as a teenager.

"You're not there yet. We'll see how this conversation goes, though." Her tone was even sharper now.

"Okay. Well, what exactly is it you want to know?" I asked, putting some lettuce on my sandwich and stifling a smile as I thought about Jayda asking if I ate vegetables.

"I'd like to know more about this situation with Jayda from the other night," she said, her eyes shrewd.

Man, she just went right there, didn't she? Thinking carefully, I put the other piece of bread on top and carried my plate to the table. "What about her?" I said, trying to keep my tone casual.

My mom laughed as she followed me to the table and took a seat. "The way you're acting tells me everything I need to know."

What did that mean? "Which is?" I dared ask as I bit into my sandwich.

"Which is... you like her."

Yep, she pretty much nailed it. But I wasn't going to admit it.

Of course, she continued on anyway. "And I can see why. I remember her from high school, and I always thought she was a sweet girl. And obviously, she hasn't changed much. She even looks the same."

Taking another big bite, I nodded a little when she looked at me.

"So what are you going to do about it?" she asked.

I held up a finger as I chewed, trying to buy some time. So not what I wanted to talk about with my mom. But she was acting kind of like a dog with a bone at the moment, and everyone in my family knew when she acted this way, there was no escape. My mom could be downright scary, even to my dad. Heck, especially to my dad.

She patiently waited for me to finish, not saying a word, just watching. Finally, I shrugged.

"Honestly, Mom, not much I can do about it."

"Why not?" she said, her eyes piercing me.

"Because of the distance."

She raised her own shoulders in a shrug. "So?"

"So... neither of us is going to move."

"How do you know that?" she asked, those eyes not wavering from my face.

Sighing, I responded, "Because she lives in Maine, near her parents, and I highly doubt she wants to move away." And I certainly couldn't leave my family either.

"And you?"

I moved my plate away, not feeling very hungry anymore. "Same."

"So you don't want to move because of us?"

"Right. Of course," I admitted.

She slapped the table with one hand, making me jump a little. "Well, that's just bullshit."

I felt my jaw drop in shock. My mom rarely cursed. In fact, I didn't even remember the last time.

"You heard me," she said, glaring at me.

Now, I was kind of scared. I shook my head trying to get around my sudden shock and confusion. "Okay. So you're saying you *want* me to move?"

"I'm not exactly saying that. I'm just saying don't you dare give up a chance at happiness because of us, because you think we need you here, or whatever bullshit you're thinking."

Okay, she could stop swearing any time now.

"But—"

"To be honest, your dad wants to retire, and we'd like to travel."

"Oh. I didn't know that." I had no clue. And now, the guilt started to creep in, like Gabby and I were holding them back.

"We didn't want to say anything because, well, I didn't want you to feel bad or anything. But now... I know it's early and it was just one weekend. But I saw the way she was with Gabby and the way you were looking at her."

My heart thudded against my ribcage at what my mom was saying. Was it that obvious? She also had super eagle vision when it came to her sons. "So you're kicking me out of the nest, huh?" I said, a strange feeling growing in my chest.

"Yep. Pretty much," she said, smiling. "I really think you should go check out Maine."

And something about those words made me the happiest I'd been in a long, long time.

***

That night after a fun afternoon at the beach with Gabby, I watched the time, waiting for that magic hour of nine o'clock.

I'd already done the legwork for a trip to Maine, looking ahead at my work schedule and seeing some days off in about six weeks where I could squeeze in a visit. I just needed to run it by Jayda before I booked any tickets.

My phone buzzed, and I looked down to see it was Jayda calling. "Hey," I answered, surprised.

"Hey. Beat you to it," she said. I could practically hear the smile in her voice.

"That anxious to talk to me, huh?" I teased.

Her light laughter met my ear. "If only I could throw a stuffed animal at you through the phone."

"If only," I said, wishing I could see her face. "So how are you doing? What'd you do today?"

"Just tried to write while my parents took Audrey to storytime at the library."

"Fun. Tried to write, huh? So not very successful?" I asked, flicking off the TV.

"Mm, yeah. Just not feeling it today. One of those days."

If I wasn't mistaken, her voice sounded a bit tired today. "Sorry to hear that."

"Oh, that's okay. Some days it flows better. And some days it's best to take a break. But anyway, how are you?"

"Doing well." I paused, thinking about when I should bring up a trip to see her.

"You sure?" she asked after a beat, probably wondering why I was quiet.

"Yeah. Yeah. Just..."

"Just what?"

"Just..." I felt some nerves as I thought about telling her but decided to go for it. "Well, I'm thinking about coming to Maine for a visit."

I could almost hear her surprise through the silence on the phone. Finally, she said, "You really want to come to Maine?"

"Yes, I do."

She was quiet another few seconds, and I wondered what she could possibly be thinking. "That would be great," she said, her voice a little soft, giving me that strange feeling in my chest again. "I'd really like that."

I exhaled a breath I didn't know I was even holding. "Good. Good."

"Just you or..."

"I thought I'd bring Gabby too. If you don't mind."

"Of course, I don't mind," she said quickly. "So Gabby meeting Audrey?"

"Yes. Exactly."

"Wow, that should be interesting."

I wasn't sure what to make of that. "Interesting good? Or interesting bad?"

"Ha! I guess it could go either way." She laughed. "No. But really, Audrey loves other little girls. Or I should say she loves bossing them around."

Now it was my turn to laugh. "Look out."

"Yeah, look out," she warned, humor in her tone. "Has Gabby ever been on a plane before?"

"Uh, no. I'm a little scared to be honest."

She giggled in that adorable way I craved. "Oh, I don't blame you. Then I won't tell you my horror story till you get here."

"Okay. Now you have to tell me." I put my feet up on the couch and settled back.

"Yikes. I don't know if that's a good idea."

"Jayda, please. I can take it."

She sighed. "Okay. Well, my story didn't happen till the return trip when Audrey was all exhausted and completely wrung out."

"Yeah? So what happened?" I asked, beyond curious at this point.

"Well, she got totally freaked out about landing for some reason and screamed the whole way down about how we were going to crash and she wanted *off this plane*!"

I couldn't help smiling at the way Jayda described it, complete with imitating Audrey's panicked voice. "No way. She did not."

"Yep. It was *bad*. I ended up crying too, just holding her little body. She was clinging to me, grabbing on to me like I was her life raft. Wouldn't go in her seat to put her seatbelt on. She was absolutely and utterly terrified. It was awful."

"That sounds terrible." It truly did and gave me pause about my own upcoming flight.

"I know, right? But here's the thing. We survived it. And people were actually nice about it."

That shocked me. "They were?"

"Yes, surprisingly. Everyone applauded when we landed." We laughed together for a moment. "Sorry. I shouldn't have told you that."

"No. It's fine."

"But really, just remember my story if you have any issues. I survived that, and you can manage anything she throws your way. And now, I can even look back and laugh."

"True," I agreed. "And you also have a good story to tell."

"Exactly." She paused a second, then said, "So, Alex, serious question here, do you even own a winter coat?"

I cracked up laughing. "No. No, I don't."

"I didn't think so. Guess you need to do some shopping. So when are you thinking of visiting?"

I told her the dates, and luckily, she didn't have anything going on and would be in town. We didn't talk much longer because Jayda's mom called her, but we made a "phone date" for the next night as I wondered how I'd make it for six long weeks until I could see her again.

One day at a time, man. One day at a time.

CHAPTER THIRTEEN

Alex

Six weeks later...

As I balanced a sleeping Gabby on one shoulder and our carry-on bag on the other, we walked down the aisle of the plane, my heartbeat starting to accelerate at the thought of being with Jayda again in just a few minutes.

I couldn't wait to see her, face to face, and hold her in my arms. After all of our late-night conversations almost every day for the last six weeks, I felt like I genuinely knew her now. We'd talked about pretty much everything—family, religion, parenting, politics, and almost every topic in between.

There were nights we talked so long that Jayda practically fell asleep on the phone. She said writing this last book was wearing her out.

But there were still a few things we hadn't discussed really. Maybe it was premature. I didn't know. However, she hadn't mentioned much about her late husband, and we hadn't talked about any kind of future for us beyond this visit.

I guessed this trip could be a big turning point.

After waiting a few minutes for our suitcase at baggage claim, I looked for the pick-up area where Jayda said she'd meet us. Somehow, even with the jostling, Gabby was still out like a light.

I found the exit and walked out the door, a blast of cold air hitting me in the face. Damn, even though I knew it was coming, I wasn't prepared for it. Glancing at Gabby, she didn't even stir from the change in temperature.

"Alex!"

Jayda stood a little way down the curb, next to a black SUV, waving at us, her face lit up with a big grin.

That smile did something to my chest, something I'd never felt before, something that grew the closer I walked. God, she looked cute *and* sexy in her winter hat. What did they call those things anyway? Beanies? Well, whatever they were, she looked *hot* in her cold-weather get-up.

"You made it," she said, sounding a little breathless when I reached her. Her eyes darted from me to Gabby. "Aw, she's sound asleep."

Holding on to Gabby with one hand, I couldn't resist leaning down and kissing Jayda. I had waited six long weeks to see her again and to taste those lips. I brushed my mouth against hers. And holy heck, I could kiss this woman forever. And she seemed to love it as much as I did.

I had to stop myself. Now was not the time. But I couldn't wait to get her alone. It might be complicated with two little kids involved, but we'd figure out a way. I had saved up six weeks of wanting her, of aching for her, and I was dying to sink into her heat and feel that passion between us.

She swallowed hard. "So... you, um, ready to go?" she asked, peeking up at me, that sweet look in her eyes that made me want to pull her to me and not let go.

"Yeah. Sure."

My voice was rougher than usual, but she didn't comment, just went to work opening the trunk where I tossed my suitcase. Once the conked-out Gabby was situated in her car seat, I settled into the passenger side, and we took off. Jayda looked so tiny in the huge car, and she was pulled up so close to the steering wheel that it made me laugh.

"What?" She glanced over at me.

"Just kind of a big car for ya, shorty." I grinned. She reached out and lightly shoved my arm.

"Well, first of all, it's not my car, all right? I rented this SUV because it's four of us, including two humongous car seats. *And* it's supposed to snow this weekend—way earlier than usual—and I haven't put the snow tires on my car yet."

"Wait a minute. It's going to snow?" I couldn't believe it.

"You didn't check the weather before you traveled?" she asked, that teasing tone in her voice.

"What do *you* think? Do I seem like I'm that organized to you?"

She giggled and looked at me again. "Well, you did manage to buy a coat at least."

"I did." I pulled at my seat belt, trying to get comfortable with all the extra bulk. "So how'd I do? You like it?"

We stopped at a light, and she gave me a once-over. When her eyes finally returned to my face, I swear there was heat in her gaze. I held my breath at what she could do to me with just one glance.

She gave me a shrug. "Not bad, Alex. Not bad."

Man, she cracked me up. Her words may have been nonchalant, but her flirty smile afterwards gave it away. Clearing my throat, I asked, "So where's Audrey? With your parents?"

"Yeah, she's spending the night." She sighed. "I don't know. I just decided maybe it was better to wait till tomorrow to introduce her to you both, you know, when we have a full day and everyone has more time to adjust."

She sounded a bit unsure of herself. "I think that's actually a good idea," I reassured her.

Nodding, she turned a corner and jumped the curb. "Oops, sorry about that. So that's another thing I'm not very good at."

"Driving?" I asked, gripping the edge of my seat.

"Um, yeah. I do okay. But I get flustered easily."

"Really? You seem to be doing all right. Well, except for that poor curb you just murdered," I teased.

Shooting me a quick glare, she said, "I think it's because I didn't drive much for a very long time when we lived in New York, and I sort of lost my confidence. But I'm loving this SUV. I feel much, much safer."

"Maybe *you're* safer—" I started to say, grinning.

But her sudden hand on my knee stopped me. "Don't you dare finish that sentence!"

The sound of her laughter went straight to my chest, and I couldn't take my eyes off her.

"Hey," she said, "so how'd it go on the plane? How was Gabby?"

"Great actually."

She narrowed her eyes at me. "Are you freaking serious?"

"Absolutely." I nodded, feeling proud that we'd made it through unscathed. "She played with all her stuff the whole time and did great changing planes, taking off, landing, all of it. She was just excited about everything."

"Show-off," she said under her breath, giving me a sideways look and nudging my knee with her hand. "I'm just kidding. Really. I'm glad to hear that. She's a little trooper."

"She definitely is."

I took a second to glance around outside and realized how gorgeous Portland was—kind of quintessential New England with lots of brick buildings and old trees. Definitely no palm trees here.

Jayda looked over at me as we entered a residential neighborhood. "So this is the West End area where we live. It's an older area with quite a few historic homes. And what's great is we're near downtown *and* the water."

"Wow, it's really nice."

"Yeah? You like it?"

"I really do." Honestly, I did. Surprisingly. It was different but stunning. She slowed down at a beautiful house covered in weathered wood shingles. "This is where you live?" I asked.

Pulling in to the brick-paved driveway, she answered, "Yep. The ol' homestead. Would you believe it was built in 1835?"

I shook my head, amazed by the history contained in such a home. "You're kidding me."

"Nope. Pretty cool, huh?" she said, putting on the parking brake.

"Very cool. I love it."

Right when I opened my door to get out, Gabby made some noises, and I realized my respite was over. I sighed, wishing she had slept a little longer because seeing Jayda... I just wanted to kiss every inch of her delicious body. But I guessed that would have to wait.

To say Gabby woke up cranky would be an understatement. "At least you're not on the plane right now," Jayda said as she struggled to take a screaming, flailing Gabby out of the car seat.

"That's so true. Thank God." I laughed over the noise and grabbed my luggage from the trunk. "You want me to get her?"

"Nah. Take a breather, Alex." Finally getting Gabby from her seat, she swirled her around. "Hi, wee one. Should we take a little tour?"

Bouncing Gabby on her hip, Jayda headed for the front door, pointing out a little hidden fairy house along the way. "Here we go," she cooed. "Let's check out all the goodies inside. So many new toys for you to play with."

I followed, beyond curious to see how Jayda lived. Once she opened the door, the first thing that struck me was how bright and airy everything seemed, sunlight streaming in through the many windows. The layout was so open I could see into the kitchen and dining room at what looked like the far end of the house.

"Well?" Jayda asked, her eyes lit up. "What do you think?"

"Honestly? It's beautiful here."

I could see touches of Jayda everywhere—flowers, artwork on the walls, neutral calm colors, plush cushions on her couches, even a large fireplace that set off the entire room.

Feeling her gaze still on me, I added, "It feels like you... like home."

I stopped looking around to meet her eyes, and damn, if someone else was watching, even they would have seen the sparks flying between us. Her chest rose and fell as we stared at each other. God, I had missed being with her so much.

Not able to ignore any longer the intense need to touch her, I closed the space between us and pulled her into my side since she still held Gabby.

Her free arm went around my waist as she squeezed in. "Group hug," she said to a now-quiet Gabby.

Something leaped in my chest as my arms went around them both. This was how it was supposed to be. This was my heaven.

We stayed like that for a few moments as I breathed in Jayda's scent—a mix of vanilla and strawberries, probably her shampoo—her head fitting right below my chin and resting on my chest. The way her body fit into mine... I couldn't even describe it.

It just felt right.

Gabby could only handle so much of the group hug and began to fidget. "Okay," Jayda said. "Let's show you your room and all the toys. And Alex?"

"Yeah?" I said, shrugging out of my coat and

grabbing the suitcase.

"This place is totally baby proof. Believe me, Audrey has tried to get into absolutely everything." She waved toward the fireplace which was surrounded by safety panels. "Someday, I'll be able to take down all the gates everywhere and put out my vases."

I laughed. "Hopefully. Although it's hard to imagine."

"Exactly. But it's actually getting better now. I think age two was the trickiest. I had to put clamps on every single drawer, the fridge, the toilets. Oh, and the little plugs for the sockets weren't even enough. I had to take some out completely and put those monstrosities on." She pointed to a large outlet cover in the corner.

"Well, they say curiosity is good, right?"

"Supposedly." She shook her head, laughing, and started toward the stairs where there was another gate at the bottom and one at the top. "I probably don't even need these anymore for Audrey. She's pretty good at steps now. But it just keeps her on the same floor as me. I don't need her going upstairs while I'm trying to cook down here."

"That makes sense. Especially if you're going to burn something," I teased.

"Not funny," she said with a laugh. "But definitely true."

I was soon distracted by her hips swaying as she went up the stairs in front of me. I'd never seen her in jeans before, and they hugged her body in all the right places. As she unlocked the top gate and held it open for me, I took a deep breath.

This was going to be a tough weekend.

The guest room was perfect, a huge bed with a little crib for Gabby nearby, plus tons of toys and board books in a big bin that Jayda had brought in for our visit.

After we dropped off our stuff, we toured the rest of the house and then headed to the kitchen to start dinner. Jayda grabbed a bunch of toys, and Gabby hung out on a large plush rug, thrilled to check them all out.

"So," Jayda began, "what do you think we should have for dinner? Mac and cheese?"

I couldn't resist her anymore and grabbed her to me. "You think you're so funny. I'm never going to live that one down, am I?"

Peeking up at me with those beautiful eyes, my heart lurched inside my chest. Her body was flush with mine, and I had to fight the urge to take her right there.

Damn, I wanted her. I couldn't get enough of her.

She reached her hands up to wrap around my neck. "Alex," she whispered, her sultry voice making me want her even more... if that was possible. I pulled her in tighter, her soft breasts crushed against me. Our breaths mingled as our chests rose and fell together.

Crash!

Gabby's little tower of stackable cups fell over, and she let out a roar.

Laughing, Jayda and I broke apart, and she rushed over to help Gabby. I let out a sigh. Of course, I loved my daughter dearly, but I was dying to get Jayda alone. And I realized I'd have to wait till Gabby went to sleep for the night.

And then... then I'd do everything I'd imagined for those six long weeks that had been filled with cold showers.

CHAPTER FOURTEEN

Alex

For dinner, we decided on a Thai noodle dish with vegetables.

"I've never burned noodles before," Jayda joked as she stirred the boiling pot of water. "I mean, I'm sure I could find a way."

"Maybe between the two of us we can manage to make a decent meal."

"One can hope."

After I picked up a fussy Gabby, I walked around the kitchen and helped as much as I could with my one free hand. I also couldn't keep my eyes off Jayda as she cut up a few carrots.

Something was different about her, something I couldn't quite figure out. I'd had that slight feeling right away when I'd first spotted her at the airport. But I'd pushed it to the back of my mind. But now, watching Jayda, the feeling grew. Maybe it was her hair? Maybe she was waiting for me to notice?

"Did you get a haircut?" I asked.

She glanced at me sideways. "Um, yeah, like a month ago I think."

"Ah, okay." So that wasn't it.

"Why are you looking at me like that?" she asked, a small frown on her face.

"Like what?" I said, trying to buy time.

"I don't know. Like you're trying to figure something out I guess." She stared at me, a wooden spoon in her hand.

"Just... just there's something different about you, and I can't figure out what," I admitted.

She spun around, her attention back on the stove in front of her, stirring the noodles with determination. A few seconds later, the buzzer went off, and she dumped the noodles and hot water into a colander, the steam making her cheeks pink.

I still couldn't make out what it was, but I decided to drop it. Maybe it'd come to me later.

Together, we finished making dinner, and before long we were sitting at the table, a curious Gabby picking up a water chestnut to munch on. I sipped my water, glancing at Jayda who had been rather quiet since my haircut question.

"Everything okay?" I asked.

She nodded quickly. Too quickly. Maybe she

needed some wine to relax or something. I remembered how she'd been so nervous around me at the reunion for some reason, and the wine seemed to help her be more comfortable.

But she hadn't been anxious all these nights of talking to me on the phone. Maybe it was something about being together in person?

"No wine tonight?" I asked.

"Um, yeah, no, not for me. Just kind of not feeling it tonight."

I noticed she was twisting her wedding band, something she had done a lot at the reunion.

"That's fine. It's not like we're in high school and I'm going to peer pressure you into drinking," I teased.

She let out a nervous laugh. "Well, that's good. Do *you* want some?"

"Nope. I'm good."

While we ate, we talked about our big weekend together. Jayda was definitely an organizer and had everything all planned out. And as she talked about the history of Portland and some of the spots she wanted to show me, I had to be honest, I half-listened but only because I was so distracted by her, by the way her lips moved and her eyes lit up.

Jayda had this way of showing every emotion she felt on her face, something I loved, something my ex had been very good at hiding. And right now, Jayda's face was all excitement and nerves, animated... but almost too much so, I suddenly realized, like there was an energy about her that was different, and I couldn't put my finger on it. Almost like she was trying to deflect my attention elsewhere.

I hated being suspicious. God, I'd had enough of that with Fiona, always guessing what she was thinking, not being sure of her true feelings. And with Jayda, that had been something so refreshing, that she never tried to hide herself from me.

Sure, she'd been a little shy and uncomfortable around me at first. But there was an honesty and openness about her that I'd never seen in any other woman I'd been with. Ever.

I'd actually noticed that honesty from her way back in high school... even though I'd been an idiot and hadn't realized what a beautiful and rare trait that was at the time. But now I knew. And my heart sunk a bit that there was something off right now.

As we finished our meal, Jayda suddenly stared wide-eyed at me, a finger to her lips, and nodded toward Gabby. I had to stop myself from laughing because Gabby was slumped down in the high chair, her head nodding forward then jerking backward as she fought sleep.

"Poor thing," Jayda whispered as she scooted away from the table.

But I reached Gabby before her and tried to gently remove her from the seat. In my head, I said a silent thank you because I really wanted...

no, needed to talk to Jayda and figure out what was up.

Luck was not on my side, though. The minute I put Gabby in the guest room crib, she rose up, wailing her little head off. And she didn't stop.

We both took turns walking her around, rocking, listening to music. Every single time she seemed to calm down, we tried to put her in the crib or even let her play on the floor. But nope, she was *not* having it. She just wanted to be held, and she wanted movement. So that's what we did—for hours—Jayda wondering if Gabby's ears were bothering her.

I couldn't be sure. But one thing I did know? It was killing me inside as the minutes dragged on and on. Of course, my daughter always came first, but right now, I just wanted to talk to Jayda, touch her, be with her.

Finally, at about eleven, with Jayda nearly asleep on the couch next to me, Gabby shut her eyes and stopped fighting sleep. I waited a few extra minutes to let her fall deeper as I also watched Jayda's eyes closing. And then, like I was performing the most delicate surgery, I walked carefully up the stairs and put her in the crib, tiptoeing away and swearing at the creaky hardwood floors.

Thank God she stayed asleep as I crept back downstairs, now concerned about waking up Jayda. I stared at her on the couch, sound asleep, and my heart sped up at how beautiful she was to me. How long had I admired that face? How long had I dreamed of that body?

The way her long lashes rested against her skin, the flush in her full cheeks, the way her wide mouth curved.

But more than that, I'd dreamed about *her*. Just her. How she always made me feel good. Something about her... I didn't know. It was like she gave off a vibe, if that was the right word, that made anyone around her happy and positive. She was genuinely the *best person* I had ever known.

I rubbed my forehead, not sure what to do. Traveling with Gabby had wiped me out. And obviously, Jayda was tired too. I had been dying to talk to her, dying to kiss every inch of her soft skin, and damn, what I wanted to do with all those curves of hers.

Just thinking about it made me hot. Ever since that weekend, I couldn't get her body out of my mind—her soft lips, her incredible breasts against my bare skin, how her hands had explored my own body, shy at first but then gripping me with need.

Holy heck. I needed yet another cold shower.

Letting out a shaky sigh, I walked over to her and pulled up the blanket to cover her. More than anything, I was disappointed we couldn't just talk. I'd never felt so comfortable with anyone in my life. No one. Asshat that I was, I had even felt that as a teenager. She was someone I didn't have to pretend with.

I stared at her a few more minutes, watching her chest rise and fall, noticing the way her skin was almost calling out for me to caress it.

Should I wake her? Would she be upset if I did? Or if I didn't?

Not only did I want to be with her right now, I had really been determined to dig a bit deeper and try to figure out if I was just being paranoid earlier or if there really was something going on that I needed to worry about.

In the end, she looked so peaceful, I decided to walk away, swallowing my bitter disappointment.

CHAPTER FIFTEEN

Alex

I n the morning, Gabby stirring in her crib woke me up. And for a split second, I wondered where I was. Alone in this large bed in Jayda's house. Not exactly how I had pictured it.

With two little kids around, I hadn't been expecting a repeat of the sex-fest we'd had six weeks ago. But I'd at least like a minute to kiss her, talk to her, and be alone with her.

Releasing a breath, I tried to recover from my disappointment about the night before which had seeped into the bright morning sunshine peeking through the windows next to me. I heard noises and voices downstairs like a little kid was trying to be quiet but not exactly being successful at it.

I smiled, realizing it must be Audrey.

Crap, what time was it? Had Jayda's parents already come and gone while I was up here lazing in bed?

Reaching for my phone, I saw it was almost eight-thirty. Wow. I hadn't set an alarm because I figured Gabby would wake me up at her usual time. But I hadn't counted on her being so exhausted that she'd sleep this late.

Now I wasn't sure what to do. Wake her up so she didn't get too much rest and have trouble napping? Or let her sleep?

But she made the decision for me when she opened her eyes and smiled at me, helping all my frustrations disappear. Thank God she slept so well. A well-rested Gabby meant a better day for us all.

After we were both ready for the day, we headed downstairs to finally let these girls meet in person. They had "talked" to each other over video a few times, but of course it was nothing like hanging out in real life. And I couldn't wait to see how they got along.

Before we could even make it all the way down the stairs, Audrey ran over to the gate, Jayda not far behind.

"Gabby!" Audrey shouted, holding out her arms like she wanted me to hand her over.

"Hi, Audrey," I said as Jayda undid the latch.

But she completely ignored me as all her focus

was on Gabby, making me feel like I held a little rock star in my arms. While Jayda laughed, I put Gabby down, and she toddled right up to Audrey who grabbed her hand.

"Come here, Gabby. I want to show you..."

Her words were lost as the two girls disappeared around the corner. I glanced at Jayda who laughed once more, shrugging those beautiful shoulders. God, just seeing her this morning took my breath away.

"She's been begging me for a little sister for the last year since her best friend—" Jayda's cheeks flushed that adorable shade of pink. "I mean, not that... well, you know, of course Gabby's not her little sister. Just... well..."

I decided to rescue her. "I know what you mean, sweetheart."

She flashed me a grateful smile as she took a deep breath, her spectacular breasts rising and falling. I forced my eyes away from her chest and back to her face.

"So," she breathed, glancing up at me. "Did you sleep okay?"

I nodded. "Slept great actually. Sorry we were so late. Gabby usually wakes me up before seven."

"Oh, no problem. She was probably exhausted from all the excitement yesterday."

"Exactly. But I'm bummed I missed meeting your parents when they dropped Audrey off. Think I'll get another chance?" I asked, trying to remember if that was something Jayda had mentioned last night during dinner.

"Um, I'm not sure actually. They're exhausted. I guess Audrey kept them up late and then woke up super early."

"Oof, that's brutal."

Jayda started twisting her wedding band. "Yep. And plus, they have this idea that they don't want to intrude on us this weekend. Or something like that. That's what my mom said anyway."

That was thoughtful of them, but I wasn't surprised since they were the ones who had raised such a kind soul in Jayda.

We paused and listened to the girls playing in the other room, Audrey clearly taking charge.

I couldn't resist the moment of being somewhat alone, and I reached out to pull Jayda to me, not exactly sure how she'd respond. But she seemed more than willing to meet me halfway and melted into me, her arms going around my back, her chest crushed against me.

Maybe this was all we needed... a moment of physical closeness to bring us back together, to squash that weird feeling I was having.

I kissed the top of her head. "I've really missed holding you."

She let out a sigh. "Me too."

I rubbed her back, and she leaned backward a bit to look up at me. "I've just really missed *you.* I mean, talking every day was wonderful. But there's just something about...

well, just something about seeing you in person, you know?"

"I know. Believe me, I know."

Those eyes seemed to turn blue as she stared up at me. And then her gaze went to my mouth, and I knew I had to taste her.

Our lips met, hesitant at first. Except for the brief kiss at the airport, it had been so long. So many nights of thinking and dreaming about her. Her arms went to the back of my neck, her hands in my hair. I grabbed her closer to me as our kiss grew into something raw, something hungry.

But still, something inside me held back, not just because I knew it couldn't really lead anywhere but because something still felt... off. And I couldn't be completely comfortable about Jayda and I being together until I knew what it was.

But damn, she tasted good. And my body immediately responded to her.

A loud noise in the next room broke us apart. Seconds later, Audrey and Gabby came crashing around the corner.

"Mama, I'm hungry, and you promised pancakes!" Audrey said.

Jayda let go of me and laughed. "You're right. I did."

Swallowing down my passion, I said, "Pancakes sound great."

"So, Alex," Jayda said, glancing back at me,

"you up for a little pancake making contest this morning?"

I couldn't resist her sexy, teasing smile. "You ready to eat the best pancakes you've ever tasted?"

"Oh, you mean mine?"

And with that, Jayda and her flirty grin disappeared around the corner with me and the girls following behind. The kitchen was already prepped with ingredients all set up on the counter, and I pulled up my favorite recipe that I had saved on my phone.

"It is so on," I said, my competitive side coming out. "Although you do have home stove advantage, so I'm not sure how fair this is exactly."

Jayda giggled as she pulled out a griddle from a low cupboard. "This ought to help you. I'll even tell you what setting to put it on for the best results."

"You'd do that?"

"Well, I wouldn't want to have to eat your undercooked or burnt pancakes, would I?"

"I'm not the one who burns everything," I joked.

She smacked me on the ass with a spatula as we laughed, the girls pausing to stare at us. I cleared my throat and got to work on making my batter, Jayda and I both quiet as we concentrated and the girls started to play with a big container of kitchen utensils.

As I stirred in the ingredients, I thought back to how competitive Jayda was in high school and realized she hadn't really changed much in that aspect. She'd also been almost shy and embarrassed about how smart she really was, but sometimes her inner shark had appeared, like the time we had competed for the top physics prize.

"Remember when you beat me on the final exam to win physics student of the year?" I asked.

Her face turned pink again, and I loved the way I could do that to her.

"Yes, I remember. I remember it like it was yesterday. And I also remember how you pretended to trip me as I walked up to the stage to pick up my award."

I grinned because of course she would bring that up. "Hey, I was just trying to help you out and make you laugh."

Her eyes narrowed at me. "Oh, yeah? And you thought that was a good time to make me laugh?"

"Honestly, you want to know why I did that?"

"Yes, I *would* like to know actually... making the whole school laugh at me."

I put down my measuring cup, not sure if she'd believe me. "Well, first off, they weren't laughing at *you*, doll. They were just laughing at the situation."

"You think?"

"Yeah, I don't just think. I know," I assured her.

"Okay. So Mr. All-Knowing Alex, why did you

do that?" she asked.

"I... well, I knew how much you hated being the center of attention and how much you hated having to cross that stage with everyone watching you. And I was just trying to make you laugh and trying to make you forget about all those eyes on you."

She stopped stirring to stare at me, quiet for a minute as she studied my face. "Honestly, that's pretty sweet, especially for a seventeen-year-old..." She glanced at the girls and came closer. Standing on her tiptoes, she whispered in my ear, "asshole."

Now it was my turn to smack her ass with my spatula, and she danced away laughing. Shaking my head, I started to pour my batter onto the griddle that Jayda had set up for me. "You didn't sabotage this thing, did you?"

She shot me an innocent look. "Me? Never."

I wasn't so sure, so I kept a close eye on the pancakes as Jayda used three different pans on the stove.

Once she had poured her pancakes, she looked at me with apologetic eyes. "I'm really sorry I fell asleep like that last night."

"It's okay. I get it. I must be boring company," I teased.

"Yep, just *so* boring." She shook her head, her eyes lighting up with her smile. "You know I'm kidding, of course. I'm, well, disappointed because... "

"Because what?"

She carefully slid the spatula under one of her bubbling pancakes. "There's just a lot to talk about."

I felt a rush of nerves with those words. "There is?"

She kept her eyes on the stove as she shrugged. "Well, I mean, I wanted to talk to you, you know, be with you."

Damn it, there it was again. After laughing so much only a minute ago, I had forgotten my worries from before. But just now, it really seemed like she was downplaying something. And I had no idea what.

Was she going to say this whole thing wasn't working for her? Did she want me to go? I had no clue what was going on. And it was driving me batshit crazy.

If there was something we needed to talk about, why hadn't she brought it up on the phone? We'd talked for hours, and I mean *hours*, over the last six weeks. Why hadn't she mentioned whatever this was?

As I flipped over one of my own pancakes, my stomach churned as I realized something. Whatever it was she wanted to speak to me about must be big, like huge, something that she needed to discuss in person and not over the phone. And that's why she wasn't quite being herself, because *this thing* had to be on her mind, weighing on her.

Pouring more batter onto the griddle, I vowed to find out today what this thing was. Somehow, I would find a way to be alone with her, without interruptions. Maybe it wouldn't be until tonight.

But I told myself even if Jayda fell asleep on the couch again, I would wake her this time... because we needed to get this out in the open. Whatever it was. Even if it destroyed me.

CHAPTER SIXTEEN

Alex

"You definitely win," I said as I bit into another one of her delicious pancakes. "These are far superior to mine."

Jayda grinned at me from her seat at the small table in the corner of the kitchen. "Want to know my secret ingredient?"

"Nope."

"No?"

"You'll just have to be the pancake maker whenever we're together."

She shook her head at me as Audrey came back into the kitchen then snuck away with two pancakes in her hands.

"I hope one of those is for Gabby, at least,"

Jayda said, taking a sip of her tea.

"Don't worry. Gabby isn't shy about letting me know she's unhappy about something."

"And thank God for that." Jayda laughed. "I love these little strong-willed girls. It's so different from how I grew up, you know?"

"It's definitely a different era from our childhood," I agreed.

"Gosh, that makes my parents sound like they were horrible," Jayda said. "And they definitely weren't."

"I know what you mean, baby." Jayda flashed me a thankful look. "And for what it's worth, I think you're an amazing mom."

She inhaled sharply. "You really think so?"

"Yeah. I know so."

"That really means so much to me. No one ever tells me that. And God, do I worry about that."

"You do?" That surprised me because she seemed like such a natural and so confident.

She nodded, her face serious. "Only all the time."

I shook my head, confused as to why she would feel that way. "But you really *are* amazing. Why would you doubt yourself like that?"

"I just..." Staring down at her plate, she let out a deep sigh. "It's—I guess..."

Seeing how much trouble she was suddenly having, I reached my hand out to grasp hers on the table, hoping she would look at me again. And when she finally did, I could see the pain in her eyes.

"What is it?" I asked, squeezing her soft hand beneath mine.

Biting down on that plump lower lip that I ached to bite too, she took a few more breaths. "I guess I was so consumed by grief during those first months—or years probably—of motherhood, I'm not even sure what kind of a mom I was. It's a blur now. Just days and days of crying almost all the time."

"Of course," I said, my throat suddenly dry.

If I was being honest with myself, there was something in me that was jealous, a little envious of what Jayda had with Blake. Even though he was gone now, he still had a hold over her that I didn't know if I could ever compete with. Not that it was a competition. Just... I didn't know. Sometimes it really sucked to try to live up to the ghost of the love of her life.

Jayda stared at me, and I realized I had missed something she'd said. "Sorry. What was that?"

"Well, I worry sometimes about how my grief affected her. My only hope is that she slept so much that she didn't really notice it?"

I thought back to how much Gabby slept as a newborn when I was going through my own difficulties. "That's my hope too with Gabby."

Jayda reached out her other hand now to cover my own. "You went through something similar at the same time, didn't you?"

I nodded. "It wasn't the same as having a

spouse die, though."

"I don't know. It had to be pretty traumatic for you. Having a newborn is hard enough."

"You can say that again."

She laughed. "But you don't seem as worried about it as I do."

I shrugged, not sure what she was getting at. "I guess I'm just not a big worrier."

"You are such a guy." She squinted her eyes at me in a way that reminded me of a ferocious kitten.

"Thanks?" I chuckled at the vicious little cat in front of me, thinking she might hiss at me any minute. But instead of hissing, her eyes turned a beautiful shade of green that reminded me of hot summer days. And that swell in my chest returned.

Then her squint turned flirty. "I like that."

"Good. I'll keep trying to be a guy then."

As she laughed, I put my other hand on top of hers so now we had a stack of hands on the table. And I remembered the old game probably at the same time she did because her hand that was on the bottom suddenly slapped mine on top. I did the same with mine, both of us cracking up like little kids as the game evolved into a fast and silly slapping of hands, each of us fighting for the top spot.

Finally, I claimed both her small hands in mine and stood up, pulling her to me, hoping to get my chance to nibble that sweet lower lip of hers. But Audrey and Gabby had another idea as they reappeared in the kitchen, running up to show us what they'd made with big lego blocks.

After we admired their creation and they ran off again, Jayda turned to me and said, "Is it horrible of me that I can't wait until certain someones go to sleep tonight?"

Laughing, I said, "Not at all. I'm right there with you."

"And don't let me sleep tonight, okay?" she said, peeking up at me with those sexy eyes.

That was something we could both agree on for sure. "Okay."

"Promise?"

"I promise." Hell, yeah, did I promise.

She moved away to start cleaning up the kitchen, but I held onto her hand and brought her back to me, leaning down close to her ear. "Don't you *ever* forget what a wonderful mom you are. You did the best you could at the time. And Audrey is the luckiest little girl in the world to have you in her life."

Those green eyes filled up with tears right before I captured her lips with mine.

***

"You know, I made all these plans," Jayda said. "But we don't really have to do anything. I'm just enjoying being with you. And look at these girls."

Gabby and Audrey had both abandoned their jackets to storm up and down the play structure in Jayda's backyard. Well, Gabby more toddled her way around, trying to keep up with a wild Audrey.

"That's some serious energy," I said.

"I'm wondering if Audrey got into the candy stash. Or maybe your pancake recipe had a lot of sugar in it," she teased.

"Yep, just blame it all on me and my crappy pancakes," I joked, glancing down at Jayda who looked so hot in that little winter hat and her coat. I didn't know what it was about that hat, but I loved it on her.

I put my arm around her, squeezing her into my side as her arm came around my back, her hand gripping my waist. Man, even that tiny gesture set me off. Everything about this woman's touch made me lose it. For the millionth time, I mentally cursed my teenage self for not grabbing her up when I had the chance.

"Can't you just feel the snow coming in the air?" Jayda asked between the girls' shrieks.

I glanced up at the blue sky, the weak sun shining on us. "Um, no. I can't say that I do."

"You can't, Miami boy?"

I gave her arm a squeeze. "No, former Miami girl."

"Well, I guess I'm a Maine girl now... because I can *feel* it, smell it, almost taste it." She bounced up and down on her toes. "First snow of the season."

"How did I get so lucky?"

Eyes narrowed, she studied my face. "I can't

tell if you're being sarcastic or not."

I couldn't resist laughing. "No, actually, I'm excited. I don't have much experience with snow, except the rare times when I've traveled someplace cold during the winter. And of course, Gabby's never seen it."

"Oh, I really hope we get a good amount and not just a dusting."

"When's it supposed to hit?"

"Tonight. I'd love to wake up to a couple inches even. They say it should be three to four." Her enthusiasm was downright contagious. "And I have Audrey's old snow pants that Gabby could wear."

"Do you have snow pants for me? Or maybe one of those hats you're wearing?"

She glanced at me sideways, giggling. "I never know with you... whether you're kidding or not."

"Good." I laughed. "But seriously, I'd like one of those hats."

"Really?"

"Yeah. I'd like to see if I look half as cute as you do in one."

Despite the cold air, a flush crept up her cheeks. "So you like the beanie hat?"

"On you, yes." I whispered near her covered ear, "It's hot."

A shiver went through her as I nipped her neck. "Whew, okay. I'll have to remember that," she said, a mischievous look in her eyes that made my imagination run wild thinking about

Jayda wearing the hat and nothing else.

Mentally sighing, I realized I shouldn't even go there right now. Tonight was still many hours away, and I could only take so much torture. I wondered if Jayda felt the same. Through my arm, I could sense a tenseness to her body and noticed her breathing was ragged.

"You okay, sweetheart?" I asked.

Staring straight ahead at the girls who had quieted down a bit, she nodded and dropped her arm from my waist. And then the ring twisting began. "Alex, I need..." Her face turned pale. "I'll be right back."

She ran off inside, leaving me bewildered. But I didn't get a second to even think about it because suddenly a screaming Gabby hurdled her little body my way.

"She fell," Audrey shouted, running after her.

"Where does it hurt?" I asked, swooping her up into my arms.

But obviously, she couldn't tell me.

"Her knee," Audrey answered, hovering by my legs.

I inspected both knees to find a new hole in her pants that revealed a few scratches. Okay. It wasn't anything too awful, and her crying had already started to quiet.

Squatting down, I smiled at Audrey. "You know what? Thank you. You were a big help."

She puffed out her little chest. "I was?"

"Yes, you were. Gabby can't really say much

yet, and I never know where she hurts herself. But you knew and could tell me."

"Of course, I could. I'm literally four."

I almost died laughing. "Literally?"

"Literally," she repeated, mangling the word.

Man, was this kid Jayda's or what?

Gabby struggled out of my arms and took off toward the small slide. Glancing back at the open door, I wanted to check on Jayda. But I didn't want to leave the girls, so I waited, wondering what on earth had happened. She'd looked kind of sick. Or nervous. Or both.

What the heck was going on?

Walking to the back door, I looked in to see Jayda in the kitchen not too far away. "You okay?" I asked, my voice competing with the noise of the microwave.

"Yeah, just needed the bathroom real quick. I'll be right out after I make some tea."

I shook my head, trying to make sense of it all. Was she sick or something and too embarrassed to tell me? I could definitely understand that. But I wished she'd just tell me whatever it was because the not knowing was killing me, and I wondered if I'd have to wait till tonight to find out.

Gabby burst out crying again, making me realize it was probably about time for a nap. I walked over to pick her up.

"I don't know what happened," Audrey said.

"Aw, don't worry about it, Audrey. I think she's

just tired now."

"Does she need a nap?"

"Definitely. And I think she's extra tired trying to keep up with a big four-year-old."

I opened the door wider for Audrey to go inside with us, and we kicked off our shoes by the mat.

"Mama!" she yelled. "Gabby needs a nap."

Jayda looked up after putting a teabag into a steaming mug. "Do you feed her first or..."

"Usually. Yes." Gabby rubbed her eyes and yawned. "But today, maybe not. I think the Jenkins ladies are wearing her out."

"Oh, poor thing," Jayda said, still looking a bit pale.

"Mama, I'm hungry!"

"I figured. All that running around. Okay. Well, why don't we let Gabby take a nap, and I'll make you something."

"I'm going to head up and see if I can get Gabby to stay in the crib," I said, wondering if this was all going to be too exciting for her to get herself to sleep.

And after about ten minutes of her crying every time I put her down, I realized, yep, it was definitely too exciting. And I completely understood. We were *all* excited, I thought, rounding the corner back into the kitchen.

Her hand occupied with plates, Jayda glanced at the annoyed child in my arms. "Do we just need some chill time? Maybe watch a movie and see if she falls asleep in your lap?"

"Yeah! Yeah!" Audrey said. "Frozen."

Jayda put her free arm around Audrey. "Well, I know that's what *you* want. But what about you, Alex?"

"That actually sounds perfect."

Jayda loaded up the ottoman with a heaping platter of sandwiches, cheese, fruit, and pretzels that we all helped ourselves to. And soon after, with a drowsy Gabby lying up against my shoulder, I settled back onto the large sectional couch that was perfectly positioned to take in both the fireplace and the TV.

"Have you seen Frozen?" Jayda asked me as the iconic Disney castle appeared on screen.

"First-timer here. Probably first of many, I'm guessing."

"Definitely." Jayda laughed as she grabbed a few pretzels.

"Shh. I don't want you to miss it," little miss Audrey ordered.

Patting Gabby on the back, she fell right asleep, her tiny body warm on my shoulder. And a few minutes after the movie started, Jayda snuggled in on my other side, leaning against me with her legs curled up beside her. As her heat seeped into my body, my heart swelled up with a happiness that I'd never felt before, not even close.

This was what I'd dreamed about. This was the definition of my heaven. And I wanted this... forever.

In that moment, I vowed to do whatever it took to make it happen, to make this my family, to make this my life. Till death do us part.

CHAPTER SEVENTEEN

Alex

Before long, I noticed Jayda's breathing slow down and realized she was also asleep, cuddled up next to me, her sweet face resting on one shoulder and Gabby on my other. I wasn't sure how anyone could sleep with Audrey bouncing all around the rest of the couch, grabbing food and spilling half of it on the floor.

Audrey kept glancing at me, making sure I was watching the TV and pointing out her favorite parts. And with every song, she sang along, her off-key little voice butchering the words and tune in the cutest possible way.

I couldn't help but feel honored that she was so excited to be sharing her favorite movie with me. And she didn't seem at all bothered that her mom lay sound asleep between us.

"I'll show you my Elsa dress after the movie," she whispered.

"I can't wait," I whispered back, shaking my head at the amazing world that little girls seemed to inhabit, something I hadn't really yet experienced with my one-year-old, but something I was looking forward to diving into.

Jayda didn't stir the entire rest of the movie, and I wondered why she was so tired all the time. Six weeks ago, she'd had no problem staying up with me most of the night. Well, the second night. The first night, she'd pretty much passed out after the amazing passion we'd shared. As did I.

The credits started to roll, and I wondered what to do with the two sleeping beauties resting against me. But Audrey took care of it, shouting, "Mama! Wake up! The movie's over, and I need my Elsa dress."

A drowsy Jayda sat upright. "Oh, sorry about that," she said, glancing my way and stifling a heavy yawn.

As her warmth left my side, Audrey scrambled over to the now empty space. "Did you like it?" she asked me, her eyes wide, the open expression on her face reminding me of Jayda.

"I loved it."

"You did?" Jayda asked, eyeing me.

"Yeah. I really did. It's a great story." It really

was.

"Well, now you have to see the sequel and the shorts. It's a whole world, Alex," Jayda said, coming to life now.

"I'm gathering that."

"Mama! I need my dress."

"Okay, lovey, let's find your dress." Sighing and stretching, Jayda rose up from the couch. "And maybe when Gabby wakes up, should we get out of here? Maybe go see the lighthouse?"

"That sounds perfect."

Moments later, Audrey came rushing down the stairs to show off her ice-blue dress complete with a ripped hem. I couldn't help but laugh as she twirled around and sang at the top of her voice.

All the noise and excitement woke Gabby up. But instead of being cranky about it, she stared at the very excited Audrey who was now creating her own ice castle in the air with a smiling Jayda standing nearby.

"Mama, I want Elsa hair!"

"We can ask Santa soon. Okay?"

"You always say that."

Jayda laughed and rolled her eyes at me before turning back to Audrey. "I know. Hey, why don't we take a ride in that big old car you've been wanting to see, and we can show Gabby the lighthouse?"

"Can I wear my Elsa dress?"

"Sure, why not? *And* your coat and shoes."

Audrey grumbled about a jacket, but she went anyway to grab it off the hook. "What do you think, Alex?" Jayda asked. "Are you and Gabby up for that?"

"Absolutely. Just need to change a diaper here probably. We'll be ready in a few."

I carried Gabby up the stairs with Audrey and Jayda soon following to look for some kind of Elsa crown. As I changed Gabby's diaper, I thought about how it'd be nice to see a bit of the area, and I kind of hoped Jayda would wear that hat again. I laughed at myself as I also switched out Gabby's pants for a new pair that didn't have a hole in the knee.

Setting Gabby down on the rug in our room, she immediately went to town on all the toys Jayda had brought in, and I took the free moment to brush my teeth in the bathroom across the hall. It was then that I heard footsteps rushing past toward the end of the hallway where Jayda's room was and a door slamming shut.

What the heck? Why was Jayda practically running to her room?

I hurried to finish and decided to investigate after I saw that Gabby was still busy. But as I neared Jayda's open doorway, I hesitated, seeing that the bathroom door in her room was shut.

If she was sick, would she even want me near? Wouldn't she be embarrassed? Knowing Jayda, of course she'd be mortified if I knocked on her bathroom door.

And then I heard the gagging. Like she was trying not to be sick. And I felt awful. Was she attempting to hide some kind of stomach bug and just didn't want to tell me? I could see how she wouldn't want me to know.

But I didn't care if she was sick in front of me. If we were going to have any sort of future like I dreamed about, it would be in sickness and in health. And if she was ill, well then, I wanted to take care of her. That was the kind of thing that had been lacking between Fiona and me. And damn it, I couldn't handle another relationship like that.

Determined to make things different this time, I walked toward the bathroom and the intermittent gagging noise. For a split second, I hesitated, my hand raised to the door, not sure this was the right thing. But screw it, I forged ahead and did it anyway. I knocked. And the gagging immediately stopped.

"Jayda, are you okay in there?"

Complete silence. And then the sound of water running.

"You don't have to be embarrassed, you know, if you're sick."

Still nothing.

"Will you let me help?" I asked. "Please?"

The water shut off, and I heard the sound of her footsteps on the creaky floor. I held my breath, wondering what the hell was going on and whether she would actually let me help. The door slowly opened to reveal Jayda, her whole face pink, the wet trail of tears evident down her cheeks, her watery blue-green eyes capturing mine.

"Are you okay, sweetheart?" I asked.

She licked her lips and nodded, her stare faltering, like she was afraid to meet my eyes. And in that moment, *I knew*.

The gagging, the exhaustion, the refusal of wine, the *big thing* she was hiding... it all snapped together in my mind as my heart pounded in my chest. And before I could think about the wisdom of asking, the words blurted out of my mouth. "My God, are you pregnant?"

CHAPTER EIGHTEEN

Jayda

My heart in my throat and my stomach churning, I nodded, beyond nervous about his reaction. Scared to look into his eyes, I finally dared to glance upwards. I watched as the expression on his face turned from shock and disbelief to confusion and finally to joy—a pure and utter joy that lit up his entire being.

The tears spilled down my cheeks again, this time with emotion... with release from finally telling him, *finally* not holding this secret inside of me anymore.

"You're really pregnant?" he asked me, his own eyes filling up.

"Yes," I whispered, not trusting myself to speak

with the nausea that was overwhelming me.

All the sudden, Alex's arms were around me, holding me tight to him, and he began to twirl me around in circles, laughing. "Oh, my God, Jayda! Once again, you've made me the happiest man alive."

I gagged near his ear, and he quickly put me down. Clamping my hand over my mouth, I mumbled, "I'm sorry."

Those brown eyes I loved so much creased with concern as he put both hands on my cheeks. "No, no, no. *I'm* sorry. I'm so sorry."

A giggle escaped me at how sorry he could have been if I'd been sick on him. And then, we both started laughing, the tears flowing freely down my face now as Alex's thumbs wiped them away.

"You have no idea how happy I am right now, sweetheart."

His words shocked me. "Really? You are?"

"Happy doesn't even describe it. I don't know of a word that describes it, honestly."

He pulled me to him again, but this time in a gentle hug, his arms so tender around me, the tears came down even more. I felt him tremble against me. Or maybe it was my own trembling I felt.

I nuzzled my head into his solid chest, appreciating the feel of him more than I ever had before. Just having him hold me like this was all the answer I needed right now.

"I can't even believe it," he said against my hair. "This is absolutely incredible."

In my wildest dreams, I couldn't have imagined this reaction. I thought maybe he'd be upset, maybe worried, or just completely freaked out. I didn't dare hope for any kind of happiness. And it absolutely blew me away to have Alex acting like this.

He pulled back to stare into my eyes. "Are you sure? I mean, how? When? You're really sure?"

"I'm sure. I missed a pill. Or maybe two," I squeaked out.

"Are you okay?" he asked, his eyes softening even more.

His face showed so much concern that relief flooded through me, and my nausea vanished. For the moment anyway. But God, the emotions washing over me were just too much right now.

"Jayda?"

I could barely nod. And before I could say anything, Alex lifted me up into his arms and held me close to him. And like I was the most precious thing in the world, he carried me over to the bed and gently laid me down, adjusting the pillows behind my back.

He disappeared into the bathroom, soon returning with a cup of water and a cool, wet washcloth that he put on my forehead.

"Here," he said, holding out the glass. "Would a sip of water help?"

I wasn't sure what would help the overload

of feelings thrumming through my body, but grateful, I took a tiny sip, and it seemed to go down okay.

We both turned to the doorway as we heard noises down the hall. Alex glanced at me. "I'll be right back. Don't move."

I couldn't move a muscle even if I wanted to. Shock held me still. Shock that he knew. Shock at his reaction.

And in a flash, he returned. "They're fine. Just playing together in the guest room."

I smiled as he sat on the edge of the bed, keeping his eye on me like that small movement might set me off again.

"Thanks for that," I said, still overwhelmed with emotion. "So you're really actually happy about this? For real?"

He grabbed my hand in both of his with his strong grip. "Yes, absolutely, one-hundred percent for real. I am absolutely thrilled. But I'm worried about you. Are *you* okay?"

I smiled at this sweet man in front of me. "I am. Just having some morning sickness lately. Or all-day sickness really."

Those brown eyes narrowed. "Did you have that last time?"

"Yeah. It's normal. I had it the whole time."

He looked surprised. "The whole nine months?"

"Yep. But it's not that bad. Just nausea and lots of gagging. I don't actually get sick much. Only if

I let it get too far."

Shaking his head, he said, "That sounds awful. Is there anything that helps?"

"I have ginger gum that I pop any time the feeling comes up. I just..."

"What? What is it?" he asked, his eyes beyond intense.

"I just haven't been chewing it since you came because, well, because it would have been pretty obvious. And I..." I took a second to straighten the comforter next to me.

"You what?" Alex prodded. "You didn't want me to know yet, right? Is that it?"

"Well, I *was* going to tell you last night. I wanted to be alone, you know, just the two of us, where kids couldn't interrupt us. And not do it over the phone."

"I get that. So were you going to tell me tonight?"

I nodded. "I've been so nervous waiting for the right time to tell you."

"Nervous?" He leaned closer to me. "Why on earth were you nervous about it?"

I looked down, unable to meet his eyes. "Because I've never had to tell anyone that I was accidentally pregnant."

He surprised me by laughing. "No? Not a regular occurrence for you, huh?"

Thank God for this man because his laughter had a way of helping me with my crazy emotions right now. "Not exactly."

But he turned serious again. "Were you afraid of how I'd react?"

"Terrified," I admitted.

His eyebrows shot up as he squeezed my hand. "Are you serious? What'd you think I'd do?"

"Honestly, I had *no idea*. I guess I assumed you'd be upset about it."

"Upset? In no way am I upset." He paused a second, deep in thought. "How long have you known? Have you told anyone else? Your parents?"

"Well, the only person who knows is Kaileen because she was there on the plane when I—"

"Wait a second," Alex interrupted. "You knew on the plane? Like the plane from Miami?"

I pulled on a little thread that was escaping my jeans. "Mm-hmm."

His hand reached to my chin, lifting my gaze back to his. "Jayda, I'm not going to get upset at anything you tell me. I promise. Please believe me."

Those words from him... wow, they were an absolute dream. For six long weeks, I had held in all this worry, all this anxiety, about telling him, about his response. And to have him here reassuring me, acting so sweet, it made me want to cry.

"Do you hear me, sweetheart?"

"I do."

"I'm just shocked you knew on the plane, that's all. Not upset."

I swallowed against the lump in my throat. "I know it's weird. I didn't know for sure. I just had the same little cramps I had with Audrey."

He began to slowly rub my leg. "So you've been worrying about all this for six weeks?"

I nodded, watching him climb up onto the bed to sit next to me, his back against the padded headboard, his big arm coming around me and holding me tight.

He kissed my head as I turned into his side, so grateful for this man beside me. As I inhaled his comforting scent, the emotions swirled around inside me... honestly, so many emotions I couldn't even name them. Except one. One rose up above all others. An emotion so strong it threatened to rock my entire existence.

With Alex's unbelievably sweet and caring reaction, it cemented something I already knew, something I hadn't acknowledged yet and didn't dare think about, something that lurked in the back of my mind that I was afraid to admit to myself because I had no clue what lay in front of us.

After everything I'd been through with losing Blake, I didn't think my heart could hold any more love. But I was wrong. Apparently, my heart was capable of an infinite amount of love... because this man beside me now carried my whole heart in his hands.

I was totally and completely in love with Alex.

CHAPTER NINETEEN

Jayda

A lex reached for my hand with his and lazily traced the lines on my palm with his index finger, giving me tingles all throughout my body.

The love I felt flowed through me. And while it was exhilarating, it also calmed me... which was weird and unexpected because I had no idea how Alex felt, if we even had a future. But I would relish this feeling that I thought I'd never have again.

It had been so incredibly long since I'd felt that rush of a new love. And I never dreamed it'd be possible to actually love a man again.

"Jayda. My sweet, sweet, Jayda," Alex murmured against the top of my head. "I can't believe we're going to have a baby."

Those words, my goodness, they slayed me. "Me neither."

"Have you been to the doctor yet?"

"Yes. I'm sorry. It felt so weird to go without telling you. I'm so sorry."

"Don't be sorry!" He squeezed my hand. "I'm glad you went. And now I know. Now I'll be here for you."

I wasn't sure what to make of that because one thing I really didn't want was for Alex to think he needed to be with me just because of this baby. I wanted him to want *me*. I thought so anyway. God, I was so confused right now.

Also clouding everything was the promise I had said to Blake right before he died, and I wondered if that was a promise I could break. Under the circumstances, it certainly seemed like it could be. But I'd think about that later. For now, I'd just soak in this man holding me, offering me his comfort and unbelievable support.

His caresses on my palm continued, and I took a second to admire those strong hands. I had noticed and loved those hands even in high school. There was something about a man's hands that could be so attractive, and Alex's were the most beautiful I'd ever seen.

"I know it's early," he said, interrupting my hand lust. "But what did the doctor say? Was everything okay with you? With the baby?"

Just the way he said that, the kindness in his voice, made me want to cry again. I was an absolute emotional wreck right now.

"Jayda?"

"I'm sorry. I'm having trouble talking," I managed to say.

He chuckled and pulled me in closer. "Okay. I tell you what, baby, squeeze my hand once if everything went okay with the doctor."

As I squeezed his hand once, I felt my heart squeeze too. Oy, I had it so bad right now. Hormones, emotions, love, uncertainty, guilt. They all swirled together to make me one big bundle of craziness.

I buried my head in his chest. "You know I'm not normally like this," I muttered against his shirt.

"I know, sweetheart. I know. You've been through a lot. God, you've been through a lot."

Oh, now he was really going to make me cry, but he just held me. For how long, I wasn't sure. We sat there, his thumb making circles on my hand, calming me, infusing me with his own special brand of Alexness... until the girls made an appearance around the corner, probably wondering where we'd been for so long. Audrey had always been great about playing by herself, thank goodness. But that had been a marathon even for her.

Alex patted the bed. "Come on up, girls. We're just having a little rest."

"But didn't Mama already have a nap?" Audrey looked skeptical as she climbed up then hoisted Gabby up next to her.

I laughed as I realized Audrey wasn't going to go easy on me, which was probably a good thing.

They crawled over to us, Audrey tearing the hem of her Elsa dress even more. "Aren't we going to the lighthouse?" she asked.

"Oh, right. I forgot all about that."

She narrowed her little eyes at me. "Why's your voice funny?" She didn't wait for an answer, instead poking my leg. "Come on, Mama!"

I felt Alex's chest rumble with his laughter. "No rest for you..." He leaned closer to my ear, which I was beginning to think was his signature move. "Hot Mama," he whispered.

Giggling, I elbowed him. Making me laugh was Alex's specialty, and I appreciated it now more than ever. "All right. Maybe some cool, fresh air would be nice. I shouldn't sit around all the time anyway."

With great reluctance, I tore myself away from Alex's warm side and stood up from the bed, stretching out my muscles. I looked back at Alex who followed, and the look in his eye melted me, like we had a special secret together, like we were the only two people in the world. Well, except for these two little ones scrambling to get off the big bed.

Alex swooped down to pick up a laughing Gabby, and we all went down the stairs together to grab our jackets. After a few minutes of chaos trying to get two kids into their shoes and out the door, we finally managed to make it to the car and situate the girls in their seats. As we both struggled to buckle them in, Alex's eyes met mine from the other side of the car, his face alight with amusement. And that feeling of being a team swept through me, something I had dearly missed, especially once Audrey was born.

A longing poured through me, right down to my toes. God, how I wanted that. How I wanted to have this man in my life. Not just for the everyday things like getting kids out the door and into the car, but for *everything*.

"Toss me the keys?" he asked, a smile on his face.

I clicked together the final clasp in Audrey's harness. "So in other words, you're scared of my driving," I teased.

"No, not at all, baby. But will you let me take care of you? Just a little?" he asked, grinning at me still from across the SUV.

Smiling and shaking my head, I heaved out a sigh as I handed over the keys and shut the door. This was weird, I thought, getting into the passenger side. I was so used to doing everything on my own. Yeah, sure, I had my parents to help. But they were getting kind of up there, and taking care of a little kid took a lot out of them. So I mostly did it on my own.

As Alex adjusted the seat backward and

started the car, he glanced at the girls who had their hands occupied with the basket of toys I had put in the car. "I know you don't need a man to take care of you, Jayda. But will you let me spoil you?"

The truth was it felt really nice to have someone drive me around. I really hated driving.

"Just a bit?" Alex asked.

This man was impossible to resist. "Well, maybe just this once. Since you love cars and all."

"You know I've been wanting to check out how this thing handles anyway."

After shooting him a faux glare, he backed out, and I began giving him directions. Not that it was very difficult to get to the lighthouse only five miles away.

"So what do you think?" I asked. "Ready to give up your fancy ride for a more family-friendly SUV?"

His lips curved up in a grin. "I'll consider it."

"I'll believe it when I see it," I teased. "So have you ever driven in snow before?"

He thought for a second. "No. Can't say that I have."

"I'm not sure what's worse, to be honest, driving in torrential tropical downpours like in Miami or the ice we get here." They both scared me.

"I love driving in the rain," he admitted.

"Why does that not surprise me?" I laughed. "I hydroplaned once in high school, and it scared the you-know-what out of me." I shuddered remembering that awful feeling and lack of control.

He gave me a concerned glance before returning his eyes to the road. "Did you crash?"

"No, thank God. I honestly have no clue what I did, but the car somehow straightened out despite my panic."

"Well, thank goodness for that." A teasing grin appeared on Alex's face. "You know, my friends and I used to hydroplane on purpose in high school."

"What? Excuse me?" I stared at him.

"Yeah, it was a blast." At my look, he cleared his throat. "Not that I'd ever do that anymore. Of course. But I did learn a lot from it."

"Hmm," I said, not too shocked by his admission actually. It really seemed like something high school guys would do. "Yeah, let's go hydroplane for fun."

We laughed as he pulled into a parking space at the lighthouse. No one else was about at the usually popular spot. Maybe the lighthouse wasn't high on most people's list on a cold December afternoon with snow threatening to fall any second.

But the park was beautiful, made even more so by sharing it with this man next to me. Alex and I held hands, the girls running off ahead... or rather Gabby trying to keep up with Audrey.

Looking at the stunning scenery before me, I

let the beauty embrace me. I breathed in the cold air, letting it fill my lungs and awaken me. And with it came a happiness that I hadn't felt in a very long time.

We all followed Audrey as she led the way through the vast and winding park to the playground, the historic lighthouse rising up in the distance. I knew we wouldn't have time to really tour the lighthouse area as dusk would be upon us soon. But at least Alex could see it from the park and take in the atmosphere.

When we reached the playground, Audrey and Gabby had their run of the place with no other kids around. We were the only ones crazy enough to be out here.

Alex hadn't let go of my hand the whole walk here, and I loved how his hand stayed warm despite the cold. That heat seeped into my body, making me crave this man more than I already did. Or maybe it was the fact that he had surpassed my wildest wishes with his reaction to my pregnancy. But Alex had crept so completely into my soul now, I didn't think there was any going back.

"How you doing over there in that cute little hat?" Alex asked, turning his attention away from the girls to glance down at me.

"What is it with you and this hat?"

He threw his head back and laughed. "I have no idea. But I can't wait to get you alone tonight."

"Me too."

"It *is* okay though, right?" he asked. "What did your doctor say?"

My heart sunk to my toes at that question. "Um, I..."

Alex surprised me by laughing. "Let me guess. You didn't discuss that, did you?"

"Darn it. No," I groaned.

Alex let out a groan as well. "You're killing me, Jayda."

"Well, from what I know it's supposed to be safe. I guess I need to think about it a bit because, I mean, I never... well, when I was pregnant with Audrey, Blake and I never..." I felt my cheeks flame.

"I know what you're trying to say." Alex squeezed my hand. "Fiona and I never did either."

Now that shocked me. And I wondered why or why not, but I didn't want to ask. To be honest, Alex and I had talked about so many things over the phone. Except our previous partners. Of all things, that might be one of the most important.

I wasn't sure why Alex rarely brought up Fiona. But I knew I didn't like to talk about Blake much because... well, because I thought it might hurt Alex's feelings in some way. I didn't want him comparing our relationship to my previous one.

Maybe that was a mistake on my part. I didn't know. This whole thing was so new to me. I hadn't "dated" anyone since the age of nineteen, and I was more than out of practice. If you could even call this dating. I wasn't sure what we were doing exactly. If we *were* dating, we were kind of going about it all backwards what with a bun in the oven already.

"Maybe it's TMI," Alex continued. "But Fiona didn't want to be touched the whole time she was pregnant."

"Ah, I see." I could understand that. Some women felt miserable the entire nine months. "Well, pregnancy can be pretty awful for certain women. Some of my friends were very unhappy pregnant ladies."

"I get that. I really do. I can't even imagine how it feels, all the hormones, the emotions, the physical changes, the—"

But he didn't get a chance to finish his sentence because a few flurries began to fall, and Audrey started to scream and dance around.

"It's snowing! It's snowing!" she cried as Gabby stared at her, wide-eyed.

"Omigosh, Gabby's first snow," I said, excited for her to witness the magic.

She toddled over, and I picked her up. "Look, Gabby." I caught a snowflake on my finger and held it out to her. She touched the wetness as it melted then stared at the light flurries floating around us.

Audrey came running over. "Gabby, watch!" She stuck out her tongue and tried to eat some snowflakes. But it wasn't really coming down hard enough to catch any, so she cried out in frustration. "I want it to snow harder!"

"I think it will, love. Just need to be patient."

And like the heavens heard us, the snowfall started to pick up.

Alex ruffled Gabby's hair. "What do you think, pumpkin?"

The wind began to howl through the surrounding trees. "We should probably get going soon," I said, glancing around.

"I agree. Wouldn't want either of us to have to drive in a blizzard. Although I wouldn't mind trying."

I laughed. "Of course, you wouldn't."

***

A focused Alex drove us home, and I couldn't help smiling at how much he'd changed from the daredevil high school boy to this man driving around precious cargo.

When we made it safely into the driveway, Alex grinned at me. "That was fun. Not much different than rain. Actually easier than the sheets of solid rain."

"Glad to hear that, Miami boy."

He laughed as we both worked at getting the girls out, snowflakes starting to stick to his dark hair and somehow making him look even sexier.

Once we were inside and the girls were unbundled, I realized I was too tired to deal with dinner. "You guys up for ordering some pizza?" I asked, watching the girls empty toys out of a bin.

"Extra cheese!" Audrey looked up to say.

Alex nodded, shrugging out of his coat. "Pizza sounds great."

"I just feel bad we're making some other poor soul drive around in this weather," I said, cringing as I hung up my coat.

Alex shook his head to get out the snow. "It's probably a teenage boy who actually likes it and *wants* to skid out."

"Hopefully, he delivers the pizza first, and then he can do whatever it is that teenage boys do."

"Yeah. You don't want to know what teenage boys do."

"No." I laughed as I took off my hat and hung it on the doorknob to dry. "I really don't."

Normally, at the first sign of darkness, I closed the curtains around the big picture window in the front room. I hated the thought of someone looking in and watching us. But tonight, I left it open so we could see the snow, the streetlights illuminating the white glow.

I actually remembered to turn on the gas fireplace, and something about the scene caused that lump in my throat to return. The girls playing together, the gentle quiet of the snow falling, the warmth from the fire.

Everything was how it *could* be, how I dreamed it could be late at night when I was by myself. I just really wished—with all my heart—that Alex and I would have some sort of future and that he could possibly return the feelings I had for him.

CHAPTER TWENTY

Jayda

Several hours later, with the girls asleep upstairs, the house was finally quiet, and I made a cup of tea, the smell beginning to calm the hint of nausea in my stomach. I knew the first sip would take care of the rest.

Alex came into the kitchen and surrounded me with his body, his chest to my back, his arms coming around to caress my belly. "Can't believe our little tiny baby is in there," he whispered by my ear.

His words, his body, his warmth... all made it hard to breathe.

"She or he is probably the size of a pea at this point," he added. "You don't even have a bump yet, sweetheart."

He was so incredibly sweet because there was definitely a bump, or I was just bloated. I turned around to show him, lifting my shirt a bit. "There's a bump. See?"

His Adam's apple bobbed up and down while I raised my shirt even higher. Then he reached out a hand. "May I?"

"Of course."

The warmth of his hand on my stomach made me shiver as his eyes looked into mine. "Maybe the tiniest of bumps," he confessed.

I could tell he was nervous about saying it, and I could understand why. No man with any sort of brain wanted to comment on the size of a woman's stomach—pregnant or not. "You're totally scared to admit it, aren't you?"

He grinned at me. "Terrified."

The look on his face cracked me up.

"And you made me break my rule earlier today," he said.

That caught my attention as I let my shirt drop back down. "Which is?"

"I have a rule to never, and I mean never, ask a woman if she's pregnant."

I laughed so hard at that. "You're a smart man, Alex Hernandez."

The timer on the microwave went off, and I took out the teabag, putting it into the sink.

Alex sniffed and said, "What do you have there anyway?"

"I'm sure you know all of this already, but

there's a ridiculous amount of things to be careful about with pregnancy. That alone is exhausting. So when I stopped drinking coffee..." I let out a pretend sob. "Well, I have a midwife friend in Brooklyn who makes her own tea, pretty much just dried fruit and ginger, and she sent me some. Because you also have to be careful about tea apparently."

Alex squinted his eyes at me. "Really? Tea? I didn't know about that one."

I took a sip. "Yep. Tea. And you know what?"

"What?"

"This time, I'm considered *old* to be pregnant." Alex shook his head, but I was sure he wasn't shocked at this bit of information. "And that's why tonight," I continued, truly depressed at what I was about to say. "Well, I'll call my doctor tomorrow and discuss it, but I've decided, until then, we probably shouldn't..."

Ugh, I couldn't even say it.

Because the reality was I wanted to jump his bones. The way he was standing there, his brown eyes soft with tenderness, his shoulders and arms straining against his shirt in a way that made me want to touch every inch of him. I bit down on my lip. This man and what he did to me.

He swallowed, probably feeling the heat and hormones coming off me, then sighed. "Are you trying to tell me I'm not gettin' to home base tonight?"

I stared at him, not sure if he was joking.

"So no rockin' the Casbah?" he continued. "No joint session of Congress? I don't get to tap that?"

I couldn't stop laughing as he lightly smacked my bottom. Shaking my head and giggling, I snatched up my tea and tried to escape him. But he only chased me into the living room, still trying to grab my ass.

As quickly as I could, I sat down on the couch, trying not to spill my drink. "You are incorrigible, you know that?"

He laughed as he collapsed on the couch next to me. "You love it."

Yeah, I did. More than loved it. I loved the way he could make me laugh and lighten me up.

The video monitor made a crackling sound, and we both looked at Gabby sleeping soundly. "It's nice you still have that," Alex said.

"Well, I keep meaning to get rid of it, but it's one of those things I never get around to doing... along with all the clothes Audrey's outgrown just sitting in bins in the spare closet, you know?"

"Yeah, I get that."

I set my tea down and snuggled in closer to his side, both of us facing the window and watching the snow falling down, surrounding us with its hushed magic. We were quiet for a minute as I enjoyed the feel of him next to me, my softness sinking into his hardness.

"Alex, I..."

"Jayda, I..."

We both started to talk at the same time.

"You first," I said.

"You sure?" he asked.

"Mm-hmm," I murmured as his hand found mine, our fingers intertwining.

He took a deep breath, and I felt a flutter of nerves about what he had to say. "So I've been thinking a lot today about... well, about the future."

I swallowed hard, the nerves shooting throughout my body. "Okay?"

"And I don't really know what the future holds, but I want you to know something."

"What's that?" I managed to say, my throat suddenly dry.

"I don't know how yet." His thumb caressed mine. "But I want you to know I'm going to be here for you. I'm not going to let you go through this all alone."

I closed my eyes at those words, the pain of my last pregnancy sweeping through me. God, I had felt so alone. I had tried so hard to be strong. For everyone. For Blake. For Audrey growing inside me. For my parents. Even for myself. But every day, while Blake had been struggling to recover, it had all been so incredibly hard.

"Okay? Do you hear me, sweetheart?"

Overcome with emotion, I buried my head in his shirt, which somehow still held that scent of sun and heat. I breathed him in, trying to calm myself, trying to stop the tears from flowing.

"I just need to go home and figure out what to

do, figure out how."

I didn't say anything because even the thought of him leaving soon destroyed me inside. But I couldn't say that. It wasn't fair. Of course, he had to leave. He had family. He had a career, a home. And there was no way I could ask him to stay.

"But somehow, in some way, I'll find a way to be here for you."

I nodded into his shoulder, not sure if he could even feel my movement. As I swallowed against the pain, I realized I was going to have to trust him. I didn't know how he'd manage to be here for me.

With this child growing inside me, I felt so vulnerable. And the painful memories threatened to overwhelm me. I just didn't think I could manage it all by myself... again.

"Jayda? Are you okay?"

What was wrong with me? I was strong. I was tough. I had survived through so much. I had somehow managed to get on with my life. So what was happening to me right now? What was it that made me completely useless?

Alex's other hand started to caress my hair, and somehow I managed to sink into him even more.

"I'm not going to let you do it alone."

I tried to fight the onslaught of emotions, but it was too much. This man promising to be here for me, saying he wouldn't let me be alone through this. Those words meant so much to me, while at the same time, they were a stark reminder of everything I'd been through.

And it was more than I could handle, more than I could bear. The tears came, a full-on assault of tears, right on Alex's strong shoulder. I kept my face buried into him, not wanting him to see me fully.

Usually, I stuffed down my tears until I could cry by myself. But something about Alex must have made me feel safe because they kept on coming. Or maybe it was the way he comforted me, the way he gripped my hand in his, the way he stroked my hair.

"I'm so sorry," I finally said, once I'd regained some control. Reaching for a tissue in my pocket, I edged away from him, completely embarrassed at what I'd just done.

But he pulled me back, his hand on my face. "Please don't apologize."

I searched his eyes, and all I could see was concern, which threatened to set me off again. *Get it together*, I told myself.

"Are you worried about the future?" Alex asked, his thumb caressing my wet cheek. "Or thinking about the past?"

His questions made me think for a heartbeat. But truthfully, I already knew the answer. "Both."

He dropped his hand to my leg, where he gave me a gentle squeeze. "Will you talk about it with me? Tell me more about what happened with Blake?"

That surprised me. I hadn't been so sure he'd want to hear about Blake. It's not like he had said anything to indicate that, but it just felt like something he wouldn't want to hear about. "You sure?"

He nodded. "I think it's important to talk about it, baby, and not hold it all inside. Don't you think?"

I thought about the two years I saw a therapist, and she had said the same thing. And it *had* made me feel much better. But after that, I hadn't really discussed it much.

"I suppose you're right," I admitted. I looked down at his hand, not even sure where to begin. But I supposed I should start with *that* night, the awful night it had all started. The beginning of the end.

Alex patiently waited, his thumb now moving on my leg, making a pattern. I reached down to hold his hand, needing to feel his strength, grabbing onto his solidness.

"So I think I told you I was two months along," I sighed, realizing it was about the same place in my pregnancy as now. "I was in Los Angeles for a book signing, and he called me one night right after dinner..."

Alex leaned his head down to try to capture my eyes. "What happened?"

"He was at the hospital in the ER. He'd felt an excruciating ripping in his chest, and his legs went numb. He thought he was having a heart attack. So he called an ambulance."

Shaking his head, Alex squeezed my hand as if encouraging me to go on.

"And it took a while for them to figure it out. They ruled out heart attack. They thought it was a blood clot. And Blake kept calling me and texting me, keeping me updated."

"Where were you? In a hotel?"

"Mm-hmm."

"By yourself?"

I nodded, and Alex swore under his breath. "And then after a CT scan, they figured it out and had to take him right into the operating room. And just before he went in, the surgeon had him call me..."

Chills went through me at the thought of that phone call, the one I would remember for the rest of my life, the one I hated to even think about but now found myself discussing with this man in front of me.

"Call you?" Alex prodded, his eyes so sweet and tender.

I couldn't even look at him because he might make me cry again. "The surgeon told him he should say goodbye to me," I said, my voice cracking.

Alex shut his eyes, and I watched as he took a slow breath. "I can't even imagine, sweetheart."

The kindness behind his words gave me the much-needed fuel to continue. "It was awful. I mean, what do you say? After being together for all those years, it just..."

I realized right then that it was maybe something I didn't need to delve into with Alex. Those words between Blake and me should remain between the two of us. And the last thing I wanted to do was hurt Alex in any way. So I decided to move on.

"And then he had the surgery," I forged on. "And it was a very long surgery."

"What about *you*? What did *you* do?"

I was amazed that Alex asked so much about *me*. Usually, the focus was on Blake and what he was going through. Which of course it should be. But I appreciated Alex also wondering about me.

"I cried. I lay awake all night. I prayed that my baby would have a father."

Alex rubbed his forehead. "Oh, God, Jayda. I'm so sorry."

Inhaling sharply, I attempted to get through the rest of the terrible story. "And he did make it, of course, as you know."

Alex nodded.

"And the next morning, I flew back home. He spent a week in the ICU and another in a regular room on the cardiothoracic floor. But he somehow made it, and everyone was rather optimistic."

"You must have both been so relieved, but I bet the recovery was rough."

"Definitely," I agreed. "He could barely move

for a while. I did everything for him for a long time."

"While you were pregnant," Alex said, his voice deep with empathy.

I nodded, that ever-present lump in my throat growing larger. "He was a ghost of himself. He was literally the color gray for months."

"That must have been so hard on you."

Looking down, I played with the border on the plush pillow next to me. "It was," I whispered, hating to remember that time, the physical exhaustion, the worrying about Blake, the worrying about being pregnant. "I tried to focus on the future, you know, getting the baby stuff all together. But it was hard because Blake felt awful, and he was so scared. So I was terrified too."

Alex's brows drew together. "Why was he so scared?"

"Well, they said he still needed more surgeries in the future because he had multiple aneurysms all along his aorta that needed repair. And while they were optimistic, they also warned him that the aneurysms might rupture and he might need another emergency surgery."

He let out a loud exhale. "God, that's terrible. What an awful thing to live with. For both of you."

"It sucked, to be honest. Every twinge, every pain, it was just kind of a panic, looking at each other and saying, 'Is this it? Should we call an ambulance?'"

Shaking his head while caressing my hand, Alex said, "That must have been so stressful, sweetheart."

Nodding, I took a deep breath because the worst part was still coming up. "So even though it was tough, he made it through and really seemed to be doing okay when Audrey was born."

Those brown eyes stared into mine. "At least, he got to meet his daughter."

"Yes, he did," I said, smiling a little, remembering how happy we both were, how excited our entire family was at the time. "It was an exhausting but blissful three weeks. You know how one little baby completely changes your whole world."

He chuckled. "Yep, sure do."

Sighing, I kept going, and Alex's grip tightened on my hand, encouraging me. "And then... well, then..."

With his free hand, Alex put a finger under my chin, returning my gaze to his. "You don't have to go on if it's too much for you, love."

Closing my eyes and exhaling, I shook my head. No, I needed to finish the story so Alex could know, so we could move on from this. Opening my eyes again, I looked into his, determined to continue. "Thank you for that. But I want to tell you everything so we can get this out in the air between us."

"I appreciate that."

He gave my hand another squeeze, and I went on, remembering *the* night, the night that Blake died.

Another deep breath. And then another. "So one evening... three weeks and a day after Audrey was born, well, it happened. What we were dreading. The thing we were so scared of."

Alex didn't say anything, just let out a sigh.

"Audrey was asleep. Blake was watching TV, and I was reading. He stood up to get a drink or something, and that's when... that's when it happened. He doubled over in pain. The doctors always said he'd know. And he knew. Even I knew." I breathed through the horrific memories. "I called 911."

I looked away to watch the quiet snow still falling outside, amazed at the peacefulness just outside the window, a peacefulness that went on despite the pain in my heart. Alex's hand on mine brought me back, brought me back to the present, away from that terrible night.

Fighting the sudden swell of tears in my eyes, I said, "But he was gone before they could get there."

Alex pulled me to him, bringing my head into his hard chest. "I'm so sorry, sweetheart."

Breathing in my Alex, I remembered those final few minutes as Blake lay on the floor, clutching his chest, the life draining from his face, the agony pouring through me, the terrible helplessness I felt, those last few spoken words between us as we realized that *this was it*, that he was going to die.

I'd never spoken about that time with anyone, not my parents, not my best friends, not even the therapist.

And I wasn't sure I could speak about it with Alex. It almost felt like something so intensely private, something no one else should ever know about, the whispered words between us, the final goodbye.

But even though I wouldn't discuss the entirety of it, I knew there was something I needed to tell Alex. I needed to tell Alex about my promise to Blake. I knew that I owed this amazing man next to me that much.

"Alex, there's something else I need to tell you..."

CHAPTER TWENTY-ONE

Alex

There was more? I didn't know how she'd even managed to tell the whole story. It was more awful than I'd ever imagined. And I could read between the lines of what she hadn't said, fill in the blanks of that phone call, those last moments as Blake lay there dying.

How could she even stand to talk about it?

To live through that and then carry on the way she had took so much courage, so much strength. And my admiration for her grew stronger, if that was even possible. All these strange feelings rose up inside me as she spoke, an envy of the relationship they'd had, a sympathy for her like I'd felt for no other person before in my life, and a deep desire to comfort her, to take away her pain.

I held her as close to me as possible as I waited for her to go on, waited for her to gather herself. And in that quiet moment, I wondered what else she could possibly say. Her tone had been... well, the way she said it made me feel a little sick.

And the way she had trouble meeting my eyes, I knew I had to help her—or try to help her—through whatever this was. "You know you can tell me anything, sweetheart. What is it?"

Her eyes filled with unshed tears as she glanced at me and took another long breath. "Oh, God, this sucks."

Those words sent dread throughout my body, and I didn't know what to say, so I gave her hand another squeeze, hoping she'd tell me, even though part of me really didn't want to know.

"It's just..." She put the top of her head against my shoulder and sighed. "In those last moments, I kind of... well..."

I waited again, my heart starting to pound in my chest.

"Sorry. It's so hard to even say." She finally lifted her face to meet my worried stare, her eyes in agony. "I promised Blake I'd never be with another man. Never marry again. Anything."

Damn. What could I say to that? What did that even mean? Be with another man? We'd already broken that promise, hadn't we? So that explained where her deep guilt came from.

And never marry again? I'd be lying if I said I hadn't thought about it. Of course, I had. I'd thought about marrying Jayda Jenkins for years. Since the age of sixteen. Maybe even fifteen. And most definitely, I'd thought about it recently.

That was the hope. That was the dream.

But it was too early to discuss it. I didn't want to scare her away. Sometimes, she seemed so skittish with me. I didn't even want to talk about love yet, let alone marriage. But it was always there in the back of my mind.

"Alex?" she asked, her hand gripping me. "What are you thinking?"

I let out a sigh and looked out the window at the beautiful scenery without really seeing it. My mind was a mess. I knew Jayda. And if she made a promise, she meant it.

But part of me was pissed off, I mean, *really* pissed off. What the hell kind of man would ask that of his wife? Particularly a wife who was made a widow so young? That just didn't sit right with me. And it didn't seem like there was a damn thing I could do about it.

I wanted to get up and walk away to clear my head, to clear this cloud of anger. But I couldn't do that to Jayda, especially not after everything she'd just told me. Meeting her eyes, not sure if I was successfully hiding my anger, I shook my head. "Honestly, I'm not sure what to think."

Her tears spilled over then, and I felt like the world's biggest asshole. Clearly, she'd felt my anger. I closed my eyes and counted to five in my head.

Let's try that again. "I'm really sorry, Jayda. But it's upsetting to me to hear about that promise."

She nodded as she swiped at some of her tears. "I'm the one who's sorry. I should have told you before. I was just being selfish."

"You were in no way being selfish," I said, attempting to reassure her.

But really, I wanted to shout. I wanted to yell. However, *she* wasn't the one I was angry at. I was pissed off at a dead man. Pissed off that there was no way to talk to him. No way to reason with him.

We were caught in the middle of this awful promise that had been spoken in someone's final moments, without thought maybe, without really thinking about the consequences, without thinking of how that would affect the rest of this woman's life, this woman who had so many years ahead of her, who was now pregnant with our child, *our* child. This woman I had been wanting since high school.

You know what? I wasn't going to let it stand. This was one of those promises that could be broken. It had been totally unfair to ask that of Jayda.

With that thought, I felt some relief. I'd do my best to convince her of that. I'd die trying to convince her of that. I would never give up. I just needed to go about it carefully and not freak her out. I needed to act with the precision of a surgical procedure. Time was what I needed most to figure it out.

In the meantime, I had to keep doing what I was doing, trying to convince Jayda that I was worthy of her, worthy of a life together.

Then a teary-eyed Jayda surprised me, glancing up at me, saying, "I mean, really, I already broke the one promise, didn't I?"

She smiled, and I couldn't resist smiling back. "Yep," I said. "Five times."

"Are you counting, Alex Hernandez?" She shocked me by laughing.

"Maybe." I grinned as I shrugged. "You're not?"

She giggled and moved in closer to me again. "I'll let you keep track."

"Oh, so you think there'll be more?" I asked, half-teasing and half-probing to see what she'd say, holding my breath.

Sighing and nuzzling back into my shoulder, she said, "I think I have a lot of thinking to do about that promise."

I let out that breath, my anger from before dying down as I felt her warm body melting into me, the intimacy of everything we'd shared making me feel so close to this woman beside me, closer than I'd ever felt to another soul on this planet. And I vowed once again to do whatever it took to keep her by my side.

**

The snow stopped falling, leaving behind stunning scenery right out of a painting, the whiteness taking away the darkness of night.

Jayda was quiet, and I wondered what she was thinking, whether that promise was still on her mind or whether she was reliving Blake's death again. I didn't know about her, but I was exhausted. The emotions of the day had been unreal from the absolute high of finding out that Jayda was pregnant—pregnant!—to the tears and anger just now.

"Are you all right?" I whispered against her hair, that scent of hers making me want to inhale her... all of her.

But she didn't answer. And I noticed her breathing was deep and even. I had to stifle a chuckle. Yep, I'd say she was even more exhausted than I was, which of course made sense with all the pregnancy hormones she was dealing with currently. I didn't want her to sleep on the couch tonight and have a bad night of rest, so I nudged her a little and she sat up.

"Oh, sorry," she said, sounding confused. "I didn't even know I was falling asleep."

"Let's get you upstairs."

She sighed and stretched before getting up from the couch. "That was a pretty emotional day, right?"

"Just a little," I said as she closed the curtains and checked the locks on the front door. "You definitely know how to entertain houseguests."

She shook her head, laughing at me, as she headed up the stairs with me following, trying to smother the intense physical reaction I had just from watching her go up the stairs in front of me. I felt like a horny teenager again.

At the top of the steps, Jayda reached for my hand. "Will you sleep with me tonight?" she asked me, her voice quiet.

For a second, I couldn't breathe. But as she watched me in the dim glow from the hallway nightlight, I realized exactly what she meant. "Of course. If you're sure."

Smiling, she leaned up close to my ear and whispered, "If I can't have you in me, at least I can have you around me."

God, what those words did to me. "Jayda, Jayda, Jayda. I'll be right in as soon as I take a cold shower."

She put her hand over her mouth, her eyes bright with laughter. "See you in a minute." And then she tiptoed down the hall to her room, leaving me thinking seriously about that cold shower.

A few minutes later, I headed to her room, the monitor in my hand, to discover Jayda already in her bed under the covers. I swallowed hard because this was going to be rough for sure.

Of course, I wanted to hold her in my arms all night, but I was also desperate for more. *Desperate.* I knew that for most pregnant women, sexual activity was completely safe. But there was no way in hell I was going to pressure Jayda into doing anything until she felt comfortable. And if that meant waiting for her to speak to her doctor, then so be it. I would wait.

Jayda smiled at me as I turned off the lights and headed over. "That was quick," she said.

"Didn't want you falling asleep on me." My eyes adjusted to the dark as I slid in next to her.

In an instant, our bodies melded together, her back to my chest. "This is torture," I groaned against her neck.

"Alex, will you let me—"

"No," I choked out, harsher than I intended. "Sorry. Didn't mean to sound so rough. I just want you so badly right now."

She rubbed against me as her hand moved down my stomach. "Please, let me—"

"I don't feel right about taking and not giving." Jayda rolled over, and I sighed with relief that her sweet ass wasn't nestled up against me anymore.

"I get that. But I want to," she said. "I can't even tell you how much better I feel right now."

My mind was still stuck on the first part of what she'd said as she settled into that perfect spot, her head on my shoulder and hand on my chest. But eventually, the rest of her words hit my lust-filled brain. "You feel better?"

I felt her full breasts against the side of my body as she inhaled and exhaled. "I really do. Everything is out there now. Keeping this pregnancy from you was the worst. But I wanted to tell you in person. And now, it's such a huge relief to share that with you."

"I bet, sweetheart," I said, kissing her head.

"And then, finally telling you all about Blake..."

At the sound of his name, I felt a jolt of anger, still not one-hundred percent over that insane promise, apparently.

Her sweet mouth against my chest, almost making me wish I hadn't worn a t-shirt to bed, Jayda continued, "It's such a release. I can't even tell you. I seriously feel like a huge weight has been lifted off me, like I lost a million pounds."

"I'm glad to hear that." I stroked her back, trying not to think about what being this close to her body was doing to me.

"You're a good man, Alex," she murmured against me, her voice fading slowly.

Those words filled my chest with a warmth I'd never felt before. No one had ever said that to me. And to have Jayda say it? Well, it made me want to be the best man I could be... for this woman, for these girls, for this family I was determined to build.

She yawned. "And I have the worst case of blue balls," she said, barely audible.

Did she really just say that? My Jayda? My whole body shook with laughter. I couldn't help it. There were layers to Jayda I'd never dreamed about. And the more I knew, the more I loved it.

"That makes two of us," I finally said, grinning, even though I knew she was already asleep.

As I lay there, still holding her trusting body, her heat flowing into me, the events of the day worked their way through my mind. I didn't think sleep would be coming anytime soon.

Thinking about how thrilled I was to welcome a baby with Jayda to feeling the sadness of what she went through with Blake's death, I realized something that blew my mind. Just when I didn't think I could feel any *more* for this woman, it dawned on me that she had, without even trying, fulfilled that marriage vow I'd so desperately wanted to experience.

Jayda and I had doubled the joys and halved the sorrows.

CHAPTER TWENTY-TWO

Jayda

When I woke up in the morning, Alex was gone. The sheets around me were cold, and the door was shut. Weird. Bright sunlight streamed in through the edges of the curtains. Feeling completely disoriented, I glanced at the clock.

9:52?

Are you kidding me? I didn't remember the last time I'd slept that late. Definitely not since Audrey had come into my life. And I actually felt amazing, no nausea and well-rested. Very strange. But the strangest thing was the quiet. I couldn't hear any noises, no little kids running around, yelling, and playing.

As quickly as I could, I threw on some clothes

and brushed my teeth, wondering what on earth was going on.

Downstairs, I turned the corner to the living room and stopped, my jaw dropping. There they were! All three of them were lined up on the couch, cereal bowls in their laps, watching Tangled.

Alex turned and grinned at me. "Let you sleep in, hot Mama."

Those Alex butterflies took off deep in my belly. Could I possibly love this man any more than I already did?

"Shhh," Audrey said, shooting me a look, not having any interruptions.

I didn't even say anything because nothing could take away from the wave of love washing over me right now as I stared at Alex. Not to mention the wave of lust. These pregnancy hormones were making me crazy. Or it was just the gorgeous, sexy man in front of me.

Like he could read my thoughts, Alex put his bowl down and walked over to me, quietly taking my hand in his and leading me to the kitchen. He spun me around, putting his hands on my hips and bringing me in close. "Good morning," he whispered, those deep brown eyes staring into mine.

I shivered, wanting his hands all over me. "I need to call the doctor."

"Wait," he said, his voice low and husky, making me melt all over.

And then his lips were on me, drinking me in, heating me up, his hands roaming my body, making me somehow want him more than I ever had before. That mouth of his and what it did to me. I shuddered at the memories from six long weeks ago.

Why, oh, why hadn't I asked the doctor about sex? I was kicking myself right now. Hard.

Alex's kisses sent shockwaves all the way to my toes, and I had to pull back, my lungs thirsting for oxygen. He rested his forehead on mine. "Call the damn doctor," he said, his voice strained.

Laughing, I skirted away from him, needing to put some distance between us. "I'll call the damn doctor. But first, I'd like to know... how on earth did you manage that?" I waved toward the living room.

"Ah, easy actually. You were snoring away when Audrey busted into the room. Just so you know, she had a few questions about why I was sleeping in your bed, but I deflected."

I grimaced, thinking of the conversation we'd have to have later.

"Anyway," Alex continued, "I woke up, but you didn't budge. So I snuck out and thought I'd try to let you sleep. And it actually worked." He smiled like he was proud of himself.

"Well, I'm seriously impressed. I don't remember the last time I slept that late. And by the way, I don't snore, Doctor Hernandez."

"No. Of course not." He raised a brow, making me unsure whether he was kidding or not, but also sending tingles through me at the hot way he was checking me out.

"I need to call the doctor," I mumbled. "And take a shower."

He swatted my bottom as I walked past him, and I laughed my way back up the stairs.

***

Of course, the doctor didn't answer, so I left a message, asking her to call me as soon as possible. *Please.*

Feeling like a different person than I did yesterday, I rushed through the shower, wanting to get back downstairs, hoping to spend as much time as possible with Alex before they left tomorrow morning.

I couldn't believe how happy I felt today, like so much pressure had been lifted from me. When I had told Alex last night how great I felt, I hadn't been exaggerating. Truly, all the stress of keeping everything to myself had made me miserable. And trying to be a good mom to Audrey, dealing with pregnancy hormones, and writing my book amidst all that was absolutely exhausting.

But between Alex's excitement about the baby and his empathy while talking about Blake, he had shown himself to be an amazing man. Combing out my tangled hair, I shook my head, not quite believing how sweet he'd been.

I mean, what man wanted to hear about someone's past husband? It couldn't have been easy for him. But he had actually *asked* me about it. And the whole time, he had been so incredibly supportive of me and so caring.

My heart gave a little squeeze as I remembered how he'd held me in bed last night, how he'd caressed me and held onto me like I was someone to be treasured, how I'd woken up a few times and he'd always pulled me back to him, keeping me downright hot during the cool night.

Somehow, I'd fallen even harder. Somehow, I'd fallen even more in love with him.

***

The day ended up being one of the best days of my life. We spent most of the time outside, bundled up in the snow. The girls could barely move in their puffy pants and coats. But they both loved falling in the powder which they did over and over and over, laughing and tossing clumps of snow, the bright sun shining down on us.

We'd go in to thaw and eat some food, then head right back out again. And the best part? Once Alex saw the neighbors outside with their snow blowers and shovels, he just grabbed my shovel that was leaned up against the shed in the backyard and started to clean up the sidewalks... on his own, without me even asking.

While I played with the girls, I couldn't keep my eyes off him. Something about it was so hot.

Maybe because I'd had to do it on my own for so long. Every winter, I'd swear this was the year I'd buy a snow blower or hire someone. But I never got around to it and ended up doing it by myself. Or sometimes, if I was lucky, a kind neighbor would do a bunch of houses, including mine.

But watching Alex so easily scrape up the snow and toss it to the side, it made me so... I took a deep, steadying breath, trying not to think of the way his muscles strained against his coat.

Feeling heated suddenly, I loosened my scarf and took off a glove to check my phone. Nope. Nothing from the doctor.

After I stared at Alex the entire time, he finished up and walked by me to put the shovel back. "That hat. You just had to wear the hat, didn't you?" he said, smiling and shaking his head.

So I wasn't the only one feeling it, I thought, laughing quietly.

***

Not long after dinner and an impromptu dance party in the living room, the girls fell asleep lightning fast from all the fresh air and playing in the snow. And I found myself once again snuggled up with Alex on the couch, my new favorite place to be, well, if I couldn't be doing other things with him. I let out a sigh.

"So still no word from the doctor?" Alex asked, his hand finding mine.

I stared at the crackling fire in front of us. "No.

I guess it's not surprising for a Sunday."

"I guess not," he said, releasing an epic sigh himself.

"I could have called the on-call emergency doctor, but—"

Alex's laughter interrupted me. "But it's not *really* an emergency... not to anyone but us."

"Yeah. I would have felt pretty ridiculous."

We were silent a moment as Alex studied my hand in his. "You know, you have beautiful hands," he said. "You always have. I remember that in high school."

I smiled to myself because I had thought the exact same thing about him.

"And your toes. I remember all the sandals you used to wear and those little toes with hot pink nail polish."

I had to laugh at his words. "So you're a foot guy?"

He joined in my laughter. "Only yours. You used to totally distract me in trig. Let's just say that did not end up being my best class."

"Oh, blame it on me, huh?"

"Completely."

I noticed him checking out my fuzzy pink socks. "You want me to take off my socks for you?" I teased.

He flashed that sexy smile at me. "Nah. Wouldn't want you to get cold feet."

The double meaning behind those words was not lost on me, and I swallowed because I still had some thinking to do about our future, even though I desperately wanted a future with Alex, even though—hello!—I was pregnant with our baby.

There was also something else on my mind, something we hadn't really talked about yet. And because of that, it worried me a bit, not a ton though because I trusted Alex and knew he wouldn't ever hurt me intentionally. However, I did think about his ex sometimes.

I knew they had divorced and it was officially over. But as a woman and as a mom, I had to wonder what would happen if she ever changed her mind and wanted to be a mother to Gabby. She'd only had Gabby fourteen months ago. And it was a strong possibility that she might want to know her daughter someday. Before Alex and I could forge any kind of future, I needed to know what he planned to do if that ever happened.

He was a smart man, and I was sure he'd thought about it. But being with Blake for so long, I'd seen over and over how he and his guy friends tended to avoid talking about more serious topics and just lived in the moment.

Many times, I had envied that. But sometimes, it had annoyed me when I wanted to discuss something heavy. It'd been like getting water out of a rock to get Blake to talk about the deeper stuff in life, and I had to wonder if Alex was the same way.

"What are you thinking about over there,

baby?" Alex asked, squeezing my hand.

I sucked in a breath, not sure how to even bring up the topic and also feeling bad about it. Hadn't we just had a gut-wrenching emotional discussion last night? Did we really need another tonight?

"All right. Now, you're kind of freaking me out," Alex prodded.

"Oh, I'm sorry. It's nothing *that* bad really."

"Not that bad, huh? What is it then, Jayda?" he asked, his eyes creased with concern.

"Well, I'm just wondering, you know, if... well, if Fiona ever shows up, what would you do?"

He let out a breath.

"Is that something you've thought about really?" I asked.

"I actually have." I waited for him to continue. "And first off, I can promise you that Fiona and I are completely done."

Well, that was good at least.

"And as far as Gabby goes, I know there's always the possibility that Fiona will change her mind. And I'm not sure how you feel about this, but I've thought about it a lot. And if she wants some kind of relationship someday with Gabby, I think I'd try to support that somehow and work something out for Gabby's sake."

I nodded. "I get that." And I really did.

"You do?"

"Yeah, of course. Gabby's going to have lots of questions someday I'm sure."

He sighed. "I know. I never thought I'd be in this complicated of a position."

I held his hand tighter, trying to offer some kind of support like he had given me. "Well, for what it's worth, I think you're doing the right thing."

His eyes looked into mine. "Thanks. I appreciate that. It hasn't been easy. And I just feel like Gabby's missing out."

My heart squeezed at that thought. "But she has *you*, Alex."

"But I want more for her." Those incredible eyes of his filled up.

"Of course. I think every parent wants that."

Alex opened his mouth like he was going to say something then stopped himself.

"When was the last time you spoke to her?" I asked.

"Fiona?" He took a breath. "It's been a while. I guess since the divorce was finalized. And that was just to go over details."

"Was it a complicated divorce?"

"No. It was rather amicable, and it was fast. She didn't want anything. No spousal support. I bought out her part of the house. She just wanted to get back to LA as quickly as possible where her family is. She even signed over her parental rights."

That surprised me that she'd already taken that step. "She did?"

"Yep. But that's only the beginning. It would

have to go through court for anything to be official."

I nodded, not sure how to feel. The way Alex talked, he didn't seem very emotional over it all... well, except about Gabby. But certainly not about Fiona. And I didn't know what to think. Maybe it was as straightforward as it all seemed. Maybe he really was over her.

But it *had* been somewhat recent. Plus, she was the mother of his child. Even though it had been four-plus years since Blake had died, I knew I would never get "over" him. He would *always* be a part of me.

Maybe death and divorce were different beasts. I didn't know really. I had only experienced the one, so I had no clue about the other. I had friends who were divorced, and they'd handled it in various ways, some moving on quickly, and others still grieving.

"Mama!"

The gate upstairs rattled, and I jumped up, afraid that Audrey would awaken Gabby. And then the fun would really start.

"Mama!" she yelled again before I could get there.

"Shh, sweetie," I said as I unlocked the bottom gate and rushed up the stairs. "We don't want to disturb Gabby."

But it was too late. A cry came from down the hall. Dang. I should have cranked up the white noise even more I supposed.

Neither kid would go back to bed, and I had no clue what to do. If it were just Audrey, I'd let her go to sleep in my room and read on my phone until I conked out.

Whenever she had nightmares, she had an awful time going back to sleep and usually ended up in my bed. And I totally understood. I had been the same way as a kid. I still remembered some of the awful nightmares I'd had, most involving clowns.

But it was also the excitement of this visit that was keeping them awake. So we ended up back on the couch, all four of us, covered up with blankets and snuggled together, watching Tangled again.

Sitting right next to me, Alex glanced at me. "Hand me the remote?" he asked, grinning.

"You want the remote, huh?" I returned his grin. "I'm not sure I can do that."

He whispered in my ear, "I'm willing to pay a price for it."

At that, my pulse picked up. "What kind of payment are we talking about?"

"You'll have to wait to find out. But I promise I'll make it worth it." He paused for a second then went in for the kill. "And you'll be thanking *me* after I make you moan my name."

I slapped the remote in his outstretched hand as he chuckled. And I sat there smiling through my misery again, wondering exactly how long I'd have to wait.

CHAPTER TWENTY-THREE

Jayda

S ometime in the night, we had all fallen asleep... except for Alex. At least there was one responsible adult watching out for us all.

I awoke to him gently picking up Gabby in one arm and taking her up the stairs. And a few minutes later, he returned and gathered up a sound asleep Audrey. I watched, a lump growing in my throat, as he carried her so effortlessly.

That got to me—totally and completely— seeing Alex acting paternal to Audrey, filling a hole I thought I'd never, ever see filled.

Soon, he was in front of me again. "Want me to carry you too?" he asked, that smile of his making my breathing ragged.

I wouldn't mind being carried. But that might be a bit much with the gates and stairs. Before I knew what was happening, though, Alex reached down and lifted me in his arms like it was nothing, giving me a sweet, lingering kiss that made me melt.

I sighed as he carried me to the gate, setting me carefully on my feet. "I like watching you go up the stairs," he said, swatting my ass.

All I could do was shake my head as I went up the steps in front of him, fully aware of his eyes on me in the dim light. And then, it was a repeat of last night—Alex joining me in my bed, holding me up against him, his soft t-shirt on again, which was smart. I didn't think I could handle it otherwise.

"Maybe I need a new doctor," I mumbled. "One that gets back to me in a timely manner."

"We can look into that," Alex said.

I loved how he said "we." With that thought in my mind, that Alex would be a partner in this pregnancy, I let myself drift off, Alex's chest rising and falling beneath my hand.

***

In the morning, Alex's phone alarm woke us up. He was nestled up against my back, his arm around me.

"Good morning," he said, his lips moving on my shoulder.

"Hey," I said, trying not to let my heart break at the thought of him leaving so soon. He had said he'd be here for me, and I was going to trust him.

Audrey came running in and jumped on the bed, kick-starting the whole morning. I sighed as Alex and I both rose up from the warm covers when Gabby made noises down the hall.

The thought of this house without Alex left me a mess. He had been here for a little over two days, and already, he'd filled the emptiness completely. I didn't know how I'd bear it when he left.

And I knew he really had no idea when he'd be back. He had a career that couldn't just be abandoned. He had actual patients relying on him, needing his care, needing surgery.

The little time we had passed in a whirl with excited girls spilling cereal everywhere, and all of us tripping over the clutter of toys that had taken over the house. Of course, we were running a bit late. It was hard enough getting one kid out the door. But two? Holy crap.

In a blur of jackets, scarves, and mismatched gloves, we somehow managed to get out to the SUV, Alex smiling across from me as we once again buckled in the girls.

"Let me drive?" he asked.

I hesitated for a second.

"Come on," he pleaded. "I really want to drive in this slush. It looks like fun."

"Fun? If you really think so, sure. Please be my guest," I said, shaking my head as I handed him the keys.

A minute later, I found myself gripping my seat as Alex backed out of the driveway and maneuvered down the street, the sun and warmer temperature making a mess of yesterday's snow. But at least it wasn't icy. I definitely preferred slush to ice.

And of course, Alex handled it like a champ. The streets in my neighborhood were always the worst, the last to get plowed, and I dreaded it during the winter. Thank goodness I didn't have to drive anywhere for my job and that Audrey's preschool was within walking distance.

"I loved that," Alex said as he pulled out onto the main street that had clearly already been plowed.

"Really? That was good for you, huh?"

"Piece of cake."

"Okay, Miami boy."

He just laughed as he kept driving the short distance to the airport. And with each passing moment, I fought the dread growing in my stomach.

I popped a piece of ginger gum, hoping that would help. But it didn't. This wasn't morning sickness. This was a special kind of missing Alex sickness, a sickness that I didn't think could be cured unless Alex and I found some way to be together... for good.

The dread spread throughout my whole body when we drove up to the departure area. I took deep breaths, trying to calm the ache in my heart as he pulled over to the curb and stopped.

His phone buzzing, he reached for it and frowned.

"Everything okay?" I asked.

He let out a sigh and glanced over at me, placing a hand on my knee, a look in his eyes that I'd never seen before. "Look, Jayda, I don't want there to be any secrets between us. And I don't know if this is even the right decision at this moment..."

My heart started to gallop. "What do you mean? What's going on?"

He drew in a long breath, squeezing my leg. "That was a text from Fiona."

Was he serious right now? He *had* to be kidding!

"She's in Miami and wants to talk to me."

Absolutely unbelievable! Despite the adrenaline pounding through my body, I somehow managed to swallow a total freak-out. "Did she say why?"

He sighed. "No. No, she didn't."

The girls started to make noises in the back, and I knew we couldn't really hash this out fully like I wanted to do. Plus, we didn't have much time before their flight. I unbuckled my seatbelt, numb with shock, not even sure what I was doing. Alex's hand on my thigh stopped me, though.

"Look at me, sweetheart." So I did, the concern in his eyes catching my attention. "I have no idea what she wants," he continued. "But I do know this."

"What?" I managed to say.

"Nothing is going to stop me from coming back to you."

Inhaling, I pressed my lips together, trying not to let out all the crazy emotions I was feeling. It wasn't the time or place. I needed to keep it together.

"Mama! Why did we stop? I want out!"

Gabby started up at the same time, but Alex still held onto my leg. "You hear me, Jayda?"

Slowly, I nodded. I heard him all right. But I wasn't so sure. He finally let go of me, and we both stepped out of the warm car and into the cold, the metaphor hitting me full-on in the chest.

And too soon, with Gabby in one hand and his suitcase in the other, Alex stepped toward me, placing his luggage down on the sidewalk. He gave me a one-armed hug, pulling me tightly to him, like he was trying to reassure me.

Gabby's bright eyes were right in front of me, and I couldn't resist giving her kisses on those sweet, chubby cheeks. "Enjoy the plane ride, little lovey," I said, holding in my tears as she gave me a gummy smile, showing off her two teeth.

Alex pulled back, capturing my eyes with his. "Jayda, I'll be back. Okay?"

My heartbeat racing, I stared at him, searching his eyes, his face.

"Okay?" he repeated, his voice rough.

I finally nodded because I knew he meant it. I knew he had the best of intentions. But I also knew from experience that even with the best of intentions, life could completely fall apart.

He kissed me then, the sweetest, most tender kiss I'd ever experienced, making me want to weep. His face close, Alex grabbed onto my shoulder, his eyes burning into mine. "I'll see you soon. Okay?"

"Okay," I breathed out.

"Dadadadada," Gabby said.

Alex gave me one last smile as he picked up his luggage and walked away, my heart breaking into a million little pieces. When he reached the automatic doors, he turned around to wave at me.

"Have a safe flight," I whispered while waving.

Somehow, I kept my tears in until I got back into the car. I cranked up the Frozen soundtrack for Audrey and put on my sunglasses, reminding me of the months I'd hidden behind them after Blake had died. And then the tears spilled down my cheeks.

How on earth had I let this happen? How had I let myself fall so deeply in love? Alex Hernandez had broken my heart once before in high school. What the hell was wrong with me that I would let that happen again?

Part of me knew it wasn't his fault. I couldn't blame him. I could only blame myself. I had let him into my life so completely, and I just wished with all of my shattered heart that he'd come back to me.

CHAPTER TWENTY-FOUR

Jayda

Despite the amount of tears, I managed to get us home in one piece. I knew dropping Alex off at the airport would make me an emotional, hormonal mess. But then that added little drama about Fiona was like a knife to the heart.

Sure, last night he had assured me that they were done. But what did I *really* know about that? Alex had never said anything to me about love, about marriage, or any sort of future really. Of course, he said he'd be here for me regarding the pregnancy. But what did that actually mean?

As I cleaned up the house in a depressed funk and tried to get a very grumpy Audrey ready for preschool, I knew there was one person above all I needed to talk to, someone who was always there for me, no matter what—Kaileen.

I just needed to make it until a little after noon, when I would get home from walking Audrey to preschool.

***

She picked up after one ring and didn't even say hello.

"Spill it. I want to hear everything," she said.

And the tears threatened to come once again just at the sound of her voice.

"Jayda? You okay?"

"I'm okay," I croaked out, sitting on the couch and reaching for a tissue in my pocket.

"Oh, Lord." She sighed. "What happened, girl?"

I drew in a shaky breath. "I don't even know where to start actually."

"Well, why don't you start by telling me how he took the baby news?" she asked, the worry evident in her voice.

"Oh, he was amazing." My eyes filled up at the memories of his sweetness. "He was so incredibly supportive. And he was actually happy, like really, really happy about it."

I heard a gasp through the phone. "Oh, that's good news, hon. You must be thrilled."

"I am," I said over the lump in my throat.

"Then why don't you sound very happy?"

I could imagine the look on her face, the crease between her brows. "Well, the weekend was great, except for the no sex part," I admitted without even thinking. "And then—"

"Wait. Excuse me. Did you just say you didn't have sex?"

"No. We didn't," I said, my voice full of regret.

"Why on earth not?"

I sighed. "Because I forgot to ask the doctor."

Her sigh matched my own. "Oh, that sucks. It's probably fine, though."

"I know. I know. I just wanted to be sure because this time I'm considered to be of advanced maternal age," I said, exaggerating the last three words.

"I hear you. Or what they used to call a *geriatric* pregnancy," she said, beyond annoyed and frustrated. "I know all about that. Try being over forty and being pregnant. They freak out about everything and want you to take every goddamn test available."

"It's crazy," I said, shaking my head, remembering everything she went through.

"I know they mean well. But if I was able to have sex, you'll probably be fine too."

"Probably. I mean, if..."

"If what?" she asked, her voice edgy.

"If things go well and he comes back," I said so quietly I wasn't sure she could hear me.

She jumped on those words immediately. "Why wouldn't he come back? What are you not telling me?"

I realized I needed to back up a bit so she could understand everything. "Well, he was so sweet and said he'd be here for me and not let me be alone through this pregnancy..."

"He is a *man*."

"He is. He really is," I completely agreed.

"But?"

Oh, I didn't want to relive this part, but I had to tell her, had to get her opinion. "But then, literally, like out of an awful movie, as we pulled into the airport this morning, he got a text from his ex."

"Are you kidding me?" She was so loud I had to snatch the phone away from my ear. "What the hell did she want?"

"Would you believe she's in Miami and wants to talk to him?"

"That's total BS." She was silent a moment, and I was so caught up in my misery, I couldn't even speak. "What did he say about it, though?" she finally asked.

I thought back to that awful moment. What had he said exactly? I mostly remembered how intense his eyes had been as he spoke to me. "Well, he kept reassuring me he'd be back."

She let out a whoosh of air. "Jayda, I know you're probably freaking out right now. But please listen to the man and don't jump to any conclusions."

"I want to. I really do. But I can't help what I keep thinking about obsessively. What if he goes back to her? What would I do then?"

"First of all, that's not going to happen. And

you know what? Even if it did—which it won't—you'd be fine. Yeah, it would be hard. But you've been through worse."

She had a point. I'd experienced worse. And yes, I'd waded through it somehow. But the pain of it... the pain had been more than I could handle at times. And the thought of facing that kind of pain again destroyed me inside.

"And why on earth do you assume that he'd choose her over you anyway?" she asked.

That was a good question actually. "I guess because she was the one that left him in the first place. So maybe he still has feelings for her?" I groaned. "I don't know. It's just bringing up all kinds of crazy I haven't felt in a long time. I forgot how agonizing being in a relationship can be."

"It can be hell," she admitted.

"Especially in the beginning when you don't know where you stand. At least with Blake, I felt pretty sure... I mean, you can never be one-hundred percent sure I guess. But I, at least, was ninety-nine percent confident that he'd never leave me or cheat or anything."

"I'm at about ninety here." I smiled at her tone of voice. "But I remember how it really sucks at the start when no one has committed to anything."

"And I feel so old to be doing all this again. I just don't have the energy. Like with Blake, in the beginning, I'd sneak out of bed in the morning and brush my teeth, comb my hair, wipe away the drool, and sneak back into bed, pretending I woke up like that."

She laughed. "Please tell me you didn't put on makeup."

"No. I didn't go that far. But over the years, there was such a comfortableness there, you know?"

"I do know. Yeah. I'm only at year seven. But I'm trying to think, what year did I stop holding in my stomach? Or start having hairy legs all winter?"

I had to laugh. And that's why I loved my best friend. I knew she'd make me feel better. "You know how much I love you, right?"

"You know how much I love you? And you know you have nothing to worry about?"

Sighing, I propped my feet up on the ottoman. "I guess I'm just reverting back to some high school insecurities being with him."

"That makes sense." She paused for a moment. "And what else? Did you talk about your future at all or either one of you moving?"

"No. No, we didn't. I just don't see how it's ever going to work." The whole thing was so hopeless. We had no chance of a future together. "I can't move. My parents are actually starting to need *me* now. And I seriously doubt he'd move. I don't know..."

"Well, maybe he *would* move. You don't know that."

"Maybe." But I doubted it. "Maybe he's going to visit a lot during this pregnancy. Maybe that's what he meant by being here for me. I didn't want to ask too much about it. I mean, the poor guy just found out about it all. He has to be in shock."

"I get that. But I also saw the way he looked at you. That was a man that will find a way to be with you, pregnant or not."

Something about the way she said that gave me a teeny tiny bit of hope. "You think so?"

"I *really* think so. I don't think you have anything to be insecure about, hon. Even I could see how much the man cared about you. And that was six weeks ago, before six weeks of talking every day and then seeing each other again."

"I suppose so," I said, twiddling with the string on my hoodie.

"So just chill. Let the man take care of his business in Miami and figure out how he's going to be there for you."

"Okay. I'll try." I heard the faint sound of someone else's voice on her end. "Hey, I'll let you go. I know you're probably busy with work."

"All right. You know I'm only a phone call or text away. Always."

"Same here."

"And Jayda?"

"Yeah?"

"Try not to worry. Please try," she pleaded. "I know you. But just try. Do something else, like maybe some writing."

I laughed at her not-so-subtle push to get some chapters from me. "Right. I'll try that. Thanks for listening."

"Of course. I love you."

"Love you too."

Hanging up, I definitely felt better. Kaileen knew me so well, and maybe I'd take her advice and let Alex figure out his way back to me. Perhaps I was throwing all my insecurities at him, insecurities I hadn't felt since my teenage years.

I'd pretty much outgrown them in college when I hit my stride. Then, in my twenties, I was a married woman and finding my passion in writing. And my thirties, so far, had been filled with an actual writing career and single motherhood.

But being with Alex took me back, way back, to *that* place.

While I made some tea for myself, I realized it wasn't necessarily insecurity I was experiencing. It was something close, though, so no wonder I had mistaken it. The actual feeling was vulnerability.

I had placed my heart in this man's hands. But could I trust him with it?

And not only my heart, but also my daughter's, whose heart was even more precious than my own. She was my *everything.* And this child growing in my belly would be the same.

Could I take the chance that Alex would be here, *really* be here, for us... for life?

CHAPTER TWENTY-FIVE

Jayda

The rest of the day went by in a blur, except for a brief call from my doctor. After she reviewed my chart and we discussed my reproductive history, she gave me the green light for sex.

Great. A day late and a dollar short. I shook my head at the irony of it.

All day, I hoped to hear from Alex, even a short little text. I checked on his flight status and found out that the second leg had been delayed for hours. Poor guy. I knew how fun it was to entertain a little one in the airport for a long period of time. So it wasn't surprising that he hadn't reached out to me.

Once Audrey went to bed, I tried to write a

bit, waiting for that magic hour of nine o'clock. I typed all of two words before I let myself get distracted by my work email and then tortured myself with random searches about men getting back together with their ex-wives, which seemed to happen quite frequently.

Sometimes, I really hated the internet. I put my phone down and watched the news. And that was even worse.

Sighing, I noticed it was almost nine, and I decided to just try him instead of sitting here in agony. With shaky hands, I picked up my phone and called him. With each ring, my heart sped up.

One... two... three... four... five... and voicemail.

Hanging up, I shut my eyes against the frustration coursing through me. Why hadn't he answered? Even with the delay, his flight had landed hours ago. He should definitely be home by now. And he had never, not even once, missed our nightly phone call.

Of course, my mind took off, imagining him with Fiona, ripping each other's clothes off and tumbling into their old bed together.

No, no, no. Don't even go there. He said they were over.

And then my stupid brain started to worry about everything else—a car accident, a heart attack, Gabby getting deathly ill, something happening to his parents.

I hated this. Why hadn't I heard from him all

day? Why?

Heading to the kitchen, I tried to make some tea to calm my crazy. I decided I'd try him again soon. Maybe text him.

Why did he have to be so far away? Why did I ever think it was a good idea to sleep with him in the first place? What the hell was wrong with me?

I had a daughter to think of. I couldn't be selfish like that. How many times had Audrey asked me today when she could play with Gabby again? She'd even asked about Alex, breaking my heart when she called him "that nice man." And tonight after dinner, she'd finally found her Elsa crown and sobbed because she wanted to show it to them both.

Trying my best not to cry too, I comforted her and wondered how I'd get through this pregnancy in one piece. Last time, there had been no kids involved. But this time, I needed to be there for Audrey and make sure she was doing all right and not feeling my own stress.

After I finished my tea, I tried him once more, my heart sinking when he didn't answer again. After I hung up, I sent a text asking if he made it home okay. I felt like such a stalker—especially if Fiona was there sitting next to him, wondering who the crazy chick was that kept calling.

And that was it. I wasn't going to call again. Or text again. Well, at least not tonight. And maybe not ever. I had some pride. I had self-confidence.

If Alex wanted me, he'd have to show up.

***

I woke up in the morning on the couch again, my phone in my hand. Nothing. No calls. No texts.

What the heck?

Now, I was mad. How rude could a person be? How hard was it to send a text? I knew he was busy. He had work. He had a daughter, parents, a home... and an ex-wife in town. But still, it took all of five seconds to send me a text and tell me everything was okay. Five seconds. He couldn't spare *five seconds*?

Audrey made noises upstairs, and I closed my eyes, breathing in a lungful of air. Forget him. Forget all men. I needed to be there for my daughter. I *would* be there for my daughter and this baby inside me. Stress wasn't good for him or her either.

I could do this.

I was strong. I was a survivor. Strength didn't mean I never cried, didn't mean I never fell apart. Strength was pulling myself back together, finding new life after death, finding my way forward through the ashes of destruction. I had done that—more than done that—before.

And I would do it again.

***

We spent the day with my parents, getting a head start on making Christmas cookies even though it was still so early in December.

Silencing my phone, I stuck it in my back pocket. If he did call or text, well, he could wait. I needed some family time, and so did Audrey.

My heart broke a little at my mom's confusion a few times when measuring ingredients, mistaking tablespoons and teaspoons. It was something I was noticing more often with her. I had tried to talk to my dad about it. But he didn't want to even entertain the idea that anything could be wrong.

I hated even thinking about Alzheimer's or dementia. Maybe it was something else. Could there be something else? Perhaps it was part of the normal aging process, but I doubted that. I vowed to look into it when I got home.

This was my priority, this family I had right here—my parents, my daughter, my unborn child. Not my love life. Or lack of it.

I had no business even going there. I needed to forget the heartache and go back to my original thoughts about that first weekend with Alex. It had been a one-night stand. Or one-weekend stand.

And this past weekend?

Well, I didn't know what to call it. But it needed to fall into the background of my life where I just forgot about it, if that was even possible. I would make it happen. I *would* forget about it. It might take some time, but I would.

Hours later, Audrey and I returned home with tins full of cookies. Although my mom had a few hazy moments, she was still her generous and kind self, filling my arms with more cookies than I could carry. I thought she was making them for church friends. But she said she'd make more for them.

Even though I'd put on a smile and told them we'd had a great weekend, she must have known something was up. I supposed it was hard to hide some things from your mom... no matter how old you grew.

And still no word from Alex. Only a few texts from Kaileen asking me for the latest. I'd wait until later tonight to reply. I didn't want to even go down that road while I was with my daughter.

***

As soon as Audrey was asleep, I sprawled out on the couch, trying not to think about this past weekend when I'd shared so much with Alex in this very spot. I finally texted Kaileen and told her no word from him. I didn't even want to say his name.

We went back and forth for a while with her still reassuring me that something must have happened. I wanted to believe that, wanted to believe that with all my heart. But it was so difficult. Why couldn't he just call?

In addition to looking up stuff about my mom and coming up with a plan, I spent some time searching for death notices in Miami. Had something happened to him or one of his family members? Really, that was the only reasonable explanation I could think of, some kind of awful emergency.

Nine o'clock came and went. Nothing. Damn it. Nothing!

I couldn't believe it. Should I call him again? Oh, I didn't know. How desperate was I right now? I picked up the phone, then put it down again. Then picked it up. Then threw it down.

In the end, I sent a text... after typing and erasing it about fifty times. What did you say when you didn't hear from the father of your unborn child for two whole days after his ex showed up in town?

Finally, I decided to write, "Are you okay?" And that was it. I was done. This time, I meant it.

As I went into the kitchen, a numbness settled over me, a familiar feeling that I'd experienced all the time after Blake's death. In between the tears, the anger, the questions, and the guilt, numbness was my favorite because I just didn't feel anything, and it was such an actual relief to not have to deal with the more gut-wrenching emotions.

After I made some tea and grabbed a tin of cookies, I settled back on the couch, giving my phone one last glance. Nope. Nothing. The numbness deadened all the other feelings. And I embraced it.

CHAPTER TWENTY-SIX

Jayda

Wednesday dawned. A full forty-eight hours with no word from Alex. Numbness was still with me. Thank God.

I spent the morning devouring cookies and hanging out with Audrey, leaving toys everywhere, making a huge mess all over. Maybe it was weird, maybe it was selfish, but I let her natural joy and happiness fill me.

And it worked. Kind of. Well, not really.

But at least while I was with her, I smiled. For her. And then it was time for an early lunch and preschool. I thought about what I'd do for those four hours she was gone.

Maybe I should try to work. Writing might

help. The problem was my story was at a really dark place—kind of the darkness before the big finale and the light. And usually, when I wrote the dark stuff, I ended up crying. Not exactly what I wanted right now.

Maybe I'd actually shower. But did I even care?

I walked Audrey to school, not wearing a hat, because now a stupid hat reminded me of him. The wind was freezing in our faces, but Audrey didn't even seem to notice. I went through the motions of saying hello to her teacher and the other parents, then walked home, head down, dead inside.

And that's when it happened. That's when my phone rang. And it was Alex.

I hesitated, my heartbeat skittering all over the place. Did I really want to hear what he had to say? I noticed he had timed it for when Audrey would be at school.

Should I pick up? Just to hear him say he was back with Fiona?

After the fourth ring, I decided to answer. I might as well face whatever was in front of me. I didn't say anything, though. I just couldn't.

"Jayda?" he asked. "Are you there?"

I couldn't speak. "Mm-hmm."

"Jayda? You're really there?"

"I am," I whispered.

"Oh, my God, baby. I've been so worried about you."

What? He was worried about *me*?

"Why didn't you answer any of my emails?" he asked, his voice full of worry.

What on earth was he talking about? "Emails?" I managed to say.

"The millions of emails I sent you. Sweetheart, I left my phone at the Portland airport. Gabby had an epic meltdown."

I needed to sit down. I finally made it to my front door and keyed in, immediately collapsing onto the couch. "You lost your phone?" I squeaked out.

"I did. It was awful. And your number is impossible to track down, Miss Popular Author. And I was so crazy worrying about you."

I didn't know whether to laugh or cry. So I did a little of both.

"And then I couldn't log into my cloud, and I got locked out. Then once I finally was able to log in, I discovered I hadn't backed up my contacts."

Honestly, I didn't even hear what he was saying. I was so incredibly happy just to hear his voice and know that he was fine.

"And work's been insane," he continued. "I finally had time to go to the Apple store a little bit ago, and it took two hours for them to figure everything out, get a new phone, and finally get your number, and I just got back to the clinic. It's been crazy. And I sent you so many emails, and you never responded. I was so worried about you."

I didn't think I'd ever heard Alex talk so much.

And with every word that he said, relief flooded through me. My mind had gone down such a dark road, afraid I'd lost him, not sure I could handle another loss like that. But he'd only lost his phone. I could hardly believe it.

"You are okay, right, Jayda?" he asked, his deep voice vibrating through my phone.

I nodded then realized he couldn't see me. "I'm fine."

"Are you sure?" I could still hear that worry in his voice, and my heart fluttered that he seemed to care so much.

"I am now," I finally said.

He released a sigh. "What on earth were you thinking? Or did you even notice I hadn't called?"

Oh, I had noticed all right. "Yeah, I kind of noticed. And I thought..." Could I even say it?

"Thought what?" he prodded.

I picked up some crumbs on the couch. "I thought maybe you were, you know, back with Fiona."

He laughed so loudly I had to jerk the phone away from my ear. "You did?"

"Well, yeah, what else could I think?"

"No, baby, that's *never* going to happen." I could almost see his smile through the phone. "She already left."

Good. Thank God for that. "Well, what did she want then? To see Gabby?"

"No." He sighed again. "She dropped by the house Monday night, and we talked. She said she still doesn't have any maternal feelings. But..." Another deep breath. "I really hate telling you this. But I want to be honest."

That made my heart drop all the way down to my toes. "Honest about what?"

"Fiona said she still had feelings for me and was having a hard time of it," he admitted with a tone full of regret.

A wave of nausea overwhelmed me, and I bolted up to find my ginger gum.

"Jayda? You still there?"

With shaky hands, I ruffled through all the crap on the counter, searching. "Yes. I'm here."

"But you remember what I told you, right?" he said quickly. "That Fiona and I are done?"

"I remember," I whispered, giving up on the gum for the moment and leaning against the counter.

"I mean that, Jayda. You hear me? There's nothing there anymore. Not for me, at least."

I wanted to trust him. I wanted that so incredibly much. But could I really take that chance?

"I hope you can believe that," he added in a sincere way that made me suddenly feel warm inside.

"I'd like to," I admitted.

"You can. I promise you, sweetheart. I'm one-hundred percent yours. If you want me that is..."

A smile covered my face. So Alex was all mine, huh? Those words sent me straight from the hell

I'd been living in for the past several days all the way to heaven. "Maybe," I said, feeling a burst of happiness surge through me.

"Maybe? Really?" he said in a flirty way.

"You're a pretty smooth talker, Alex Hernandez. And I'll have to see you in person to decide that for sure and see if you really mean it."

"Oh, is that how you're going to play it?" he teased.

"Yep," I said. "So you might want to start thinking about your next visit."

"I'm so on it."

Oh, boy, I really hoped so. I was dying to see him again, especially after what we'd just been through. Talking on the phone was great and all. But there was absolutely nothing like being together in person. However, I knew it might be a while, and I tried not to let that thought crush me.

I heard another voice. "Doctor Hernandez? Sorry to interrupt, but room seven is ready for you."

"Okay, thanks," Alex said, sounding far off.

"You need to go."

"I do. I'm sorry. Work's been busy. I'll call you tonight, though. Okay?"

My heart suddenly felt so much lighter. "It's a date."

"And I'm already planning that next trip," he said in that sexy voice of his.

"I hope so. Because I heard from my doctor," I

couldn't resist adding.

"Oh, yeah?" I could practically feel his eagerness coming through the phone. "And?"

"It's a yes," I said dramatically.

He groaned. "Screw it all. I'm getting on the next plane."

***

Immediately after we hung up, I checked my personal email where I'd forwarded Alex meal ideas weeks ago. And yep, he had sent quite a few emails, each one getting more and more desperate. It was obvious he had been just as worried about me as I had been about him.

After texting Kaileen with an update—and getting the scolding of a lifetime for not checking my personal email account more often —I practically floated around the house. If anyone had seen the perma-smile on my face, they would have wondered who the ridiculous pregnant lady was that broke into spontaneous dancing while picking up toys.

The joy stayed with me all through the evening and even more so after talking to Alex for hours where he'd had me rolling with laughter describing how he'd had to create all these social media accounts just to send me personal messages on my author pages... which I rarely checked anyway and certainly not my DMs.

Poor guy. He'd really tried.

He also explained more about Fiona's visit.

I couldn't understand what she had actually hoped to accomplish. And honestly, he wasn't sure either. But it seemed she had just wanted Alex, and she was really confused and upset about the lingering feelings she'd been having ever since leaving.

He'd been clear to her that nothing could happen between them ever again. He'd also mentioned the door was open at any time if she ever wanted to get to know Gabby or be involved in her life somehow. But he admitted to me that he didn't think that would happen.

To be honest, I understood, though. Motherhood wasn't for everyone. Sometimes, it really sucked out your soul even if you *wanted* to be a mom. I'd explained to Alex that my friends and I had some very candid and hushed discussions about the dark side of motherhood that no one really liked to talk about.

Maybe I had shocked him. I didn't know. Moms were supposed to be saints in our society. But we were human too, I told him. And when a kid could ask 200 to 300 questions a day mixed in with meltdowns, well, even the most patient mom could be driven to hide in the bathroom with a can of Pringles. That had made him laugh, and he vowed to keep me supplied with chips.

But the best part of our conversation was the end when he had promised he was trying his best to come see me very soon. And unlike the previous two nights, I went to sleep with a heart full of hope.

CHAPTER TWENTY-SEVEN

Jayda

The next day, that feeling of hope and love still carried me. I didn't know how Alex was going to pull it off and be here for me, but at least, I knew he wanted to, like really, really wanted to, and that made all the difference to that beating thing in my chest.

Blake's dad called in the morning for an impromptu video chat with Audrey, and after twenty minutes of her showing him all her dolls, I asked if I could talk to him alone. He was the only family left from Blake's side, and he was a sweet man, maybe a little goofy sometimes but still very kind.

I flicked on the TV for Audrey since that was the only way to guarantee no interruptions which I definitely did not want. And then I snuck into my office downstairs and shut the door.

"What's up, Jayda?"

He was definitely curious since our conversations were usually with Audrey right there in the middle adding her two cents.

"Well..." I felt sick all the sudden. We didn't usually talk about Blake except maybe in passing but nothing serious since he had died. "Gosh, I don't know how to even start."

He smiled broadly. "Let me guess."

Hmm, that was curious. "Okay. Sure. Go ahead."

"You met someone."

What on earth? "Wow, Bill, how did you know that?"

"You just have a glow about you."

Oh, crap. A glow? There was no way I was going to tell him I was pregnant... yet. Baby steps, right? Although someday, he'd be able to do the math. I had the world's worst poker face and hoped he couldn't see right through me, making me curse video chatting.

"Well, I'm not sure about glowing," I finally said. "But that's kind of you. And you're right. I did meet someone."

This was so awkward to tell your former father-in-law that you were in love with a new man.

"What's his name?" he asked, his voice encouraging.

"Alex."

"And how did you meet?"

"Well, we met up at our twenty-year reunion about six weeks ago now," I admitted, trying not to outwardly cringe.

"Is it serious?"

I'm kind of having his baby. "Um, I'm thinking so."

He was silent a moment. "You know what, Jay?" he said, using the old nickname Blake had for me.

"What?" I held my breath.

"I think that's wonderful. You and Audrey have been going it alone for a while now, and you could really use another hand."

I let out that breath in a big whoosh. "Aw, that really means the world to me to hear you say that."

"Well, I mean it. I'm happy for you." He looked away for a second. "And Blake would be happy for you too."

"You think so?" I bit my lip, wondering how much to tell him exactly. Should I mention that promise during those last moments?

"I know so," he said, more emphatically.

In that split second, I decided not to... well, not to bring up the promise *exactly* because it might trouble him in some way. And I knew a parent's pain upon losing their child was supposed to be the greatest pain of all. So I decided to remain more general with our conversation and keep the pain of that vow to myself.

But to my amazement, Bill kind of rescued me all on his own. "Is that something that worries you, that Blake wouldn't want you to move on or something?" he asked, his brows creased with concern.

I nodded. "It does. If I'm being honest here, I feel like it's..." I sighed. "Oh, I don't know. I just feel—"

"Sorry to interrupt. I don't know *exactly* what you're feeling. But I know my Blake. And he would want you to move on, want you to be happy, and want Audrey to have a dad... or another mom if you were so inclined."

I had to laugh at Bill and his open-mindedness as relief rolled through me. He was absolutely right. I didn't know why I couldn't see it before. Blake *would* want that. That promise was made during a moment of unbelievable trauma. There was no script, no rehearsal, for the last minutes of someone's life. And we had maybe messed it up.

But it didn't erase the years of love and friendship we'd had. Blake was not the villain in my story. And overall, I *knew* that Blake had a kind heart and would always want the best for me and Audrey.

"I can't even tell you how much I appreciate that," I eventually said, feeling those tears threatening once again. Stupid hormones.

"Don't you cry, Jay, or I'll be right there with

you."

I laughed again. Blake had really lucked out in the dad department. And thank God for that because his mom had been a real you-know-what.

"All right," I said. "I'll keep the tears back."

"And maybe someday, I'll get to meet this man."

"That would be nice."

Audrey barged in. "I'm hungry!"

We chatted a few more minutes, and I thanked him profusely before we gave out virtual hugs and said our goodbyes. As I made Audrey a snack, I had that feeling again of hope, a simple four-letter word that could make a life completely turn around.

And I was incredibly grateful to Blake's dad because he had helped me think differently about the whole thing and, in his own way, reminded me to focus on my late husband's heart and all our years together instead of that crazy promise made in the last seconds of his life. In just that short conversation, he had completely changed my outlook about my future.

In the afternoon, I dropped Audrey off for a play date at her friend's house, and I actually had the urge to write. Shutting out the messy, dirty house, I closed the door to my office. I was finally *feeling* it, and I spent hours typing away in another world, music blasting, the rest of my life falling away.

And that night, talking to Alex, he told me he had some kind of surprise planned and he hoped I'd be around tomorrow afternoon for a special delivery he'd arranged. I had no clue what he had in store for me, but I couldn't wait to find out.

***

The next morning, Audrey was super annoyed that we had to wait so long to get to preschool time. And actually, I was right there with her. The afternoon seemed so far away. I was beyond excited and impatient to find out about Alex's surprise.

Would it be flowers? Cupcakes? Or maybe something I *really* wanted—a cleaning service? My mind was whirling with all the possibilities. Even Kaileen had a few guesses of her own. She thought it had something to do with the baby, like a new crib or rocking chair.

Finally, preschool time arrived, and Audrey practically ran the four blocks to school with me trying to keep up with her. But her teacher was late, a first. She texted one of the moms saying she had car trouble and would be there shortly. I tried not to fidget too much as we all waited.

Then when she did arrive, another mom tried to talk my ear off after we said goodbye to the kids. *This is not a good time*, I wanted to shout. Could I please get home already?

I had no idea when exactly the big surprise would arrive, but I didn't want to miss it, and curiosity thrummed throughout my whole body along with anticipation.

Managing to finally escape the chatty mommy, I walked home almost as quickly as our trot to school had been earlier. When I rounded the corner of my street, my eyes immediately looked to my doorstep to see if anything had arrived. I stopped in my tracks, my jaw dropping in shock at what I saw.

CHAPTER TWENTY-EIGHT

Alex

I would have sat down on Jayda's front step, but I didn't want my ass to freeze any more than it already had. As the minutes ticked by, I couldn't figure out where she was. I had tried to time it so I'd get here right after she took Audrey to preschool. And she had said she'd be home all afternoon.

Man, I couldn't wait to see her face, see her reaction. I had moved heaven and earth to arrange this visit. But after the craziness we'd both just experienced with me losing my phone, I was desperate to get back to her.

Part of me wondered if she was inside, maybe upstairs taking a nap or a shower. Maybe my brilliant plan to surprise her hadn't been so brilliant after all.

As I leaned against the railing, I heard a noise on the nearby corner, and that's when I saw her. A jolt went through my body, and the look on her face made it all worthwhile. I had completely shocked her judging by how her jaw practically hit the sidewalk.

As I rushed down the front walkway, she met me halfway. I wanted to pick her up and twirl her around, but I remembered what had happened the last time I'd tried that.

Instead, I crushed her to me, pulling her in as close as humanly possible, lifting her up high in the air. And suddenly, the cold left my body to be replaced by a fire raging through me. I had never wanted anyone more than this woman right here in my arms.

She pulled back to look up at me, wearing that damn hat. Jayda opened her mouth to say something, but I didn't let her. Crashing my lips down on hers, I kissed the hell out of her until we were both breathless.

Without a word, she grabbed my hand and pulled me toward the front of the house where she fumbled with the key. She led me inside, slammed the door, and attacked me. Where was the shy girl from high school? She was gone, and I loved every second of it.

Within a heartbeat, she had my coat and shirt off, her cool lips on my hot skin making me gasp with want. Good God, I was close to exploding just from her reaction, not to mention her kisses that were sending a fever through my veins.

I tried to keep up with her, practically ripping her clothes from her body. And when her shirt came off, I came completely undone at the sight in front of me as she nearly busted out of her bra.

"I keep meaning to get some new bras," she murmured as she returned to kissing her way up my chest, her moans against my body fanning the flames inside me.

I couldn't even say anything as I fumbled with the clasp, my fingers clumsy like a teenager unhooking his first bra. But finally, I ripped it off. And oh, God...

Damn, I needed to do something to slow myself down. Miami Marlins lineup. Now.

Alberto Garcia.

She reached up to take her sexy hat off. "Leave the hat on," I said, my voice coming out rough. Jayda laughed, making those fantastic breasts bounce.

Pablo Castaneda.

Still standing by the door, our pants came off next, and I felt such relief from the straining against my jeans. When I spotted that sweet little baby bump as she pulled off her panties, the ache I felt, the intense need to be inside her, threatened to overwhelm me.

Chuck Nolan.

I so badly wanted to take her against the wall, but I couldn't, not when she was pregnant, even if she was barely showing. I'd save that for after. I shuddered just at the thought of pushing into her, her legs around my waist, holding onto her hot ass, gravity pushing me deeper inside her.

Kendrick Vaughn.

I kissed my way down her neck as our hands were all over each other. She stopped to grab me, leading me to the couch, the view of her backside in front of me, all that naked skin, the promise of what was to come...

Rowan Sanchez.

Then she pushed me down on the soft couch cushion and straddled me, putting those stunning legs on either side of me, her breasts in my face so close I could almost taste her sweetness.

Damn.

Dax Gregory.

She wasted no time and sat down on me, taking me inside of her instantly, both of us letting out loud groans as I sank into her tight heat.

Wade Robinson.

She leaned forward, rubbing her breasts against my chest. Kissing me, she started to move, finding an easy rhythm that felt like heaven. I squeezed my eyes shut, trying not to feel the blast of pleasure as we swallowed each other's moans.

Wade Robinson.

My hands explored her breasts, plying the soft

skin, before moving to her hips, where I gripped her flesh as she ground her body against mine in a hot rocking motion that had the blood roaring in my ears.

Wade Robinson.

"Oh, God. Alex..."

I felt her body start to shudder around me already, squeezing me again and again—God, that was fast—sending me completely over the edge in a shock wave of pure ecstasy as we came together.

"Fucking Jesús Guerrero!"

Wow, what the hell had just happened? Trying to catch my breath, I opened my eyes to find her staring at me.

"What did you say?" she asked, breathless, a confused expression on her face.

I wasn't sure what I had said. She'd completely wrung me out. I had never in a million years expected that kind of response from her.

"It was probably a baseball player," I finally admitted.

She laughed, her amazing chest catching my attention once more. "So it's true then that guys think about baseball."

I glanced back up to those stunning eyes of hers. "That was a first for me. But yeah. I was trying hard not to be a two-pump chump."

Our bodies still joined, she giggled again. "I already know you're not normally a two-pump chump. Believe me. And besides, I only needed one pump."

I joined in her laughter, and because I just couldn't resist her, I squeezed her tight against me, loving the feel of her naked body against mine. In all my experience, I had never felt *so right* with anyone before.

"I think we might have made another baby," she whispered near my ear.

Laughing, I eventually answered, "You might be right."

"I can't believe you're really here." She pulled back to look at me, those beautiful eyes wide. "How on earth did you manage to come back so soon?"

Her eyes seemed to turn a blue shade that practically hypnotized me. "I told you. Nothing's going to keep me from being with you."

I swallowed as her chest rose and fell again with a deep breath. "I was expecting flowers or chocolate or the thing I really—"

Jayda's cheeks flushed as she glanced away quickly, making me wonder what she was going to say.

"What? The thing you really what?" I asked, bouncing her with my hips to make her look at me again.

With that flirty little smile and a light in her eyes, she said, "The thing I was really hoping for was someone to clean."

Now that surprised me.

"I mean," she continued, "the thing I wanted

most was *you*, of course, but that never even entered my mind as a possibility."

An idea popped into my head right then. "Baby, I can make all your dreams come true."

CHAPTER TWENTY-NINE

Jayda

I had no clue what he had in mind. But he had that teasing look in his eyes that I'd loved since high school. He kissed me then, a sweet, tender kiss that made me melt.

Pulling back, he whispered against my lips, "You ready, hot Mama?"

"Ready for what?" I asked, wondering what he could possibly have in store for me.

I tore my body away from his, finally standing up as he pinched my ass.

"Hey!" Both of us laughing, I swatted his hand away. I guarded my rear while I picked up my underwear. "So where's Gabby this time?"

Alex walked over and helped me sort through the pile of clothes on the floor. "She's with my parents. My brother's in town with his kids."

I paused to glance at him. "And you came here instead of hanging out with your family?"

He didn't even look up as he handed me my shirt. "Hell, yeah. I've had a lifetime with my brother. I'm good."

Stifling a laugh, I asked, "So how long are you here for?"

"Till Sunday afternoon. I need to be back to work Monday morning."

Both of us standing up, clothes in our hands, I gulped at the hot specimen of all man in front of me. Something about the sunlight pouring in from the windows highlighted his muscles, making my mouth water. I just wanted to jump on him again.

Whoa, what was wrong with me? Was it too soon to blame pregnancy hormones? Or was it all because of this beautiful man?

Gulping, I tried to swallow down my lust. "So, um, what was that? Sunday afternoon?"

He nodded, grinning at me as he handed me my bra. "Mm-hmm. Sunday afternoon."

I mentally did the math. So two whole nights together. And this time, a yes from the doctor. I didn't think there'd be much sleeping. It occurred to me maybe that was the reason Alex was here so soon.

"So tell me this, Alex Hernandez. Did you just come back because of what my doctor said?"

That grin on his face grew even wider. "No,

of course not. I've been working on this since the minute I got back to Miami." Those sexy eyes narrowed. "Jayda Jenkins, I'm surprised at you. Your mind sure is in the gutter. Not even saying hello to me, just attacking me right on the doorstep for all your neighbors to see."

Giggling, I tried to hit him with my bra. But he grabbed the other end of it and pulled me closer to him.

"And I loved every single second of it," he said, his face close to mine.

My heart stuttered, and I closed my eyes for a second because there was something I meant to say, but just his nearness made me forget everything. Oh, yes, right. "If I recall, I started to say hello, but you were the one who stopped me with that kiss."

He looked thoughtful, but his flirty grin gave him away. "Hmm, that's not the way I remember it."

Rolling my eyes, I shook my head at him and grabbed my bra. "I'll be right back."

I headed for the bathroom because, well, the bladder. Unfortunately, I knew this was only the beginning of the bladder annoyances. I spent a few minutes getting cleaned up and dressed again, the whole time in complete awe that Alex was really here.

My phone kept buzzing, and I saw it was Kaileen, demanding some answers. I finally texted her the scoop and said she might not hear from me for a while. Her reply? Ten surprise face emojis plus ten eggplants.

Still smiling from her response, I arrived back in the living room to find a steaming mug of tea and a tin of cookies on the ottoman.

"Have a seat," Alex said, fully dressed which was a real shame.

"All right," I said, feeling a bit skeptical. I pointed to the tea and cookies. "Is this for me?"

"Yep." He grinned then started to pick up toys, tossing them into the nearby bin. "Just sit back and relax, baby, because your personal cleaning service has arrived."

I let out a laugh. Was he seriously going to clean right now? "You're kidding me."

"Nope. You've had a lot on your plate, and I'm going to wait on you hand and foot."

He stepped around a pile of broken-up, trampled-on Cheerios that Audrey had spilled right before we'd left then stomped on accidentally a hundred times.

"I swear I'm not normally such a slob. I just got into writing mode, and I feel such pressure to get that done. And so when the mood hits me, I ignore everything else and write. I mean, I don't ignore Audrey. But if she's not here—"

"Sweetheart, I'm not judging. You have a kid. You have a career. You're pregnant. Even if you had just one of those things, or none of those things…" He shrugged as he tossed the last toy into the bin. "Come on. Grab the cookies and tea while I clean the kitchen. And then I'll vacuum last."

Oh, my heart. He was going to vacuum? I didn't know if my ovaries could take it. Good thing they were inactive right now.

I followed him into the kitchen, cookies and tea in my hands, stars in my eyes as he started to fill up the dishwasher. "Can I help?" I asked.

"No. Just sit," he ordered, the sexy way he said it making me hot all over.

When he started to wash the pots and pans, I might have drooled a little bit from my perch at the table, especially because I had such a great view of his rear in the jeans he was wearing.

"So how's the book coming anyway?" he asked.

And now he was going to ask me about my writing? That love in my heart just about exploded, and I wanted to tell him so much. I came close to blurting it out. But I bit down on my tongue.

Not yet.

I wanted to wait for the right moment... sometime when he didn't have his back to me, sometime when his hands were on me. I didn't know exactly when I'd tell him but definitely at some point this weekend.

"You said you were in writing mode?" Alex prompted.

"Oh, right. Sorry. You're just distracting me."

He turned around to look at me, slinging a dish towel over his shoulder. "I am?" he asked, that grin back on his face.

"Yes, you are." I returned the smug smile he was throwing my way then took a sip of tea. "But anyway, yes, I've been in full-on writing mode. And I knocked out the rough drafts for a bunch of scenes. I'm almost to the big finale."

"Good for you. I'm really glad to hear that." He turned back to the dishes. "So are you going to let me read it?"

Alex had caught up on the other books, something we had talked about often during those six weeks apart. His encouragement meant everything to me, something I had missed so much after Blake had passed.

"You're not going to make me wait, are you?" he asked.

I thought about that for a heartbeat because, of course, I was going to let him read it. I *wanted* him to read it. I really wanted his input. "Mmmm, I won't make you wait, but you might have to earn it."

"Aren't I earning it now?"

"It's definitely a start," I said, both of us laughing as he dried the last pan.

"All right. Where do you keep the vacuum?"

"You really don't have—"

Alex's eyes narrowed. "I'm going to."

Oh, wow. "It's, um, in there." I pointed to the tall cupboard by the back door.

After he grabbed the vacuum, he nodded towards the living room. "Let's go. I want you to tell me just how you like it."

Giggling, I grabbed the cookies and followed him out of the kitchen, settling onto the couch again.

He managed to get one of the ridiculous outlet covers off and plugged in the vacuum. Just before he turned it on, he caught my eye and grinned. "I'm getting hot. Do you mind if I take off my shirt?" he asked.

Uh, did I mind? "Please, be my guest."

He may have been joking around, but this was serious foreplay right here, and I intended to enjoy it thoroughly. Chuckling, he took off his shirt and tossed it onto a nearby chair.

While he turned on the vacuum, I bit into a cookie, savoring the sweetness on my tongue and the hot sight in front of me. I watched him as he focused on sucking up every last crumb, moving with both speed and efficiency.

The way his biceps bulged as he lifted a chair to get under it, the way his broad shoulders tensed, plus the deep tan on his torso from hours in the hot Miami sun... oh, God. I might have an eyegasm just from looking at him. As he came closer to the couch, I could see the sweat glistening on his chest, and I picked up a magazine from the ottoman to fan myself.

The vacuum passed right in front of me, and he smiled at me. Did he know what he was doing to me right now? Judging by the sexy look in his eyes, yeah, he did. He definitely did. Without taking my eyes off him, I reached for another cookie as he kept going past me, reaching into all the corners, every hidden crevice, doing a much more thorough job than I ever did.

Sweet mercy.

Alex turned off the vacuum after he did the last bit of the living room. "Can I do the kitchen with this vacuum or should I just sweep in there?"

I was busy licking the frosting off my fingers while ogling his abs. "Um, yeah, it works on rugs and hard floors."

He laughed and disappeared into the kitchen for a few minutes, the sound of the vacuum not loud enough to drown out my lusty thoughts. Exactly how much time did we have till preschool was over? I did the math, and we still had an hour.

Thank goodness... because the raw need flowing through my veins absolutely consumed me. I was a woman on fire, and the only person who could put out the flames was Alex.

He rounded the corner just then, wiping the sweat from his brow, his arm muscles popping. I hadn't even realized that the vacuum had stopped. "Take a shower with me?" he asked.

CHAPTER THIRTY

Alex

Her chest rose and fell along with that look in her eye like she was going to pounce on me. Man, I was loving this side of Jayda. Had I really missed out on years of this?

I didn't know what she was thinking about our future, but I was more determined than ever to make this woman mine. And this weekend, we were going to discuss it. I didn't give a damn about that promise she had made to Blake.

Those few days where I'd been worried to death about her and couldn't call her, that had been *it* in my mind. That had been the clincher for me. There was too much wasted time between us, and I was going to convince her that we had a future together if it was the last thing I did.

I loved this woman with all my heart, soul, and mind. And there was no way in hell I was going to let her go this time.

"A shower?" she asked, those blue-green eyes making my chest squeeze.

I nodded. "I'm hot and want to wash the sweat off me."

She stood up and walked over to me, putting her arms around my neck, pushing that plush body of hers into mine. "I don't care about that."

Damn. Images from our shower together in Miami flashed through my mind—her soaped-up body, the way her wet skin had felt against me.

She stared up at me, and I leaned down to kiss her, but first, I sucked that plump lower lip of hers into my mouth. God, she tasted so incredibly sweet. But when she moaned against my mouth, I knew I needed to get us upstairs. This time, though, I was going to take charge and make slow, sweet love to her.

I pulled back from the kiss. "Come on. Let's go upstairs."

"We have about an hour, Doctor Hernandez."

I followed her up the stairs, enjoying the view as usual. "An hour? That should be enough time for a shower and round seven."

She giggled and took my hand, leading me to her bathroom, where we quickly shed our clothes again, smiling and staring at each other like two teenagers.

"I have to draw the line at any sex in the shower while you're pregnant," I added as she adjusted the water.

"What? Why not?" She glanced at me as she stepped into the steamy stream of water.

I joined her, trying to look at her eyes and not the rest of her. At least for now. "I've seen my fair share of shower sex injuries."

She laughed as she grabbed the body soap. "Really? What kind of injuries?"

"Broken limbs, injured hips, a fractured coccyx." Covering her mouth with her hand, I could tell she wanted to laugh again. "Go ahead. You can laugh."

She did, and I couldn't resist chuckling as well.

And then all words between us were lost as she began to rub the soap over my chest, the delicious scent of Jayda rising up between us as her hands moved over me, making my breath catch.

I watched as her eyes roamed my body, and I finally let myself look at her, *really* look at her, and the changes in her body—the small swell of her belly, her beautiful breasts that overflowed from my hands, those hips, her gorgeous legs.

She was stunning. Just looking at her brought me near to bursting. Something about Jayda made me completely lose it in a way I never had with any other woman before. It was like her luscious curves were made especially for my hands.

I finally returned my eyes to her face as her fingers continued to spread soap all over my shoulders and arms. She moved closer, pressing her body against mine, her hands reaching to my back. I let out a shudder at the feel of our wet bodies melding together, those bare breasts of hers on my hot skin.

Had I really said no to sex in the shower? I knew it was for the best. But maybe we needed to hurry this along a bit.

When she was done with my back, I reached for the body wash and spread it across her shoulders as she stared at me, her breathing as heavy as mine. As my hands moved over her slick skin, I was awed by the beauty in front of me, and I realized I couldn't wait to see how her body would change as our child grew. I couldn't wait to see her belly ripen, her curves fill out even more.

Above all, I was excited to actually experience this pregnancy with her.

Something about the look in her eyes as my hands explored her made me so hot. Or it was the smoothness of her skin. Or it was the lush feel of her.

We took turns rinsing the soap off, staring at each other, and I wondered what she was thinking right now, if she wanted me as much as I wanted her. I wasn't sure that was even possible. As hard as it was, I was determined to take my sweet time with her and kiss every inch of her beautiful body.

After we dried each other off, Jayda handed me some lotion, and I happily spread it all over her as she did the same to me, the vanilla fragrance filling the air between us, making me feel like I was drowning in her scent. And damn, if I wasn't thrilled to drown in her, drown in her heat.

Still naked, she grabbed my hand and led me to the bed, the soft sunlight shining on the white sheets. I was amazed at the transformation of my sweet, sweet Jayda, remembering back to the night of the reunion when she'd been so shy with me. And now, she walked nude in front of me, leading me to join my body with hers.

I tried to catch my breath at the anticipation running through my veins. Something about this moment felt huge, felt monumental, and I wondered if *this* was the time, if I should finally admit my feelings for this amazing woman.

But just as Jayda sat down on the bed, her phone rang out from the bathroom, and she looked at me with apologetic eyes. "I should check that. In case it's Audrey's school or something."

I nodded. "Of course."

While she rummaged through our pile of clothes looking for her phone, I sat down on the edge of the bed and sighed. *So damn close.*

She stared at her phone, frowning. "It's my dad." Reaching behind the door, she grabbed a robe and threw it on. "He rarely calls me."

As she answered, I felt her concern and worried for her as well. I watched the emotions flash over her face, praying that nothing awful had happened. She listened for a minute and nodded. Finally, she said, "I'm so glad you want to talk about it. Can you give me just a quick sec?"

She pressed mute on her phone and looked up at me. "I'm so sorry. I don't know what to do. He's finally wanting to talk about my mom and her issues. He thought it'd be a good time because Audrey's at school and my mom's out. And knowing my dad, if I don't talk now, he might change his mind and never want to discuss it again."

I released a breath, relieved it wasn't some kind of emergency. "It's fine, sweetheart. You should talk to him. You *need* to talk to him about this."

On the phone the other night, Jayda had discussed the whole problem and told me about her plan to go to the doctor with her mom at her next appointment in a few weeks. She'd also been so frustrated that her dad wouldn't even acknowledge the issue.

Her eyes changed from worried to grateful. "Thank you, Alex. You are truly amazing. You know that?"

I had to smile at that. Jayda calling me amazing felt pretty damn good.

"Dad? Sorry about that," she said, bringing the

phone to the bed as I stood up to grab my clothes.

The timing sucked, but I knew we still had tonight and tomorrow. And I knew now that we had the doctor's okay, we'd definitely make the most of it.

CHAPTER THIRTY-ONE

Jayda

After getting dressed, Alex sat on the bed next to me, holding my hand through the entire conversation. The phone call wasn't easy. It broke my heart to hear my dad finally admitting that he was worried about my mom. Part of me was relieved, though, because I really needed his help if we were going to try to figure this thing out.

And Alex sitting beside me and stroking my hand? His support meant the absolute world to me.

We had talked about this on the phone, and he knew how hard it was to be in the so-called "sandwich generation," where we had to worry about our aging parents while raising our own kids. Thankfully, his parents were in great health. And my parents had been relatively healthy... until now it seemed.

But I knew that others had it worse. I had a good friend in New York whose mom with COPD had moved in with her, and she already had her hands full with a husband and three children. And other friends had already lost one or both of their parents.

As Blake used to say, "It could always get worse," a weirdly comforting thought and reminder that you better appreciate what you had now.

My dad wasn't the biggest talker, and he certainly didn't go into details about his feelings and worries, but we settled on a plan that the three of us would go to the doctor's appointment together. And maybe between us all, we'd be able to get to the bottom of it with her doctor.

When I hung up, I felt completely wrung out and emotional. My dad acting vulnerable and needing my help was something new to me. And I hated to see it.

To top it all off, I still hadn't told them about my pregnancy. I just didn't know how to handle it. I knew they'd worry. And I was waiting to tell them about it when I was hopefully a little more certain about where Alex and I stood.

But right now, I didn't know. I didn't know anything. All I knew was that Alex wanted to be here for me through the pregnancy. But I still didn't know what that meant. For now. Or for the future.

"I bet that was hard," Alex said, his hand still gripping mine, his voice laced with empathy.

"Yeah. It was." I sighed. "But at least we're moving in the right direction. I just hate seeing my dad like that. He's always been the strong one, taking care of us, helping me."

Alex let go of my hand to wrap his arms around me and hold me. "I'm so sorry."

I let his strength pour into me and comfort me. Something about his body surrounding mine made me feel better, making my thoughts turn back to Alex.

Alex.

My heart literally ached with how much I loved him. But while I desperately wanted to tell him, I was also gun-shy to say those three little words to him, words I hadn't said to a man since that night Blake had died.

"You know I'm going to be here for you," he said, "and help you through this too."

I pulled away to look up at him. "You are?"

He nodded. "Absolutely, I am."

"But how?" I didn't want to interrogate him or seem too needy, but damn it, I was ready to hear some specifics.

He reached up to sweep a lock of my hair out of my eyes. "Well, I've been talking to the powers-that-be at the clinic and they're working with me to move some patients, reschedule others, so I can have big chunks of time to come up here and be with you."

That sounded amazing, but I wanted more, and I didn't know what to say.

"And in a few months, maybe even weeks," Alex continued, "my patients will be mostly phased out so I can move up here."

I felt my jaw drop at those words. He'd just kind of slipped it in there like it was nothing. But it was everything. *Everything*. Did he really mean that? I couldn't quite take it in.

Alex was seriously going to move to Maine?

"What did you just say? You're actually going to move up here?" I somehow managed to ask even though my heart was lodged in my throat.

He smiled at me, those brown eyes locked onto mine. "That's my plan. I want to be with you, Jayda."

I could barely breathe through my shock. My heart didn't even know what to do. It was beating right out of my chest.

"But I still have one concern," Alex said, his serious tone of voice capturing all of my attention.

I held my breath, waiting to see what he'd say.

"Are you ready to move on from that promise you made to Blake?"

That one question revealed so much about Alex, that he would even think about that, and I knew in my heart, in that moment, I was completely ready to love again, to live a full life once more, and give all of my heart to Alex.

I would never forget Blake. After all, he was the biological father to Audrey. It was more than that, however. He was a part of my history. But I realized I could find a way to honor both of these men, honor the past, honor Blake, while forging ahead with a new life... with Alex.

Looking back up into his eyes, I said, "I am."

"You really are?"

I nodded, all the emotions inside me bubbling to the surface and making my eyes fill up once again.

He embraced me tight against him. "Thank God," he said, releasing a breath that tickled the top of my head.

I still couldn't believe it. Alex was moving here. Like really moving here to be with me... or us... or his baby growing inside me.

"Alex, can I ask you a question, though?"

"What's that, sweetheart?" he said, his lips moving against my hair.

"Do you..." Ugh, how could I even ask this question? Did I really *need* to ask this question?

"Do I what?" His arms relaxed around me, and he slowly pulled away till our eyes met.

I sighed. Yes, I did need to ask—just this once —because I really wanted to know the answer, really wanted to see what he'd say. Staring into that incredibly handsome face, I finally asked, "Do you just want to be with me because I'm pregnant?"

He surprised me by smiling. "Are you kidding me right now?"

His own question confused me to no end. "Um, no. I'm definitely not kidding. I'd like to know."

"Jayda, Jayda, Jayda," he said, shaking his head, still grinning. "You do remember I've wanted you since high school, right?"

The light of amusement in his eyes made me smile. "Yeah, I guess."

He had a point, but I wanted the words. *The* words. And I wondered if I should just say them myself first. But my fear held me back.

"You guess?" Alex's face turned serious again. "You have no idea how much I—"

The shrill sound of my phone alarm startled us and interrupted whatever he was about to say.

"Oh, sorry. It's time to get Audrey," I said, grateful that I'd set a recurring alarm since that one afternoon when I'd fallen asleep and almost missed pick-up time.

As I started to move away, Alex grabbed my arm. "Wait."

I glanced up into his eyes. "What is it?"

"Tonight. You are all mine."

Holy cow. The intense way he said that made me a quivering mess, and I could hardly wait to be alone with him again.

CHAPTER THIRTY-TWO

Alex

Picking up Audrey from preschool was a blast, and I loved holding hands with Jayda the whole walk there as she talked about the neighborhood. I had visions of our future, doing everyday things like this together.

She pointed out the nearby elementary school where Audrey would be going to kindergarten. And I almost had to pinch myself at how lucky I was, how excited I was to start this new life with Jayda here.

Audrey had been thrilled to see me, and as I swung her around in my arms, she laughed so much that everyone stared at us. But there were a lot of smiling faces, and I knew that all the surrounding parents and teachers here loved

Jayda just as much as I did. Well, maybe not quite as much as I did. I wasn't sure anyone could.

And tonight, I was determined to tell her.

Thank God the evening flew by with a quick dinner, a lasagna that Jayda had already "thrown together" last night, and a movie with Audrey—Tangled once again.

But this time, I found out that Jayda was obsessed with one scene in the movie, the one where they released the lanterns, lighting up the night sky. And sure enough, mother and daughter sat there together, captivated by the glowing lanterns on screen, both smiling and singing along.

It was a moment I knew would live forever in my mind. And I couldn't wait to add Gabby back to the mix and meet this new little being that would be part of the family soon.

My God, the family, *my* family, *our* family. I was so close to getting everything I'd dreamed of having, something that had always been frustratingly out of reach for me. But with Jayda, it was so easy. She was so easy to love, so easy to be with.

How had my life turned out this way? I could hardly believe it.

As I waited for Jayda to help Audrey get to sleep upstairs, I paced in the living room, wondering how I'd tell her I loved her. I wished I had some grand gesture—candles, flowers, something. But I felt so unprepared even though

I'd thought about this moment for so long.

I hoped just the words would be enough for her.

It was unbelievable how nervous I was. I'd only said I love you to one other person in my life, and that hadn't worked out so well. And now, the stakes were so incredibly high. I didn't remember the last time my heart had raced this much.

When she came back downstairs, those stunning eyes locked with mine, and I couldn't even breathe for a long moment.

This was it. Now was the time.

Jayda's face transformed with her soft, sexy smile as she reached out her hand. "Follow me," she said.

And I did, my heart pounding in my chest as we quietly climbed the steps, our hands clasped together. We walked slowly down the dark, creaky hallway toward her room, what I hoped to make *our* room soon.

I was surprised to find a single candle lit on her dresser, illuminating the space in a soft glow. I managed to shut the door behind us, and she turned to face me, the flickering light somehow making her even more stunning.

"I was hoping we could just pick up where we left off this afternoon?" she said, turning it into a question as her smile grew. "If that's okay with you."

"What do you think?" I teased.

I was already more than ready for her if she

was looking, and I found her eyes grow wide as she took in my entire body. Needing to feel her softness against me, I reached for her, but she stepped back, a seductive look on her face as she started to take off her clothes in front of me.

Damn, who exactly was this woman?

All thoughts left my head while I watched her slowly remove everything, one piece at a time, her eyes searching mine, her cheeks turning an adorable shade of pink as she came closer and closer to being naked.

As she stood before me in nothing but her bra and panties, I held my breath while remembering a similar moment not too long ago, the night of the reunion. She had been so nervous then. But now, my Jayda had become bolder with me, and I absolutely loved it.

She reached back to take off her bra, and as she revealed herself to me, a jolt shot through my whole body. It took everything I had inside me not to reach out and touch her. But something told me she just wanted me to watch. And watch I did as she took off her panties next, revealing all to me.

Stepping back toward me, she reached for my clothing now and repeated her unhurried movements, leisurely undressing me, making me feel like I was going to jump out of my skin. But I was still determined to take it slow this time.

Taking off my shirt, her hands traced my chest

then my arms, and I could smell the vanilla-scented lotion from earlier as the room seemed to heat up. Her eyes explored me along with her hands, and it made me so hot to see her looking at me like that. She held her naked body just away from my heated skin, making the anticipation rise to an almost unbearable level.

I desperately wanted to feel her against me. "What are you doing to me, sweetheart?" I said.

Jayda flashed me a smile as she reached for the button on my jeans next, and I closed my eyes at the sensation of sweet torment as her fingers barely brushed over me in her quest to completely undress me.

And then, I heard her gasp as I was free, the sound making me pulse. She brought her hands up my legs all the way to my stomach, not touching me where I wanted it the most. But two could play that game, I thought, as she grabbed my hand and led me to the bed.

She sat down, pulling me close to her, and I finally touched my lips to hers after what felt like a long drought. Those luscious lips of hers tasted so goddamn sweet, just like the rest of her, and her tongue began to tangle with mine, making me almost lose it.

Damn. Did I need to think about baseball again?

Breathless, I kept going, determined to take over now and show this woman with my body how much I loved her, how much I wanted her, and how much I desired her, all of her, and wanted to make her mine. For life.

Our kisses turned from slow and sensual to raw and hungry. As her body fell back against the pillows, I crawled over her, my arms making a cage around her, my lips capturing hers again and again, making me wonder if my whiskers would rub her raw. But she didn't seem to care. She met me with equal passion, kiss after kiss after kiss.

I didn't want to put any weight on her, always aware of that beautiful bump, a sign of this amazing miracle that had happened between us.

Leaving her mouth behind, I kissed her neck, finding that sensitive spot that made her gasp in the way that I craved. Chills broke out on her skin, and I couldn't get over how responsive she was to me.

"Do you know how beautiful you are right now?" I asked against her silky skin. "You are so damn sexy."

She shivered, and I placed kisses on her collarbone, her breaths turning ragged as I worked my way down her chest. God, if just slow kisses did this to her, what would it feel like if I...

And then her breasts were in front of me. I licked the valley between them before my tongue moved over to take her nipple into my mouth, licking, teasing, sucking, until I didn't know who was moaning louder.

Carefully putting my weight to one side, I

used my free hand to touch and caress her other breast, amazed at the feel of her soft flesh in my hand and the changes in her body already.

Her breaths came out in gasps, and I paused to glance up at her. "Are you okay, baby? Is it too much? Just tell me, and I'll do anything you want."

She sat up on her elbows, her dazed eyes meeting mine, her lips swollen from our kisses. Her gorgeous smile sent a jolt straight to my heart.

"Alex Hernandez, do you have any idea how much I adore you? How much I love you?"

My lungs stopped working. I couldn't breathe. Or move. Or speak. I stared at her like an idiot, wondering if I'd really heard that. "W-what?"

Her smile grew even wider as she stared into my eyes. "I love you."

Did she really just say that? Shock hit me. Goosebumps shot down my arms. And I couldn't even swallow anymore. Jayda loved me? I could hardly believe it. The whole world seemed to stop.

She covered her mouth with her hand, her eyes wide. "Oh, gosh, I'm sorry. I didn't mean to just blurt it out like that."

She was sorry? For saying she loved me? "Don't you dare be sorry. My God, Jayda, do you know how much I love *you*?"

Her eyes filled up with unshed tears. "You do?"

"I do, baby. I love you with all my heart."

As the tears spilled over, she reached for me and tried to pull me closer, but I hesitated, not wanting to crush her even though her bump was so small. But, God, the need to feel her whole body against me was overwhelming.

This woman loved me, and I loved her back. And the desire for her raged inside me.

Lying down on my side next to her, I grabbed her to me, face to face, her entire body flush against me. Finally. Her eyes stared into mine, and I saw such emotion there that my heart lurched in my chest.

"I love you so much, Jayda."

More tears escaped, making a path down her cheek to the pillow, and I kissed them away, the wetness on her soft skin my undoing. And the salty-sweet taste of her. And the feel of our bodies touching, the swell of her stomach against me.

"I can't even believe how much I love you, baby," I said as my chest squeezed at the look in her eyes.

She gave me a watery smile as she lifted her leg over mine and guided me into her. "I love you too," she gasped as I slid into her, filling her.

"God, you feel amazing."

We both moaned as our hips ground together and found a slow rhythm. I captured her lips with mine, and she sighed into me. Every part of her was crushed up against me, her fingers digging into my back as we moved our joined bodies.

"Say it again," I demanded, my voice so thick with desire I barely recognized it as my own.

She wrapped her leg around me tighter, bringing me in deeper. The sensations were unbelievable. "I love you. I love you. I love you," she said in breathy whispers as we moved together.

This was truly what they meant when they said making love. Because this feeling was something different from anything I'd ever experienced. I had never felt so close to anyone in my life. My God.

In this position, with our faces so close, I felt like I could see right through those beautiful eyes all the way to her beautiful soul. And I wanted to drink in every part of her.

As the passion swept through us, I felt our movements grow more erratic, and I knew she was close. I held on, using one hand to explore her, wanting to touch her, taste her, consume her, everything all at once.

My back tensed, pressure building in my whole body. She closed the small gap between our lips and kissed me so passionately, I almost burst. But I was determined to wait for her and make this sweet torture last as long as possible.

And then I felt it. I felt the amazing sensation of her starting to clench around me, and she pulled her mouth away to look at me.

"Oh, my God, Alex..." she breathed.

"I love you so much, baby."

My heart pounding out of my chest, the pressure inside me built even more, becoming almost unbearable as she let go, and I felt her squeezing me over and over again.

"Alex," she moaned, her face awash with pleasure as she made the sexiest sounds in the world.

Hearing her moan my name like that, that was it for me. My hips locked into hers as a rush of the most intense pleasure I'd ever felt shot through me, making me explode inside her and fill her, the feeling overpowering me to the point that I couldn't breathe, couldn't think, couldn't anything. Everything else fell away except for this woman in my arms whose body joined with mine kept me tethered to this earth.

Good God. What had just happened?

"Fucking Jesús Guerrero," she said against my lips.

It took me a moment to come down from my high. But her words eventually sunk in, and I laughed till I was even more breathless.

"Fucking Jesús Guerrero is right. God, Jayda, that was like... otherworldly." I struggled with how to even describe it. Staring into her eyes, we breathed each other in. "I don't know. You're the writer. What's the word for that, for what just happened between us?"

Still with that intense eye contact, I felt her chest rising and falling with mine as she thought for a moment. She reached up to stroke my cheek with the most amazing look on her face. Inhaling deeply and with a soul-shattering smile, she whispered just one word, "Love."

EPILOGUE PART ONE

Jayda

Seven Months Later...

I was so hot. Everything was so hot. Always. All the freaking time. And I felt like I'd been pregnant forever. I was so ready to get this little being out of me. When you knew you were pregnant from day one, forty weeks seemed like an eternity.

But really, it was just a minor inconvenience, I thought, as I watched Audrey and Gabby splash together in the sprinkler one scorching Saturday afternoon. Sure, the electricity bill might have been a little higher so far this summer. But that was okay. More than okay. Because I was happier than I'd been in a very long time.

And I owed it all to the amazing man that had moved all the way to Maine to be with me, to support me, to love me.

Sitting in the cushioned chair in the front yard and sipping my icy lemonade, I thought about Alex and how we'd just slipped into this wonderful life here together. He'd officially moved in a few months ago, his whole family coming to help us, and he'd hardly brought anything, saying he was more than happy with my choice of decor. Good man, I had told him, laughing.

But what was really nice about this house was it held no memories of a past for either of us. There were no ghosts to haunt us here. It was a neutral space where we could start our future together.

Blake's dad had visited with us as well, thrilled to have two "bonus" grandkids, only adding to my joy at seeing how our families blended and interacted together. I thanked God every day that my mom was back to her normal self now after switching her bladder medication several months ago, eliminating the harmful side effects that had caused her confusion.

At that reminder, I did another round of Kegels, thinking about my mom's upcoming hip surgery. While of course Alex wouldn't be operating on her, he had settled in nicely at a new practice and was making sure she had the best care possible. I couldn't be more grateful for Alex in my life, not just for his expertise, but for his partnership as I navigated having parents who were growing older and relying on me more and more.

I squirmed a bit in my chair, trying to get comfortable. *A few more weeks till my due date.* Not that that meant anything really. When I found the right spot, I set my drink down on my big belly, wondering if the little soccer star inside would kick it away.

We had decided to wait to find out the gender, something neither of us had done the last time. Although of course I'd be happy with either, I liked to tease Alex that we were having another girl because I loved to imagine this former player someday dealing with three teenage daughters in the house at the same time.

I laughed out loud just thinking about it.

"What's so funny, Mama?" Audrey asked, running over to get her own drink of lemonade from the small table next to me. "Does baby have the hiccups again?" she asked, reaching out to touch my bump.

"Nope, not—" My belly jumped, and I grabbed my drink just in time. "Oops, I spoke too soon I guess."

She felt the little jumps for a second but then quickly ran off again to join Gabby.

I wondered what was keeping Alex. He said he had an important errand to run, and I needed the bathroom yet again.

He had been so incredibly supportive these last months, going to every single doctor's appointment, getting up with the girls if they woke in the night, doing the bulk of the housework all while encouraging me to finish my book. And all while making me the most satisfied woman in the world.

At some point, even Alex had lost track of how many times we'd been intimate. He'd made me feel beautiful this entire pregnancy, practically worshipping my body throughout every stage, taking delight in all the changes along the way.

I could hardly believe how much this man had changed since high school. Sometimes, I had to pinch myself at how happy I was now.

Alex had even mentioned marriage to me several times, but I'd told him I didn't want to make any plans until I had seen how he acted when he was upset. A man who turned nasty during arguments was an absolute dealbreaker for me.

I never actually thought Alex would become a jerk when he was mad, but I had been fooled once before by my first boyfriend in college, and I'd vowed never again to put up with anything like that.

So recently, when we'd finally had our first real argument, I was beyond relieved to see that Alex hadn't turned into a jackass... not even close. Thank God he had passed my test because I really, really, really wanted to marry him.

Looking at my phone again, I checked the time. He'd really been gone a while, and worry started to creep in. Jiggling my leg, I tried to focus on the girls as they screeched with delight at the cold water spraying them.

"Mama! A rainbow!" Audrey yelled, pointing to where the sprinkler spray and the sunlight collided.

"Mamamamamama," Gabby joined in, making my heart sing.

The first time she'd called me mama, I'd melted into one big emotional puddle. Good thing Alex had been there because I'd seriously cried what Audrey called happy tears.

I'd wondered how it would feel to be a mom to this little girl, if I could love her as much as I loved Audrey. And I'll admit it took a little time for that bond to fully form between us, the same thing with Alex and Audrey.

But with the passing days, weeks, and months, we'd all grown so close as a family. It helped that Gabby was a cuddler and wanted to be held a lot, the complete opposite of my fiercely independent Audrey. I was more than happy to hold Gabby as much as she'd let me, and that love in my heart had grown exponentially.

"What's that music, Mama?" Audrey suddenly asked.

I managed to get out of the chair and stand up, straining to hear this music Audrey was talking about, but I couldn't make out anything. Audrey and Gabby both stopped playing and looked off in the distance, down the street. So I did the same.

And then I heard it. The beautiful lyrics of one of my all-time favorite songs from the movie Tangled. A big black SUV headed toward us, windows down, music blasting, while the three of us all stared in confusion. Who *was* that? And what on earth was going on?

But as it grew closer, I recognized the driver which only made me more bewildered. Why was Alex driving this SUV? And what had happened to *his* car which he had taken off in?

Pulling up to the curb, I could see him laughing as he shut off the engine, glancing over at me. I held up my arms in disbelief before I walked closer, hand on my back, still with no clue what was going on.

"What is this? Whose SUV is this?" I asked him, shielding my eyes from the sun with my other hand.

"It's ours, baby," he answered, wearing that smile I loved so much.

"Are you kidding me? You actually bought this?" I really didn't know what to think right now.

"I did," he said, a little hesitant as he slid out of the car. "Normally, I wouldn't buy something like this without talking about it first, but it's all part of my plan."

"Plan? What plan?"

He leaned down to give me a tender kiss, making me forget my train of thought. Sneaky.

"Why don't you go inside for a little bathroom break real quick?" he said. "I'd like to take everyone for a ride."

"Um, okay."

He glanced at the time on his phone, a slight crease in his brow like he was worried about something. I heard him calling to the girls as I headed into the house to relieve my poor bladder. Maybe I was having some serious pregnancy brain at the moment, but something strange seemed to be happening. And not just with the new vehicle Alex had bought.

Wow, that suddenly sank in. Alex had really bought a new car? He'd finally given up the last symbol of his previous existence and embraced this new life of total dadhood with a bigger SUV to fit the soon-to-be three kids in our little world.

When I came outside a few minutes later, Alex already had the girls all buckled into their car seats, the Tangled soundtrack playing. He helped me up into my seat then ran around to hop into the driver's side.

"You're fast," I said, putting on my seat belt and arranging it just right over my stomach.

I noticed him check out the clock on the dashboard and wondered at his preoccupation with the time.

He patted the steering wheel as he took off. "So

what do you think? Do you like it?"

Looking around, I took it all in, the crazy amount of bells and whistles on the dash, the extra space in the back for our family, that new car smell. "I love it."

"Oh, good." He sighed like he'd been nervous.

"Did you think I'd be mad at you or something?"

He gave a quick glance around at a four-way stop before turning. "It definitely crossed my mind. I had a friend do the same thing once, and his wife was furious."

My laughter made my whole belly shake. "I'm not mad. Honestly, now that the shock is wearing off, I'm thrilled. Do you know how much I hate shopping for a new car?"

"Mama, you said the h-word!" Audrey shouted from behind me.

These kids sure heard every word, didn't they? "Sorry," I said as I caught Alex's grin. "I really *dislike* shopping for new cars."

Laughing once again, I felt a sharp twinge deep down in my abdomen, making me catch my breath. I looked to Alex once again, but he was busy taking us wherever we were going which... where were we going anyway?

He really seemed focused on something, and I wondered whether I should even mention it to him. It was probably nothing, though. How many times had I experienced little cramps and twinges, making me wonder if this was the moment, and it had turned out to be a passing thing?

So I decided to keep quiet and see if it was a one-off.

Taking in my surroundings, I noticed we were nearing the lighthouse. "What's going on exactly?" I asked.

"You'll see."

On a hot, summer day, the parking lot was crowded, and I wondered how we'd ever find a spot. But right when Alex drove up, a car backed out, the young driver giving us a thumbs-up as he pulled away. He looked very familiar.

"Wait, was that our neighbor Hudson?" I asked Alex, my confusion growing. Was it just me, or did it seem like the teenage boy from across the street had been holding a parking space for us?

"Strange coincidence, huh?" Alex said, grinning as he once again looked at the clock.

Okay. Something was definitely up. But I had no clue what.

"Come on," Alex interrupted my suspicious thoughts as he turned off the car. "I have something I want to show you."

I hefted my body around in the seat, ready to test out the distance to the ground. But Alex was there in a flash, holding onto my hand and helping me down.

"Thank you." I smiled at how he still managed to take my breath away, all handsomeness in a short-sleeved shirt that showed off those arm muscles I loved so much.

"Any time, sweetheart," he said, dropping a sweet kiss on my forehead.

A banging on the window startled us apart. "Let me out!" Audrey yelled.

Chuckling, Alex and I helped the girls, each taking a kid's hand as we walked through the parking lot.

"You know," Alex said, "pretty soon, we're going to have to change from one-on-one defense to a zone defense."

"God help us."

Alex laughed as he led the way to wherever it was we were going. After spending so much time here this spring and summer, he now knew this place very well, and we ended up on the grassy area near the stunning rocky beach. Other people were nearby enjoying the beautiful afternoon as well.

As the girls wandered down closer to the water and played with the smooth pebbles, we followed along to keep an eye on them. I took a deep breath, inhaling the salty air, appreciating the sun on my face.

A strong arm went around me. "How you doing, baby?" Alex asked.

"Great." I nuzzled my head into his shoulder. "This is really nice."

Whatever had been on his mind earlier, he seemed to have relaxed now. But a split second later, a buzzing in the distance made his whole body tense.

"What's that?" I asked.

I looked toward the noise and saw a small airplane headed our way, following the edge of the coastline. Gabby and Audrey jumped up and down, pointing at the sky.

"Look at the airplane, Gabby!" yelled Audrey over the increasing sound.

I noticed it had a banner floating behind it, probably advertising some local shop or festival. But as it grew closer, I started to decipher a few of the words... "will" and "marry."

"Aw, I think someone's getting proposed to," I said to Alex, keeping my eyes on the huge letters.

I gasped loudly, and my heart stopped beating altogether as the first word on the banner came into view.

Holy cow! It was my name!

My mouth went dry as I stared into the sky, breathless and shaky, until the plane flew closer and I could read it all.

Jayda, will you marry me?

Tears rushed to my eyes as I whirled around to look at Alex who was down on one knee, holding a little jewelry box in one hand. He looked up at me, smiling widely.

"Jayda, you have made me the happiest man in the whole world, and I can't even imagine what my life would be like without you. You're my best friend, and I love you more than I thought was even possible."

He looked down, rubbing his forehead with his free hand, and mumbled something that sounded like, "Not sure that came out like I practiced."

Oh, my heart. Could I love this man any more?

Shaking his head, he lifted his gaze back up to my face. "Anyway, you're my rock. You're my light. Will you do me the great honor of becoming my wife? Will you marry me, sweetheart?"

Those deep, brown eyes and that gorgeous face were blurry through my tear-filled smile, but the words were crystal clear. The lump in my throat was so huge, I couldn't even say anything. I just kind of squeaked as I held out my hands to him, needing the strength of his body to hold me up right now.

He stood and pulled me as close as he could while the people around us burst into applause. I laughed and cried at the same time as Gabby and Audrey ran over, throwing their arms around our legs, Alex and I both ushering them into our hug.

And right then, that's when I felt it. A sharper twinge and a tiny trickle down the inside of my leg.

My heart beat all over the place as I pulled back from our group hug. Staring at Alex, I whispered the words, "I think my water just broke."

EPILOGUE
PART TWO

Alex

My hands trembled as I drove us all to the hospital. I focused every ounce of my energy on getting us safely there, Jayda sitting on a towel and holding onto her stomach while she called her mom.

After a few minutes, her parents decided the best thing to do was meet us there and take the girls back to their place. And Jayda's dad would swing by our house at some point and grab our already packed bag that was waiting in the coat closet. I wished I had thought of bringing it with us to the lighthouse. But I had never dreamed the baby would come this early. And I prayed to God that everything would be okay for both the baby and my Jayda.

I was a wreck right now. But I knew I needed to be strong.

Next, Jayda called her doctor who apparently was already at the hospital finishing up another birth. The doctor confirmed once again that even though it was early, she still wanted Jayda to go to the hospital because she'd had some issues with her blood pressure the last several weeks. Just as the call ended, we pulled up to the valet booth at the hospital.

God, I loved Maine, the lack of traffic, and how easy it was to get everywhere.

I jumped down to help Jayda out, rather than the skinny teenage valet who was heading to her door. Instead, I tossed him the keys quickly as I ran around to the passenger side. As she held onto me, she moaned while sliding from the seat into my waiting arms.

"Want me to carry you?" I asked, trying to make her laugh through our nerves.

"I don't think you can carry a beached whale like me."

"Wanna bet?" I asked. "And you are in no way a beached whale, sweetheart."

She flashed me a grateful look as she clutched onto me. I somehow managed to open the back door for an impatient Audrey who had already unbuckled herself and Gabby.

As we went into the lobby, we decided I'd hang out in the waiting area with the girls until Jayda's parents could get there. And Jayda would go ahead upstairs. She'd already filled out all the paperwork electronically so she wouldn't have to deal with it now.

And after a quick check-in at the desk, they brought her a wheelchair and I helped her settle in. With a quick kiss and reassurances from Jayda that she'd be okay, she disappeared around the corner, leaving me in misery. No offense to these two little wound-up angels, but I just wanted to be with her right now.

The girls practically climbed the furniture in their excitement. Scratch that. They *did* climb the furniture, and man, they were loud. I paced next to them, keeping one eye on them and one out the window looking for Jayda's parents.

Time seemed to slow down. Where were they? They couldn't have hit traffic. But I also knew from experience that my future father-in-law was rather slow behind the wheel. It even drove Jayda crazy.

Pacing some more, my mind wondered what Jayda was up to at this exact moment. I knew sometimes the second child came into this world much faster than the first. And I really hoped I wouldn't miss anything.

Finally, I saw the familiar white SUV pull up outside, and the girls and I ran out to greet them. They seemed just as anxious and hurried as I was.

"Is she okay?" Jayda's mom asked me after a quick hug.

"So far, so good," I said, ushering the girls into the back where there were extra car seats just for an occasion like this. "I'll keep you posted. And hopefully, you'll get to meet your new grandchild soon."

She nodded, tears in her eyes. "You take care of my baby, okay?"

"Always," I said, trying not to choke up myself.

I gave her another hug, kissing her cheek, and turned to the girls who were climbing all over the seats. Where did they find all this energy?

"Hey, girls, try not to give Grandma and Grandpa too much trouble."

They didn't even glance at me, and Jayda's dad just laughed as he opened the other side door. "Don't worry about it. We got this. You just go on in."

"Okay. Love you, girls. See everyone soon."

"Give Jayda our love," her mom said.

"Absolutely. Of course."

I waved goodbye and hurried in, knowing the girls were in good hands. Jayda had texted me her room number, and I rushed upstairs, anxious to get to her. I just needed to see her, see if she was okay.

After the slowest elevator ride ever, I finally made it to her floor and, a few seconds later, rounded the corner into her room... where I almost bumped into her by the door. I grabbed Jayda's arms to steady her, studying her face. Instead of the pain and agony I expected, I was greeted by her wide smile.

"You seem to be doing okay," I said, more of a question than a statement really.

She giggled at me. "I'm fine, Alex."

"You are?"

"My blood pressure is fine. The baby's fine. All good."

I exhaled loudly. "Oh, thank God."

Grinning at me, she tilted her head. "You're so cute."

I laughed. "You're the one who's cute."

She actually did look super cute in her green hospital gown, belly poking out, her hair up high in what she called a messy bun, making her eyes seem even larger.

Jayda grabbed onto her back suddenly, bending over, taking deep breaths, and puffing air out through her nose. I moved closer, holding out a hand just over her back. And as I debated whether or not to touch her, she finally stood up, her face pink, her eyes watery.

"Whew, that was a rough one," she breathed out, stretching her spine.

"God, I'm so sorry. What can I do?"

Staring up at me, she sighed. "Nothing really. Just be here."

That I could certainly do.

The next several hours, we waited and waited as I attempted to comfort Jayda through the contractions while she continued to dilate. We had already asked for an epidural, but the anesthesiologist was super busy apparently, and it would be a while.

Damn, I had gone into the wrong field. What I wouldn't do to be able to relieve Jayda of this pain.

With each contraction, she would double over in agony, her whole body tense, not speaking, trying to breathe. I wanted to help, but she didn't want me near her. And that smile she usually wore began to fade as exhaustion and pain took over.

I paced the room, hoping the anesthesiologist wouldn't be too late. I knew we only had a certain window of time, and I couldn't imagine the amount of pain she'd endure without it. If I could take her pain and make it mine, I would do it in a heartbeat. But there was nothing I could do, and it drove me insane... especially because I was the reason she was in this situation to begin with.

Jayda stood beside the bed where she said she was more comfortable.

"Are you sure I can't do anything?" I asked from the now dark window on the other side of the room. "Cool compress? Massage?"

"If you touch me, I'll hit you," she hissed.

Oh, dear God. I kind of wanted to laugh at this feisty side of Jayda. But I knew not to let out a sound. She was totally on the edge from the pain. And honestly, she was scary. I couldn't wait till later, maybe months later, to tease her about it. My sweet Jayda had turned into a rabid tiger.

She threw her hands on the bed as she leaned over, and I knew another contraction had hit. I just stood there, feeling helpless. Her knuckles turned white as she gripped the sheets. My hands itched to touch her, but Lord knows, I knew better than to even get near her. Or she might bite my head off. I found myself breathing for her, counting.

When it was over, she straightened herself, face red, hand on her back. "Do something!" she growled.

I approached her like I would a wild animal, hand out, cautious. "What can I do?"

"Find the anesthesiologist and tell him I'll hunt him down when this is all over if he doesn't give me the damn epidural now."

"Right. Right," I said as I edged past her toward the door, looking down the hall once again.

I'd already asked about the anesthesiologist multiple times and always received the same answer. But I'd do it again. I mean, seriously, where the hell was he?

Not wanting to move far from our room, I scanned the hallway, looking for a nurse, Jayda's doctor that we'd seen earlier, or just any goddamn person. And to my great relief, I spotted a man in a white coat coming our way.

Thank God. Instead of yelling at him like I wanted to, I shook his hand as he entered the room, Jayda letting out a huge sigh.

As he approached Jayda, apologizing profusely

for the wait, she sat down on the edge of the bed, ready to go, and without delay, he went to work. I stood near Jayda and held my hand out to see if she wanted it.

To my relief, she grabbed my hand and squeezed hard. I knew part of her pain had been the worry about whether she'd get the epidural in time. And even though I knew it took a little while for it to kick in, I could already see the relief on her face.

But soon after the doctor was done, Jayda turned to me, her face pale. "I'm going to throw up," she whispered.

I scrambled to find something for her, and I rushed back, a disposable bag in my hand. When she was done, I found a wet cloth and wiped down her face. God, this poor thing.

"There is zero dignity in childbirth," she said, smiling up at me, making me chuckle.

"You're amazing, you know that?"

She took a deep breath before answering. "Thank you, Alex. You've been so incredibly supportive. And I'm really sorry if I was mean."

"You weren't mean," I lied because if there was ever a time to fib, this was it.

And now it was just more waiting. And more waiting. And even more. But at least this time, Jayda was comfortable.

I thought back to Gabby's birth. I had missed it all because I was stuck in surgery where a man went into cardiac arrest during a knee replacement. Gabby had arrived early, and thank goodness Fiona's mom was with her and the delivery had gone smoothly.

I was incredibly grateful to be here today, but all this waiting just heightened the anxiety because there was nothing to do except worry... something I wasn't used to doing.

In a hospital setting, I was used to being in charge and calling the shots. And I found myself now in the unusual position of being completely useless. Of course, I imagined all the things that could go wrong, all the terrible things that could happen.

Usually, in surgery, I could keep a cool head, keep calm, and do what needed to be done. But this was a whole different ballgame. And even though I'd read extensively on the subject, being in the actual situation now was throwing me off.

The stakes were too high. This was the love of my life here and my child, along with Audrey and Gabby, the most important people in my life.

The nurse started to come in more and more often as Jayda became closer and closer to full dilation. And then once she finally reached ten centimeters, Doctor Chabra arrived, checking Jayda out and making sure everything was okay.

"We are all set," she said, a pleased smile on her face. "Let's get this started, folks."

Get started? What had we been doing all these hours? It was now the middle of the night, and I pictured our parents dozing with their phones in their hands, waiting for the big announcement.

I hoped to God Jayda wouldn't have to push for very long.

With the doctor keeping an eye on the contraction monitor, she let Jayda know when to push. And my goodness, did she push. And push. And push. The minutes ticked by, on and on and on, all while I held her hand, encouraging her, praising her for how hard she was working.

Jayda was oddly quiet, not speaking... just silent and staring at the ceiling. And I knew she was exhausted, working so incredibly hard to birth this child of ours. Between contractions, I wiped her forehead with a cool cloth.

At one point, the baby's heart rate dropped, and I almost had a panic attack. I said a silent prayer as my eyes darted back and forth between the doctor and the two nurses to see how worried they were. I knew from my own experience that if they were freaking out, then I'd be right to be alarmed.

But while they looked concerned, they didn't seem panicked. They gave Jayda some oxygen and put an internal heart monitor on the baby. And after a minute of oxygen, thank God the baby's pulse returned to normal.

And through it all, Jayda stayed calm, stayed focused, and pushed when she was told. And pushed some more, and then some more. *Holy crap*. The woman was a warrior, badass princess, and superhero all rolled up into one.

Not for the first time, I thought it was a good thing women were the ones who gave birth because, otherwise, humans would have gone extinct long ago. I'd seen linebackers go down at the sight of a needle and women barely over four feet tall not even crying at an open fracture with a bone poking through their skin. And this experience just confirmed that.

The endurance required to push a baby out of a body... my God.

The sweat poured down her brow, and I kept wiping it away. Her messy bun turned even messier, long strands coming out and sticking to her face. I whisked her hair away from her red cheeks, wishing I knew how to fix her bun. But she didn't seem to care, just kept her focus straight ahead like some kind of zen warrior.

The doctor and nurses seemed to be enjoying themselves as they chatted, sometimes pulling me into the conversation. But I kept my attention on this woman next to me, not fully able to breathe till this whole thing was done, till I knew that both my future wife and this child would be okay.

Then finally, *finally*, the doctor said we were close.

"Baby, you're doing great." I squeezed Jayda's hand. "You're almost there. Just a little longer."

Doctor Chabra and the nurses sprung into action, marking the end of the pushing and the beginning of this new life in our world. I felt the hugest lump in my throat at the idea of meeting our little baby, this child that had been like a miracle, helping to bring us all together.

"Push hard, Jayda," Doctor Chabra said. "You're so close."

With a loud groan, Jayda sat up and pushed with all her might.

"One more and you're done, love," the doctor encouraged. "Push hard. Harder."

"Come on, Jayda. You got this," I said, supporting her back, wishing to God I could push for her. "You're a rock star. You really are."

She pushed even harder, and seconds later, the doctor said, "It's a girl! A beautiful baby girl!"

Tears streamed down my face as I held onto Jayda's hand and watched as the doctor quickly inspected our baby, soon clamping the cord.

Oh, my God, our baby girl.

"Is she okay?" Jayda squeaked out.

"She's perfect," Doctor Chabra said as she laid her on Jayda's bare chest, her little face turned toward me.

The nurses wiped her down, but all my focus was on Jayda and this tiny baby.

"She's so beautiful," Jayda whispered, staring at her, stroking her back gently.

Big brown eyes looked at me, and I stared in wonder, completely awed by the sight in front of me. My heart swelled instantly with love for this beautiful being we'd created together.

"Liliana..." I said softly, amazed by the

magnitude of this moment.

"Liliana," Jayda repeated. "Welcome to the world, Liliana."

A perfect name for a perfect baby girl. Liliana in honor of my great-grandmother who had come to this country all those years ago to start a new life for her family. And here was a new life, a product of my great-grandma's dream, that would carry on her legacy.

I wiped away my tears and took a second to dry Jayda's wet cheek as well. "Look, Liliana's the only one *not* crying."

Jayda laughed, the baby bouncing up and down on her chest with her.

"She's a warrior just like her mama," I said, my hands on both of them now.

Jayda adjusted the blanket around them with Liliana's adorable face poking out. We watched as her eyes slowly closed.

"Poor thing's probably exhausted," Jayda whispered. "She worked just as hard as I did."

I caressed Jayda's cheek. "I'm so proud of you, baby. You're truly amazing."

Her soft eyes met mine. "I couldn't have done it without you."

"I love you so much."

"I love you, Alex."

For the rest of the night, the three of us stayed in our magical cocoon, only taking breaks when the doctor or nurses needed to do something. I could hardly wait until our other little ones showed up to meet the baby.

Before I knew it, sunlight poured in through the big window, and there was a noise outside our room. I looked up to see the door open, Jayda's dad ushering in Audrey and Gabby who wore the brightest smiles I'd ever seen.

"We'll give you a minute before we meet this new granddaughter," he said, closing the door behind him.

Gabby and Audrey were already scrambling onto the bed to get closer as Jayda tried to position Liliana just right. Of course, she slept right through the noise like the newborn she was.

"I love her little hat," Audrey said. "Is she real?"

Jayda laughed. "Oh, she's real all right. But she kind of looks like a doll, doesn't she?"

Gabby reached out and gently touched Liliana's nose, making those tears come to my eyes again. Man, I'd never in my life been so emotional.

I stuffed my hands into my pockets, trying to keep myself together, and my fingers landed on something I'd completely forgotten about in all the excitement. Oh, wow. I held onto it for a few minutes in my pocket, watching these girls get to know their new sister.

But kids were kids. And Liliana wasn't very exciting to them at the moment. Their attention quickly turned to a helicopter flying by outside the window. And I decided this was the time to get the answer to that rather important question I had asked yesterday.

Standing next to the bed, I pulled the small box out of my pocket, opening it slowly and getting everyone's attention. "Jayda Jenkins, I never did get an actual yes or no from you. Will you marry me?"

She grinned up at me, those stunning eyes bright with love.

"Of course, she says yes!" Audrey shouted.

Jayda and I cracked up laughing. My God, this was our life now.

"Yes, yes, of course, yes!" Jayda said, matching Audrey's enthusiasm.

Taking the ring out, I tried to slip it onto her ring finger, but no surprise, it wouldn't fit at the moment. So she placed it on her pinkie finger instead.

"It's beautiful, Alex."

"I want one, Daddy!" Audrey said, melting me with that word I loved to hear.

Stepping back a bit, I watched as the girls looked at the ring and then again at Liliana who opened that cute little mouth to yawn. I took a mental picture in my mind because I wanted to remember this moment forever.

I had never in my life been so happy, never in my life been so complete. These girls were my world now. Filled with pride, I looked at each glowing face, one by one, as my heart burst with joy.

My girls. My family. My dream.

ABOUT THE AUTHOR

Jenna Fiore

Jenna has always had her head in the clouds, making up stories and creating characters. After years of working as a freelancer, she finally decided to put pen to paper and give this whole fiction thing a chance.

When she's not busy at her computer, she loves spending time with her husband, daughter, and insanely energetic dog who's always looking for trouble. She lives in the Pacific Northwest where she's constantly raking up pine needles in her back yard and dodging wild turkeys in her front yard.

Catch up with Jenna on her website, jennafiore.com, and stay up to date on future projects!

BOOKS BY THIS AUTHOR

Summer Of Rain

A steamy, emotional romance featuring a sexy movie star and the sweet heroine who steals his heart...

Rain had everything he'd ever dreamed about—a successful acting career, fame, fortune, and any woman he wanted. So why the hell wasn't he happy?

Addy had nothing she'd ever dreamed about with a life that lay in ruins.

On the busy streets of Los Angeles, these two souls collide, literally, and their lives will be forever changed.

The Crush Next Door

Jessica Santoro is living the life in the big city.

Well, maybe things aren't exactly perfect with her not-so-dream job, obnoxious neighbor, and long-distance fiancé. But at least she has an ocean view. Kind of.

When Jess starts watching Dodgers games with the annoying guy next door and thinking less about her fiancé, this curveball might just lead to a home run... or a strikeout with the bases loaded.

Return To Me Always

A hot Scot and an American lass pair up when the past comes back to haunt them.

Kat Ryder sets off for London, ready for the adventure of a lifetime before starting college. The very first day, she meets the gorgeous guy she's been dreaming about forever—literally the man of her dreams—and he's nothing like she'd imagined.

When Kat and her dream man are falsely accused of a crime, they're forced to go on the run together. And that's when the real adventure begins in a race for their lives as dreams and destiny collide.

The Pinkie Pact

When a bold girl meets an inexperienced law student, sparks fly in this enemies-to-friends-to-lovers college romance.

Desperate for a fresh start, Sky makes a pact with her new roommate Kara to change their lives for the better. When she meets Kara's hot brother, however, her new life gets a whole lot more complicated.

But this is it for Sky... her last chance at the college experience. And this time, she's determined to get it right. Well, hopefully.

Printed in Great Britain
by Amazon

25428361R00188